INVASION

Sympatico Syndrome: Book Three

M. P. MCDONALD

Receive a free copy of Mark Taylor: Genesis (Mark Taylor Series: Prequel) when you join my newsletter list.

MP McDonald's Newsletter

❦ Created with Vellum

Also by M. P. McDonald

The Mark Taylor Series

Mark Taylor: Genesis

No Good Deed: Book One

March Into Hell: Book Two

Deeds of Mercy: Book Three

March Into Madness: Book Four

CJ Sheridan Thrillers

Shoot: Book One

Capture: Book Two

Suspense

Seeking Vengeance

Sympatico Syndrome Series

Infection: A Post-Apocalyptic Survival Novel (Book One)

Isolation: A Post-Apocalyptic Survival Novel (Book Two)

Invasion: A Post-Apocalyptic Survival Novel (Book Three)

For my dad, who always reads my books. Love you!
Also for my grandchild, Fox Atticus, not yet born but already firmly
entrenched in my heart.

what Jenna had brought, they had a decent supply and had divided it into a couple of boxes—one for the main cabin and one for storage. That way if there was another fire or other catastrophe, their chances of losing all of it was lessened. "Who's there?"

Elly poked her head in. "Jenna and I came to see if we could help."

Cole had expected Jenna but not Elly. His initial reaction was fear for her safety, but he set it aside. They were always in danger, to some extent. Elly had proven herself more than capable and he simply waved them in, noting the sag in the front of Elly's parka. They all carried weapons whenever they left the island and he recognized the weight of a gun in her pocket.

Jenna bustled in after Elly, taking charge and issuing orders for all of them. Cole abandoned his search in the box of supplies when Jenna plopped a smaller box down on the table. She glanced at the men, her gaze locking on Mike's protectively hunched shoulders, his hand clutched against his chest.

"Hi, I'm Jenna." Cole's sister-in-law pulled out a chair from the kitchen table and patted the back of it. "Have a seat."

"Hello Jenna. I'm Mike." He staggered a little when he took a step towards the chair. "Sorry. I was drinking." For all of his size, he looked like a guilty schoolboy caught imbibing in the bathroom.

Jenna nodded and pulled a blood pressure cuff from her box. "That's okay. I'm going to do a quick set of vital signs to see where we stand, then assess your injury, okay?"

Elly moved forward and helped Mike get his jacket off, easing his injured hand out of the sleeve.

Jenna's professional tone and Elly's quiet competence were exactly what was needed. Steve stepped away from the table and took a seat on the ramshackle sofa. Cole indicated to Elly that water was heating and then moved over to the beat-up armchair beside the sofa. He couldn't suppress the sigh that escaped when he sat. He couldn't ever remember being so tired or sore. It had been a long day and it wasn't over yet.

"So, did you find a house to bed down in?"

Steve nodded. "Yep. We found one with a wood-burning fireplace and a pile of wood by the garage. There was a body in the basement, so we avoided that and the other guys got a fire started. They were heating up venison when Mike and I left."

"You didn't stay to eat?" Cole wondered if he should offer food. Manners bred into him over a lifetime dictated that he should offer a meal, but food was precious.

As if reading his mind, Steve shook his head. "No, but I brought some supplies of our own. They're out in the truck still."

"Well, you're welcome to use the stove and there are some old pots and pans in the cupboard."

Steve nodded, smiling. "I'll be right back." He still wore his parka, but stopped to zip it before he headed out to his truck.

Cole stood and watched through the window until he was sure that the truck was Steve's true destination then turned to Elly, who, with gloved hands, gathered soiled bandages, tossing them into the wood burning stove. "How's it look?"

Elly brushed her hands together. "Not good."

He peered over Jenna's shoulder, wincing when he caught sight of Mike's hand. A gaping wound sliced through his palm, opening the meaty heel part of his hand almost to the opposite wrist bone. The skin surrounding the gash seeped pus and the whole area appeared swollen. A dark red line trailed from the wound up the man's arm, disappearing into his sleeve where it was rolled up to just before his elbow. Cole caught Elly's eye and she nodded, her expression grim. The man already had sepsis setting in. The infection had reached his blood stream. It wasn't necessarily fatal, but in this setting, the prognosis would be guarded, at best.

What would happen if Mike died while they were helping him? Would they be blamed? Doubts about the wisdom of offering care raced through his mind. Should he send them packing? Then Jenna probed, gently, the area around the cut, and Mike hissed, swearing. Immediately, he apologized for the crude language. *Damn it.* Why did Mike have to seem like such a nice guy? It would be a lot easier to kick him off the island if he was an ass. As he wavered, Jenna caught his eye.

"Cole, could you go fill that big bowl with snow? And then set the pan from the stove into it to cool off the water? It's already been boiled, but it's too hot to use."

He completed the task as Jenna cut strips of tape, hanging them from the edge of the table where she could grab them easily. "While the water cools, I want to explain what's going on and how I'm going to help, okay?"

"Yes, ma'am."

There was a faint knock on the door. Cole stepped over, opening it. Steve stood on the porch with a large box in his hands. "Thanks. I couldn't get the door handle."

"No problem. Set it over there on the counter." The kitchen was tiny, but a short counter provided a little workspace. He watched, curious, as Steve unloaded the box. A can of beets, another of asparagus, a hunk of meat, presumably venison since that is what he said the others were cooking, a can of mixed fruit and a can, of all things, brown bread.

Cole had only eaten it once and it had been years ago. He couldn't even remember where he was, but thought his uncle had served it. His uncle hadn't been much of a cook and a lot of his meals had come from cans, but Cole remembered the bread as being delicious with a rich, slightly sweet taste. Steve took a can opener from the box and raised an eyebrow at Cole then nodded to the can, apparently noticing Cole's interest. "You're welcome to have a slice. It's the least I can do."

Even as his mouth watered at the idea of a thick slice of brown bread, Cole shook his head. "I appreciate the offer, but I ate already." There wasn't enough for everyone and he wouldn't eat something if they couldn't all get a piece.

"Go on. I have another can in here. You can take that one if you want."

"Are you sure?"

"Yeah. We have some stores of food and I'm sure we'll find more as we travel south."

Cole nodded and took the can. "Thank you. I'm sure everyone will be happy to have a slice." If they cut it thin, there should be enough for everyone, or they could save it for the little ones as a treat.

Mike grunted in pain and Steve glanced at him, his forehead creased. "You okay?"

Between clenched teeth, Mike managed a yes. In an effort to take

Steve's mind off his friend, Cole asked, "Do you have a specific destination in mind?"

Steve shrugged. "Not really. Some place warm. I don't want to have to spend another winter in Wisconsin if I can help it. Don't get me wrong—I love snow and cold weather—or I did—but it's not quite the same without central heat."

Cole chuckled. "True. It's been quite a challenge."

"Why don't you guys head south with us?" Steve opened the can of beans and dumped them in a pot he'd dug out of the cabinet. He started slicing the venison, adding pieces to the baked beans. It was a novel combination to Cole, but he supposed it would almost act as a barbecue sauce for the meat.

Cole took the pot from Steve and made room for it on the stove, setting the boiled water Jenna had used aside. "We're thinking of heading west."

"Yeah, I guess it's warmer there, too. What about going to the coast?" Steve checked the oven door. The small stove had been jerry-rigged out of a barrel and the oven, such as it was, had a rack. He put the brown bread, whole and wearing indentations from the can, into the oven to heat.

"Maybe eventually, but we haven't decided where we'll settle yet." He was mulling the idea of Las Vegas after Hunter had mentioned it earlier tonight, but they hadn't had a chance to discuss it in depth.

"The coast would be nice. Plenty of food, I would think."

"Yes, you're probably right." But Cole worried about the mountains. Fuel could be an issue. Running out of it at the top of a mountain would be disastrous. Not to mention, who knew if the roads were even passable? The chances were good that vehicles would be blocking most of them. It was one thing to drive off-road on the relatively flat terrain of Wisconsin, but another to drive around a pile-up on a mountain pass.

"If not the coast, then where?" Steve opened a drawer and found a spoon and made a face as he stirred the chopped bits of asparagus. "I love the fresh stuff, but I guess I can't be too picky, can I?" He shook his head and shuddered. Even so, he put them in a tiny pot Cole had found in the back of the cupboard.

Elly left Jenna's side and moved to the sink. She looked around, her hands up like a just scrubbed surgeon, and guessing she wanted to wash her hands, he plucked the pan with the still warm remains of the snow he'd melted for Jenna, and poured it into a wide bowl. "Here."

"Thanks."

Returning his attention to the other man, Cole said, "To answer your question, Steve, we haven't decided where we're going yet. We still have time. Spring is still at least six weeks away."

"You gotta make a plan, man. Build up your supplies."

Elly leaned back against the counter beside Cole, drying her hands on a dish towel. "We have some ideas but we're still discussing them."

Cole appreciated that she didn't give up where they might go. It wasn't as if it was some huge secret, but if Hunter was right about the power still running, he didn't want to have to fight Steve's group for the use of it. Of course, that was supposing some other people hadn't already claimed possession of the dam. He imagined survivors would already have it figured out.

Elly yawned and pushed away from the counter. "I'm heading back to the house. Wake me up if I'm asleep when you get back." She ran her hand down his arm and he gave her a smile.

"I will." It seemed like a week had passed since he last had a chance to really speak with her, not just a couple of days. "I'm going to check in on Joe before I head to the house."

"I can do that. I checked on him just before you got back and had brought him some stew. He said he was feeling a little better. Chances are, he's sound asleep." She waved at Jenna, nodded to the other men, and left.

Steve's eyes slid from Elly to Cole. "Feeling better? You got a sick person here?"

"Regular old seasonal flu, not Sympatico Syndrome." Cole didn't know why he was trying to reassure the guy. Letting him think they might be infectious would guarantee their speedy departure from the island.

Cole watched Jenna re-bandage Mike's hand, leaving a small wick in the wound— to drain—she said. The beans and venison concoction was starting to smell good, and Cole filed away the recipe, such as it was, for some future meal.

"Okay. I've done as much as I can do." Jenna took a bowl of dirty water and emptied it outside. "Now, we just have to wait and see." She had rigged up an I.V. using supplies they had found at a veterinarian's office. A plastic bag of fluid hung from a coat tree beside Steve. "I mixed up the antibiotics and hung them. He'll have to keep the I.V. in for a few days so I can give him several more doses, but we can cap the I.V. in between."

Steve moved over to his friend and put a hand on his shoulder. "How are ya doing, bud?"

"Like I never want to do that again." Mike's cheeks, above his beard, had a waxy pale sheen, dotted with sweat. He made a weak attempt to smile. Cole was glad he still wore his mask even though he was almost certain that Mike's condition wasn't contagious.

"Steve, come on over." Jenna waved her hand as she moved back to Mike's side. "I'm going to show you how to cap this. You just have to keep an eye on the bag. When it's empty, do this." She showed him how to disconnect the tubing and put a small cap on the part still in Mike's arm. "Got it?"

"Yeah, I guess—but I thought you would take care of that."

Jenna shook her head. "This isn't a hospital. Maybe one day we'll have a clinic set up again, but for now, people are going to have to do a lot of things for themselves and each other. I'll be by early in the morning to check on him and give him another dose."

"So I have to stay up and watch the bag? When do I get to sleep?"

"Don't worry about it, Steve. I can probably do it myself." Mike stood and moved the coat tree to rest at the end of the sofa. It was still close enough to kitchen table that he was able to sit on that side of the table if he wanted to eat there.

"That's not the point. She's the nurse, not you and not me." Steve crossed his arms. "I gave you the can of bread—"

Cole stepped between his sister-in-law and Steve. "Look, Jenna did this as a favor. She's not obligated to do anything else. As for the bread, we just used valuable supplies on your friend. I think we're more than even. You are free to leave any time you want if you don't like this arrangement."

"I can handle this myself, Cole." Jenna gathered her supplies, sending a glare at Steve, then Cole.

"I know you can but you shouldn't have to."

Steve sighed and ran a hand through his hair. "Okay, fine. I guess I'm not used to how things are yet. I had appendicitis and was treated like a prince in the hospital. The nurses were kind and thoughtful." He glanced at Jenna.

Jenna donned her jacket and mittens, shaking her head. Ignoring Steve, she addressed Mike. "Don't worry. I'll check on you tomorrow. If you feel that something's wrong, it's okay to send for me."

Mike nodded. "Thank you, ma'am."

Steve opened his mouth as if he was about to protest again, but Cole locked eyes with him and the other man blinked. "Uh, yeah. Thank you, Jenna, uh … ma'am."

Cole grabbed the can of bread and followed Jenna back to the house.

Chapter Two

"HUNTER, could you see if your dad is awake? If he is, tell him break-fast is ready." Elly drained the boiled potatoes, catching the water in another bowl and letting the potatoes sit while she stirred a bit of short-ening and flour together in the cast iron pan she had previously rehy-drated beef jerky in. The roux picked up bits of brown from the jerky and when it was bubbling, she added the water she'd drained from the jerky along with a little bit of the potato water. A generous sprinkle of pepper created a gravy that wasn't half-bad, if she did say so herself.

Hunter returned after a few seconds. "He's still sleeping. Should I wake him?"

Elly shook her head. "No, I'll set some aside for him. He was exhausted last night." She doubted thirty seconds had passed from the time Cole's head hit the pillow and he fell into a deep sleep.

"Yeah, I know. It was bad enough with the snow and hauling the deer, but those guys showing up didn't help anything." Hunter took a stack of plates and a pile of silverware out and set them on one end of the counter. They usually ate buffet style because the table wasn't large enough for them all to sit around at once. Every meal, a few people had to move to a card table set up in the living room.

"It sure didn't. I'm not too thrilled about them staying here, but the injured guy, Mike, seemed nice enough. I still haven't decided about Steve." Elly opened two large cans of pears. The kids loved the fruit and even though they were running low, she couldn't deny them the treat. "Where are the little ones?"

"Jake and Piper are making sure they wash-up and get dressed. They seemed like they were totally back to normal." Hunter shook his head, grinning. "A few days ago, they looked on death's door, now they're goofing off. Jake was even getting a little impatient with Lucas."

Elly chuckled. "It takes a lot to get him riled, but I'm happy to hear they're feeling better. They had me really worried." She put a spoon in the bowl of pears. "And speaking of worried—how's Sophie?" She was almost afraid to ask. The young woman had been spotting for days now. Jenna said she hadn't lost the baby yet, but it was the 'yet' on the end of her sentence that worried Elly.

Hunter sighed, but smiled. "She said the cramps stopped and so far this morning, she wasn't spotting."

"Is she coming to breakfast or are you taking her a plate?" Jenna had recommended as much rest as possible for Sophie while she recovered from the same flu virus practically the whole group had caught.

"No, she was almost dressed and sent me ahead. She's starving." He laughed. "We better get a plate set aside for my dad now before she fills hers up."

"Hey, I'm eating for two!" Sophie came from the hallway, her hand resting on her slightly rounded belly.

Hunter laughed and pulled out a chair for her. "That is the absolute best sentence I've ever heard in my life. Have a seat. I'll get you a plate."

Jenna entered the house just as Elly put the bowls of potatoes and gravy on the counter. "How's Mike's hand this morning?"

"A bit better. His fever is down, and he said his hand didn't hurt as much. The antibiotic upset his stomach a little though." Jenna took a plate. "Is it okay if I start? I'm famished."

"Sure, go ahead and eat while it's hot. The others are on their way." Elly scooped a generous helping of potatoes and ladled gravy over it, setting the plate on the back of the stove to stay warm for

Cole. They were out of foil but she upended a bowl over it like a dome. "I better take a plate to Joe too."

Jenna shook her head. "It's okay. He said he was going to come over to eat. I popped in to check on him on my way back to the house."

The rest of the group—excluding Cole—ate in the kitchen while Piper, Jake and Joe opted to eat in the living room. Speculation about the two men down at the other end of the row of cabins dominated the conversation.

"I don't trust them." Sean stabbed a potato, forking it into his mouth with a shake of his head.

Elly didn't comment, but she shared Sean's sentiment, if only because of Steve's erratic behavior last night. One second calm and friendly, the next, dark and suspicious. Cole had fallen asleep before she could discuss it with him and so until she had, she kept her opinion to herself.

Jenna shrugged and turned her fork to saw a potato in half. "They were friendlier today. Steve even offered me a plate of some kind of canned hash. I have to admit, it didn't smell half-bad."

"You didn't take it?" Elly scooped a spoonful of pear juice out of a small dish beside her plate. The adults all had one piece of the fruit and served Lucas and Zoë two pieces each. Their earlier antics had subsided as they ate. Elly noticed that they ate with a singular focus unusual in kids—at least from what she remembered from before the virus.

"I thought about it." Jenna chuckled. "But, it wasn't a very big can of hash to split three ways, and Mike needs to eat so he can heal quickly."

Sean shook his head. "You're helping them for free. The least you could do is take a meal."

"Sean, I wasn't expecting payment. I helped because that's what I do." Jenna slanted her husband a glance. Elly looked away, uncomfortable with their more and more frequent arguments.

After eating the last bite of her pear, she tilted the bowl and drained every last drop of juice. She would have scorned canned pears a year ago, but now they tasted like sweet nectar from the gods. While Sean had sounded harsh, Elly found herself once again agreeing with Cole's brother. "You know, Jenna, I understand your altruism, but Sean has a point. You have a valuable skill. In the coming days, you could barter it for things we need. It would be a good idea for all of us to learn skills that can be used as a form of currency if we meet more people."

Hunter nodded. "That's a good idea, Elly. I don't know what I can offer but I'll think of something."

"I know about foraging in the wild, but only around here. Cole mentioned heading out to Nevada. Does anyone know anything about growing food out there?"

Sophie looked at Jenna, who was also basically the chief gardener.

"I don't, but I guess I can learn." Jenna looked uncertain, her brow furrowed as she caught Elly's eye. "Has Cole thought this through?"

Surprised to be asked as if she knew Cole's every thought, Elly threw her hands up and shrugged. "It only came up for the first time last night. I don't think Cole has decided anything yet."

"Who died and put him in charge?" Sean grumbled as he rose and put his plate in a bin of hot, soapy water Hunter had prepared before the meal. He turned. "Dinner was good, Elly. Thanks." Then he stalked from the room.

Stunned at the anger in Sean's initial outburst, Elly could only nod at his compliment, but he had already turned his back and she doubted he'd seen it. Cole and Sean always had a bit of a prickly relationship and it puzzled her. She had no doubt Sean would give up his life for his brother without hesitation, and Cole would do the same. It was the small stuff that drove a wedge between them—little things such as when to hunt, what project was the best use of their time and even what would be the priority on any particular day. It all came down to power. Cole had it and Sean didn't.

It wasn't that Cole had ever claimed to be in charge—he just naturally fell into the role. If Sean wanted to be the leader, then he needed to start acting like one. That's all there was to it.

HUNTER WASHED the dishes after breakfast and set them in a rack to dry. Everyone had gone off to work on various tasks. Elly had taken the kids into the living room to give them some lessons in reading and math. He chuckled as he remembered Lucas's grumbling, but Zoë had been eager. She had gone to preschool, but not a real school. Of course, that would probably never happen now.

Jake took off to shovel paths to the other cabins and to the animals and Piper had joined him. They were also going to clean pens the best they could. Straw was running low for bedding, but feed was a bigger concern. His dad had brought some back with him so at least there was enough for a few more days. They would have to find some more soon or they would have to ration the little left. At least the horses were good at pawing through the snow, but it was so deep, even that has become difficult for them. He hoped they were getting enough to eat.

The interior of the island had a few clearings and he considered taking all the animals there for a few hours of foraging. He and Jake could take a few shovels and clear some of the snow away to allow the horses, goats, and chickens to get to the dead grass and weeds beneath it. With no fences Buddy would be in heaven herding the goats. He must have had some training before Hunter had found him or else he was just a natural, because when the goats were out, Buddy's demeanor changed. He was suddenly a working dog, alert and watchful, nipping any goat that strayed beyond his perceived boundaries.

With the dishes done, Hunter found Sophie in one of the storage cabins. She had insisted she was tired of lying around in bed, and was going to go through the bolts of fabric he and Cole had gathered. She wanted to cut and sew diapers. That was one item they had not scavenged, although he was pretty sure they could find some warehouse and get a lifetime supply of disposables—but it would be good to have some cloth diapers on hand too, just in case.

"Hey, Soph, do you need a hand?"

She turned from looking at a bolt of soft, pink flannel, her eyes shining. "Look at this! Isn't it pretty? Feel it." She stepped towards him, bolt extended. He pulled off his glove and dutifully touched the cloth.

It was soft, he'd give her that, but was she implying the baby was a girl? Did women know these things? He didn't care if the baby was a boy or a girl, but maybe Sophie wanted a girl deep down. Before he voiced any opinion, she turned and found a satiny soft bolt of sky blue material. "And this one. I want to make a blanket but can't decide which to use."

Out of his element, Hunter shrugged. "Use both." What difference did it make? The baby wouldn't care.

Sophie gave him a wide smile. "You're a genius, Hunter. I can make the blanket out of the flannel and use the blue stuff for the trim."

He wouldn't turn down a compliment and grinned. "That's what I was thinking…about the blanket I mean, not that I'm a genius."

"Here, take these two. I'm going to grab a few more things." She handed him the bolts, and turned to add a package of needles, threads, scissors, a thing that looked like a bracelet but with a cushion on it, and box of pins, putting those items into a basket slung over her arm.

After leaving her to sew, bored, Hunter put the dishes he'd washed earlier away in the cupboards. Free time, once something used to watch videos on Youtube, or to click away on social media, now made him restless. He couldn't just sit around. In the other room, Elly was giving Zoë basic reading instruction while it sounded like Lucas was helping his little sister.

Sean and Joe had gone to the storage cabin to check out some of the parts Hunter had brought back in the fall. Sean thought some of them would turn out useful in some way. Hunter was going to join them soon, but he wanted to speak to his dad first.

As he put the last dish away, he heard the door to his dad's room open. After a brief stop in the bathroom, his dad appeared in the doorway of the kitchen.

"What time is it?" He yawned and rubbed the back of his neck.

Hunter glanced at the clock on the wall. "Just after ten."

"What? Half the day is gone! I have to go see how Steve and Mike are doing. And go get the deer I stashed, and—"

"Relax, Dad. We can drive over tomorrow to get the deer. We have fish for dinner tonight. And Jenna checked on the guys. They're fine."

Twisting at the waist, his dad sighed. "I suppose we can wait until tomorrow then."

"Is your back bothering you?" It had looked like his dad was trying to work a kink out.

"Eh, just a little sore. Every muscle in my body aches, but I'm fine." His brow knit. "What about Joe?"

"He's better too." Hunter hedged on this. While the older man had said he was feeling better and had shown up to breakfast, he hadn't looked well to Hunter. He was gaunt and had coughed a lot. "He even ate here this morning."

"Excellent. And Sophie?"

"Stir crazy. She snuck over to the supply cabin and got material." Hunter grinned. "She's going to sew baby stuff today."

That comment elicited a grin and chuckle. "Oh yeah? Wow. I still can't believe I'm going to be a grandpa soon."

His dad appeared fit and healthy, not at all like a grandpa except for the touch of gray in his dark hair. Before, he'd always gone to the gym and had been in good shape, but now, the months of hard work and lack of junk food had benefitted them all and his dad was no exception. He was probably as fit as he'd ever been in his life.

Hunter wiped the small counter beside the stove, cleaning up a few drops of gravy. "Yeah, I'm still a little freaked out I'm going to be a dad." Just saying the words aloud made his heart pound. He shook off the trepidation. "Are you hungry? Elly set aside a plate for you. It's staying warm on the back of the stove."

"Starving." He moved over to the stove and took the plate, releasing it immediately with a faint curse. "Damn. It's hot."

"Here." Hunter whipped the dishtowel from his shoulder and held it out to his dad. "Want some tea?"

Carefully carrying the plate, his dad sat at the table. "Sure. Hey, could you hand me a fork?"

Hunter handed him the fork and poured hot water into a cup, digging out the least used looking tea bag and dunked it in the water. "Sorry. It looks pretty weak, but Jenna said there's some dried mint we can add to it."

"No, save it for later. This is fine." He took a bite of the potatoes. "Mmm… it sort of tastes like hash."

"Yep." Hunter sat opposite his dad. "Hey, so tell me about your hunting trip. Anything exciting happen?"

Shrugging as he swallowed, his dad took a sip of the tea and said, "Other than the actual hunt, not really. Didn't see anyone other than the group that Steve and Mike were with. Why?"

"Oh, no reason. Just wondered if you had seen something. It sounds like you covered territory we hadn't yet."

"I did. I was further southwest than we've been, but other than an empty barn, I didn't see much except snow. A *lot* of snow." He chuckled. "I spent the night in the barn, found the feed and then came back here. But that horse of yours saved my butt. I don't think I'd have found the barn without Red." He stirred the tea and took a sip.

"Yeah?" Hunter smiled. "He's a great horse."

"Anyway, other than almost getting lost, it was pretty uneventful." He scooped up a forkful of potatoes and stared at it for a moment as though lost in thought before eating it. After he swallowed, he went on, "I think the worst thing was how dark everything was. Being on the island, we expect it, but for some reason, I didn't count on it being so dark on the mainland. I still expected to see the orange glow in the sky from streetlights, or the beam of a car's headlights coming down a road. I want to say it was unnatural, but actually I guess it was completely natural like it hasn't been for a couple hundred years."

Hunter nodded, his throat tightening when he thought of the baby. What kind of life would his child have? What if having a baby was a huge mistake? He cleared his throat and scratched at a ragged cuticle on his thumb. "Uh, Dad, do you think it's a bad idea to have a kid now? This baby won't know anything of the world before."

His dad scraped his fork over his plate, getting the last mouthful and ate it before he replied, "I think this baby will do just fine in this new world. You'll be a great father and Sophie will be a fantastic mother, so there's no worry there."

Hunter bit his lip to hide his pleasure at the comment. "Sophie's super excited. With her own family gone…I don't know…she just wants this baby so badly." He did too, but he was almost afraid to think it, let alone say it. It was as if saying it aloud would curse the precarious pregnancy.

"And she's okay now?"

"Jenna thinks so, and she's nearing four months along. Jenna said the due date would be around the beginning of July."

"That's a good time of year." His dad sipped his tea. "Sophie deserves to have some happiness after all she's been through." He drained the cup and stood, taking his plate to the sink, and washed it, setting it in the rack to dry. "You and I...we've been lucky. We've been spared most of the devastation. If only Trent..." His dad trailed off and glanced out the window across the flat expanse of ice as far as the eye could see on this side of the house.

He knew his dad still blamed himself for Trent's death even though there was nothing he could have done to prevent it—not without being psychic. Hunter sought to change the subject. "I guess I just think the baby will miss everything I took for granted, like cell-phones and microwaves, and..." He tried to think of something else that he really missed. If he was honest, he liked the simplicity of this new life and he found he enjoyed the physicality of it. When something needed to be done, there wasn't some service to call or machine to do it.

His dad cut into his thoughts. "He or she will probably do better than any of us dealing with this new world. It won't be new to them. It'll just be normal—it'll be all they've ever known. Besides, what's the point of surviving the virus if we don't have children?"

Hunter thought on that. His dad was right. "Yeah. I guess. It would be really weird to live in a world without children." He envisioned growing old and being one of the very last people alive on the face of the Earth, and shivered. The loneliness of the scenario was too horrible to think about and he rejected it. His father was definitely right. They needed children. All of them did.

Chapter Three

COLE DROVE across the ice with Hunter beside him in the SUV. With the deer stashed in a garage on the mainland and no need to go beyond the town there was no reason not to take the car except it used some gas, but he'd trade a little gasoline for the chance to get the short trip done in a matter of an hour or so. He'd had enough of traipsing around in the snow and the warmth of the SUV felt like a luxury. He shook off the guilt of using precious fuel and reasoned there were still untapped potential sources nearby.

He was certain there were vehicles in garages and if they could get into a gas pump at a gas station, they might find a bonanza. Sean had mentioned using a generator to get a pump going, but there needed to be some kind of switch, but he was confident he could put one in if he had the switch available.

His main worry was whether there would even be gasoline in the storage tanks at gas stations. He remembered everyone filled up their tanks in the last few days when panic set in. Lines for fuel had wound around blocks, it wouldn't come as a surprise if many stations had run out of gas. The virus hit so hard and so fast most of the suppliers would have also succumbed to the virus. Hell, there had been stations where customers had died with the pump in their hands.

His mind wandered as he drove over the ice, scanning ahead to find the best place to leave the lake and drive onto shore. What would be fantastic would be finding a tanker truck full of gas. It would be like hitting the motherlode. If they found one, they would have plenty of gasoline to take them wherever they wanted to go. He made a mental note to keep an eye out for one.

None of them knew how to drive a semi-truck but they could worry about that if and when they found one. Of course, these days it was mostly a matter of just getting it going—there was no worry about rules of the road since traffic was a thing of the past. But, all of that was a job for another day. For now, the SUV had enough gasoline for a few trips back and forth from the island to the mainland. In a few weeks they'd have to drive the car back over and store it onshore when the weather warmed.

"After we get the deer, I want to drop by the house where Steve and Mike's friends are staying and give them an update. It should be easy to find. Steve said he plowed a route there." Cole gritted his teeth when the vehicle hit what must have been a chunk of ice beneath the snow. The path Steve had plowed was only a faint outline with the way the wind had blown. It was still better than the surrounding ice though, so he took the path straight onshore a little farther north than they usually went. The docks were farther south and so that was the spot they had grown used to entering the town.

Cole scanned the houses, recognizing a pale blue home as being one that marked the edge of town with the houses spaced farther apart. Lucas and Zoë's was a block south. He supposed they should stop and check if their dad ever came back. He didn't hold out hope, but they had promised the kids they would check regularly. The last time had been before Christmas, so Cole made a mental note to stop on the way back to the island.

Even though he was coming from slightly north of where he left the deer, he had no trouble locating the home. It seemed odd that with the world so different now, that finding an address was still just a matter of following the streets and house numbers. He supposed that would change in the coming years until some new rendition of a mail service started up again.

"Wow, Dad. He's a beauty!" Hunter held the rack of antlers. "We'll get a lot of meat from him."

"I sure hope so." The buck was frozen solid, which was a good thing as far as the meat was concerned, but they had to tie him to the rack on top of the SUV, one leg sticking up at an odd angle.

Hunter prowled the garage and found a few items they could use, mostly tools, but also a hose. "We can always use more hose for the garden." He tossed it in the back of the SUV.

Cole nodded, and approached the door from the garage into the house. He'd wanted to explore it when he'd left the deer but there was no time. They'd taken to marking an X on houses that they had checked already, usually leaving the mark on the front door. Hunter had run around to the front and reported no X, so they donned masks, and checked their weapons. Cole had a handgun and a rifle; Hunter just his pistol. They hadn't heard a thing since entering the garage, but they were taking no chances.

Hunter had found a crowbar hanging on a hook in the garage—another sign of the low likelihood of anyone being around. Survivors wouldn't have left a tool for breaking and entering so readily available. While his son pried the door open, Cole scanned the garage, noting a twenty-pound bag of kitty litter. He made a note to take it with them thinking it could come in useful if they got stuck in a ditch somewhere.

As the door opened, Hunter recoiled, turning away as he coughed and wiped the back of his hand across his eyes.

"What is it? Dead bodies?" Cole hated finding corpses but he was becoming used to it. At this point, the presence of one didn't automatically make a site a no-go. Most would be decomposed now and what was left, frozen.

Hunter shook his head. "No. Worse. It smells like a hundred cats pissed in here!"

Cole moved forward as Hunter grabbed a clean lungful of air in the garage. Prepared for the stench, he still blinked hard as the ammonia from what reeked like giant litter box assaulted his eyes, making them burn. Whatever was in the house was ruined by the stench of cat urine. Just as he turned to leave, a pitiful mewl caught his ear. Could a cat be living inside? There was no way one would have survived this long. Feeling silly, nonetheless, he called out a soft, "Here, kitty!"

"You heard a cat?"

"Maybe. I heard *something.*"

They listened for a moment. Nothing. But it wouldn't hurt to have a quick look around. The odor wouldn't kill them.

With Hunter close behind, Cole moved forward into the home, surprised to find everything neat and tidy except for the smell. The kitchen counters had a thick layer of grime, but unlike many of the other homes he'd been in, only a scattering of rodent droppings. Most of the other homes they had been in had been a mess.

With so much food available to mice and rats, the population of both rodents had exploded since the virus. It had been one advantage to being on the island. While mice had hitched rides to the island over the years in boxes or what have you, what they had was just a routine infestation. Occasional traps had taken care of most of them.

The mainland was a different story. The combination of dead bodies to feed on, unprotected cabinets, and pantries full of boxes and bags of food had allowed the rodents free rein. But here, it was different.

His hopes rose and he opened a cupboard. The top shelf held boxes of cereal, but all three had been opened at some point. He looked at them more closely— from the way the tops were tucked closed they had to have been opened before the virus. However, the bottom shelf held large plastic canisters of flour, sugar, and rice. He opened the canisters, alert for signs of contamination, then grinned. They looked pristine. What he found wasn't something that would last them more than a week or so, but he would never pass on padding their meager supplies. He hefted the flour canister and guessed it held at least five pounds. He did the same with the others.

The occupants of the house must have tried to stock up to some extent because all of the containers were full with about five pounds of white sugar, three one pound bags of brown sugar, and the last canister held five pounds of brown rice in bags. All were unopened and stuffed in the canister. As a bonus, he spotted a large bottle of molasses, one of corn syrup, and the best of all, a large jar of honey. These people really must have had a sweet tooth, and he imagined a dollop of honey on one of Piper's biscuits. His mouth watered as he set his finds on the counter.

Before taking anything from the shelves, he grimaced at the nasty condition of the countertop, unwilling to set good food onto a dirty counter. He checked under the sink, and sure enough, there was a spray bottle of disinfectant. He gave the counters a few squeezes, the orange scent filtering through his mask but not quite eliminating the urine stench.

A roll of paper towels still hung on a holder attached to the cabinet beside the sink and he reached for it without thinking. Until he *did* think. He thought about the person who put the roll on the wooden dowel and set it back on the brackets. He could almost feel his or her presence, imagining them hanging a roll of paper towels, making sure the roll spooled from the bottom, not over the top. It was such a mundane action and yet someone had put the roll up months ago probably with no inkling it would be the last one they would ever hang. His throat tightened for a few seconds before he shook off the melancholy thoughts. He ripped off a wad of towels and wiped the countertop.

"Hey, Dad—*cans*!" Hunter carried an armload of canned food over to Cole's clean counter. "Look." He tapped the tops of the cans one by one, reading the labels with each tap. "Beans, pumpkin, tuna, salmon, and even cherry pie filling!"

There were more but Hunter didn't recite all of the contents. He dashed back to the pantry, returning with a dozen more cans. Tuna, baked beans—large cans—and, Cole peered at three of the cans. *Butter*? He didn't even know butter came in a can. He added butter to his imaginary honey-topped biscuit. Now Cole was certain that the owners had tried to stock for at least a short time. Perhaps they had hoped to survive for a few weeks, praying the virus would have run its course by then.

"And the piece de resistance…" With a flourish Hunter set two large tins down, their teardrop shape instantly recognizable. "Ham!"

Cole laughed. "Well done." His own finds were boring in comparison. "I found flour, sugar, and rice." He opened the cabinet beside the one with the canisters and found an array of baking goods. These sort of evened the score, if they were keeping score. He slapped the back of his hand against Hunter's shoulder as his son blew dust off the tops of the cans. He pointed to the bottles in the cabinet. "Check it out."

There were a fair number of little brown bottles of various extracts and flavorings, and a large bottle of vanilla. Piper would be thrilled. He added a can of baking powder, another of cornstarch, and large box of baking soda to his collection on the countertop. They'd have to start moving these out to the SUV or he'd have to clean another countertop.

"Cool. There are more cans, too. I think I saw soups and chicken stock. They haven't even expired yet."

Cole threw his hands up in mock surrender. "Okay, I give up. You win."

Hunter's eyes danced above the edge of his mask. "I didn't know it was a competition, but if it is, then you win hands down because you picked this house to stash your buck."

"True."

The day was proving fruitful as they carried their finds out to the SUV. There were no signs of the homeowners, but Cole poked his head into an office off the kitchen dining area and noted the diploma on the wall from a medical school. Another was for physical therapy. So, the couple who had lived here had worked in healthcare—that would have put them on the front lines. Now the minor stockpiling made sense—they had an inside look at what was happening, but it also explained why the owners weren't here to use their supplies. They had probably succumbed in the first wave.

Sorrow pressed against the back of Cole's throat again. He had to *stop* doing this. Stop trying to piece together victims' last moments and what they had been like. It would drive him slowly insane if he let it. Every time he tried to fall back on his training and consider the victims casualties—statistics—he was confronted with evidence that real people with real lives were gone. And right now, he was faced with the evidence from this home when his eye landed on a photo perched on the desk of a smiling, middle-aged couple. Other pictures around it included small children. From the look of the images, some were probably their own children and the newer images, grandchildren. Cole shut the door, wincing when it slammed harder than he'd intended.

"Everything okay, Dad?" Hunter poked his head out of the pantry, where he continued to rummage through rodent damaged boxes of pasta, cake mixes, and other items.

"Yeah. Just expected the hinges to be rusty or something, I guess, and pulled harder than I meant to."

Hunter tossed aside a can of cat food then seemed to think better of it. "Buddy might like this." He reached into the cabinet and found a dozen more cans.

"I'm going to head upstairs and see if there's anything useful up there—there could be some medications in the bathroom or something." Middle-aged folks might have had a lot of medication on hand for ailments. At least, he hoped they had.

He took the stack of clean sheets in the linen cabinet. Since they had plenty of room in the vehicle, he wasn't averse to taking items that weren't necessarily important for survival, but these sheets were in great condition and it would allow them to tear some of the ragged sheets that had been on the island when they arrived, into bandage strips, or cut them down for crib sheets. He grinned at the thought.

After ransacking the medicine cabinet of the usual assortment of pain meds, left over antibiotics, sleeping aids, and ointments for a variety of skin conditions—all tossed into a pillowcase he'd pillaged from the linen cabinet, he turned to look in the bedrooms when he heard it.

This time there was no mistaking the noise. It was the sound of a cat, or possibly a young kitten judging from the weak sound. He set the pillowcase and other linens on a hutch at the top of the stairs and headed towards the meow. It seemed to come from one of the bedrooms, and from the look of it, the main bedroom.

The bed was unmade, but not torn apart. It looked as if it had been slept in just the night before, and Cole stilled. Was someone still living here? Were they stealing food from other survivors? But he hadn't seen any other signs of life and the deer hadn't been disturbed since he left it there last night. This couple was never coming home again. If they could have, they would have been here. They must have been out, perhaps at work or even out getting more groceries, when the virus had hit them. They even could have been caught in one of the many pileups on the highways. The bedroom looked so eerie though —like he had stepped into a time warp from the year before.

The covers of the bed were tossed back on each side and one of the pillows was still hollowed out in the middle. The other pillow had a matted ring of fur. There was so much, at first he thought it as a dead animal, but then he realized it was only fur that had been shed.

The moment it sunk in, he put the pieces together. A cat must have lived in here since the virus. There was no other explanation for the sound and for the ring of fur. As neat as this home was, there was no way the owners would have slept on a pillowcase coated in cat fur.

"Hey, Dad! Look what I found!"

There was a note of excitement in Hunter's voice. As he turned to head back downstairs, he caught the twitch of an orange colored tail beneath the end of the bed. He got on his hands and knees and spotted a dangerously thin orange tabby.

He held out a hand but the cat hissed and backed further under the bed. Cole straightened and sighed. The last thing he wanted to do was scare the poor thing, but he couldn't leave the animal here to starve.

Hunter entered the doorway, his arms crossed over his abdomen. "Look! I found a kitten!"

Cole did a double take. Two of them? He glanced at the little head that peeked over Hunter's forearm. A scrawny gray cat with green eyes stared back at him. "I think I found his friend under the bed."

"No way! Really?" Hunter started to enter, but Cole waved him back.

"Wait. This one is scared. Can you grab one of those cans of cat food and bring it up here? I might be able to lure it out."

It took Hunter only a minute to return, two cans in hand. "One for your cat and one for mine." Already he was claiming them. Cole chuckled as he popped the top off a can of salmon, or rather, delicate salmon pate in natural juices. He shook his head at the absurdly fancy description—as if a cat cared.

As soon as the top popped, Hunter's cat meowed and squirmed to get down, and so Cole pulled the top off the second can and set it on the floor. Hunter let his cat down and the feline went straight to the can, gulping it down.

Cole's cat meowed plaintively but it took her a full minute to finally come from under the bed and approach Cole. He took a scoop of the food out with a couple of fingers and held it out to the cat. "Here, kitty. I won't hurt you."

The cat licked its lips and finally stretched its nose out to smell his fingers, a tiny tongue darting out to get a taste. Overcome with hunger, that was all it took before the cat was literally eating from Cole's hand.

The cats slowed them down as one of them had to stay with them in the SUV while the other loaded, but they took turns and soon, they were on their way to check on Steve's group.

"How do you suppose they survived so long?" Hunter cuddled the gray cat while the orange one lay in a makeshift container created from an open plastic bin with a light blanket over the top.

Cole grabbed his sunglasses from the holder on the roof of the car, squinting as the sun glinted off the snow. "When I went downstairs to look around, I saw what was left of a huge twenty-five pound bag of food in the only dry corner of the basement. I think they ripped into it and ate that." He remembered the frozen patches of ice on the cement floor, but not all of it was frozen—there was a little bit of water melting around the edges. Even unheated, the basement wouldn't be as cold as the outside. The ground would add some insulation. "I think the basement suffered a flood recently—probably during one of those big storms we had last fall—they must have survived on that."

"I bet they caught a few mice too."

Cole nodded. "You're probably right. I guess we can thank them for some of the items we were able to salvage today."

Hunter scratched the gray cat behind the ears and the animal appeared to love it. Their former owners must have taken excellent care of them for the cats to have survived ten months in the house on their own. "These little guys definitely have used up a few of their nine lives, that's for sure."

Chapter Four

COLE WISHED he had Google maps available or, at the very least, a paper map of the town, but with roads choked with snow, vehicles, and now, the occasional downed tree limbs, he probably wouldn't be able to follow the directions anyway. He chuckled as he imagined the voice re-directing him over and over every time he adjusted his course. Instead of Google, he had Hunter, who did his best to remember what streets they had come down.

"Dad, why don't we just follow our tracks back to the lake and pick up the tracks from Steve's plow? They had to have left a big-ass trail."

"That was my plan originally, but I got turned around going to collect the deer. I'm not sure which way the path went." Cole checked out the street names, wishing he had paid more attention to the layout of the town. They'd designated areas more by what sector of town they were in rather than names. They had explored the areas closest to the lake and knew where most of the stores were located because those were the first places they had looked for supplies in the fall but since homes usually contained bodies of the dead, they were mostly avoided except for a few that were carefully explored. He'd wanted to make sure all were unoccupied before breaking in; not just to avoid the virus, but out of respect for possible survivors.

According to Steve's directions, his group was staying at a place halfway between the highway west of town and the lake. He back-tracked to where he had followed Steve's plowed path up onto the mainland, and turned onto it. The street wasn't perfectly clear, by any means, with the plowed path winding around accidents left abandoned months ago, but it was close to appearing similar to how it would after a major blizzard when there were often cars left in ditches even in the best of times.

These glimpses of familiarity were both comforting and disturbing. He knew life would never be like it had been. That world was gone, but the glimpses allowed him to momentarily forget about their current circumstances. For some reason, that was comforting.

He followed the path around a corner onto a street that ran parallel to the river for a short way. The homes that backed up to the river were slightly bigger than the surrounding homes and it was in front of one of them that he spotted several vehicles that he vaguely recognized from the night before. More importantly, they had definitely been driven recently with snow cleared from windshields and ruts in the snow leading up to them. He pulled in behind one.

As he scanned for any danger, the orange cat nuzzled his hand, hungry for attention. Absently he scratched under its chin, and glanced at Hunter, who stroked the gray cat's head. "I guess we need to put these guys in the back for now. I don't want them dashing out when we open the doors."

Hunter nodded. Twisting, he set his cat on the floor behind him. Cole handed him the orange one, and they both exited as quickly as they could. Cole hesitated. He had his sidearm as did Hunter, but he considered grabbing the rifle too. Then he shook his head. These guys could have killed him last night and hadn't. He did fish a mask from his pocket though, and nodded at Hunter when he did the same.

They cut across the lawn to reach the front door, and Cole pressed the doorbell. Nothing happened. Duh. No power. He pulled his glove off and knocked instead. While he didn't hear anything, he had the distinct feeling that they were being watched. Just as he hadn't actually seen any of these men before, they would have only seen him bundled up, so he called out, "It's Cole. I just came to update you on your friend, Mike."

A voice came through the door. "Yo, dudes. Leave your weapons on the porch."

Hunter looked at him and mouthed, "Do we do it?"

Cole shook his head. "No." Louder, he replied to the voice, "No dice. We're only here as a favor to Steve and Mike but …" He shrugged and motioned for Hunter to head back to the car. The guy's tone hadn't sounded threatening, but they had no real reason to trust him either.

What a waste of time. They could be back to the island by now if he hadn't searched around, wasting precious gasoline, just to find these guys.

A sound from the porch made him turn, one hand on his gun. The door opened and a tall blond-haired man with a bushy beard stepped out. "Wait! Come on back. I'm sorry about what my cousin asked you to do. We want to hear about Mikey."

Cole turned but studied the man, noting his stance and demeanor then swept a gaze over the house for any signs of deception. A face parted the curtains in the living room window, the man beckoning them to come in too.

"All right. Let's talk to them, but stay alert."

The crackle of wood in the fireplace drew Cole's first gaze and he noted a pot hanging over the fire. Steam rose from it as a mouth-watering aroma greeted them. He'd had worse welcomes, but he didn't let the homey atmosphere lull him into letting his guard down. Hunter stood beside him, also appearing to ignore the food as he looked at the men sprawled on the couch, the floor, and on a mattress that must have been dragged into the room. That made sense, it being the warmest room and all.

A short, stocky guy brought in a couple of kitchen chairs and set them near the fire, gesturing to them. "Be our guest."

"Thank you, but we're not staying long." Cole looked at the blond man. "I'm Cole, this is Hunter. We just wanted to update you on one of your own. Mike was doing fine this morning when Hunter checked him, isn't that right?" He glanced at Hunter, who nodded.

The blond man tipped his mug by way of greeting. "I'm Neil. Glad to meet you, Cole. And thanks for helping out our buddy."

Cole nodded. "He seems like a good man."

Hunter's gaze held steady and his voice was firm. "Good to meet you, Neil." Cole noted how Hunter was nearly as tall as the other man. His shoulders were wider and though his beard wasn't quite as thick, not that much of it was visible with the mask stretched across Hunter's face.

A hint of pride tinged Cole's thoughts as he observed his son. Anyone looking at him for the first time would not dismiss Hunter as a young kid, and the wariness Cole noted in the other men when they looked at him was based not just on his size, but the way he carried himself. In this group of men, his son fit right in. They were all survivors. It was the first time Cole had seen him in this light. Not as his son—still a kid in his mind— but as an adult. He'd not just filled out, he'd grown up.

After being introduced to the other men, who wandered in and out of the room, the stench of unwashed bodies almost over-powering the aroma of whatever was cooking in the pot, Cole just wanted to give their update and get out of there.

"Mike's a great guy. He might look like a big oaf, but don't let his act fool you. I've worked with him for years and he's one of the best."

"… best? At what?"

Neil laughed. "Sorry. He's a machinist. His dad was one too. It's like, in his blood."

"So you're one also?"

"Sure am. Fifteen years now." Neil motioned to the stocky guy. "And this guy here, Tony, is Mike's cousin. He's a plumber. "

Tony nodded but didn't step forward to speak to them. Instead, he turned and stirred the contents of the pot on the fire. When he lifted the lid, the aroma wafted through the air, pushing out the stink from the men and whatever had been in the house before they had moved in.

Cole could have sworn he heard Hunter's stomach growl, but his son didn't say anything about the food, but said to Neil, "I saw Mike this morning, when Jenna—she's the one treating Mike's hand— checked on him. She said the redness and swelling have gone way down, and he told her he's feeling a lot better, too."

"That is so awesome to hear!" Neil grinned and waved towards the pot. "Are you guys hungry? We have plenty."

The offer was tempting, but Cole turned it down. The other men weren't wearing masks and eating with them would necessitate taking off their own. "We have to be getting back. From what I understand, the treatment for Mike will take several more days. He's getting some I.V. antibiotics." He wondered, as soon as he'd said that, if he should have offered that information. Medicine was valuable now, but Neil just nodded.

"Well, we intend on sticking around for a bit. With all of the feed corn left standing in the fields, we intend to stock up on venison before we head south."

If the weather hadn't turned when he'd gone hunting, he might have had an easier time finding deer in the corn fields. Cole wasn't thrilled that they were going to stay and hunt, but there wasn't anything he could do to stop them. "Steve will probably be out here in the next day or so—he's been helping out with Mike, but is there anything you'd like me to tell him?"

"Nah, we'll see him soon." He scooped a ladle of what appeared to be stew into a bowl. "You're missing out." He set the bowl on the table, then rummaged through a box on the floor.

"Yes, it sure looks that way, but thanks for the offer." Cole turned but paused. "So, you're heading south?"

"Yeah. Florida or Alabama. Someplace warmer and near the ocean. Wisconsin is great in the summer and fall, but too damn cold in the winter. I'll go stark raving mad if I have to deal with this cold another winter."

"People managed a hundred years ago without central heat and indoor plumbing." Cole made the comment to hear their response more than because he felt differently.

Neil chuckled. "That's true. My own great-great grandfather was a farmer back in the 1800s. He had a dozen kids, but only seven of them made it to adulthood. It kind of makes the odds of surviving here a little longer than I care to bet on."

Dipping a rag in a bucket of questionable clean water, Neil used it to wipe out another bowl he'd pulled from the box, then slopped another ladle full of stew into it. It looked as if they'd dodged a bullet in refusing the offer of stew earlier.

Continuing his story, Neil looked over his shoulder as he set the bowl on the table. "Three babies died before they were two, and the other three died from accidents—two at one time when they fell through the ice while cutting blocks to send East. I'm not sure how the other one died, but I wouldn't doubt it had something to do with this god-awful cold."

His story was a sober reminder and Cole thought of Sophie, and saw from the stricken look in Hunter's eyes that he, too, was thinking of her and the baby. "Well, we have to get going. If there's any change in Mike's status, I'll come by to tell you if Steve can't for some reason. If I don't see you again, have a safe trip."

Neil nodded, holding a spoonful of stew near his lips as he blew on it. "Thanks. If we're up this way again, we'll stop by and say hello."

Cole paused. "If we're not here, we're thinking of checking out Vegas."

Hunter shot him a look. It was a combination of why-did-you-tell-him and are we really going.

"You feel like gambling?" Neil laughed at his own joke, but it was good-natured laughter.

Shrugging, Cole explained. "Nah, not much of a gambler, but we have some ideas about—" He was going to mention the Hoover Dam but decided to keep that info to themselves. "It's a lot warmer than here. Anyway, if you find yourselves that way, ask around. Maybe we'll be there."

Neil set his spoon in the bowl and thrust his hand out. "Thanks. I'll keep it in mind. I'm not sure about the other guys though. Some have family in Florida…or they did…" He resumed eating, "But if things don't work out, maybe I'll go that way myself."

Cole motioned to Hunter and they left, the deceptively tantalizing scent of the stew clinging to him even after he was in the car. "Damn. I wish we could have stayed for lunch. But, then again—that bowl."

Hunter laughed. "Right? Nasty."

Cole laughed and removed his mask. "I can't wait for the day we'll have time and resources, and not have to take precautions before we can hang out with other people again."

Hunter plucked the gray cat off the back seat and held her on his lap. "Yeah, it sucks having to always be on guard." He sighed as he scratched the cat under the chin.

Chapter Five

"MORE MOUTHS TO FEED?" Sean jabbed a potato and pointed his fork, potato and all, at Hunter. "What was your dad thinking? We barely have enough for ourselves and now we have to give some of it to those cats?" He devoured the potato as if it was personally to blame for the arrival of the cats. The orange cat, named Pumpkin by Zoë, wound around Sean's ankles as he ate, probably hoping for a scrap of food to drop.

Hunter narrowed his eyes. "They're good mousers. You saw all the mice on the mainland. We don't want to lose a shitload of food to them once we head out on the road." He didn't normally swear when speaking to his uncle, but it slipped out, not that he really cared at this point. Sean swore a blue streak, especially when he was working on some project or another.

Sean lifted one shoulder, his jaw working a mouthful of fish. "Who said we're going out on the road for sure? Besides, even if we do, are they going to save more than they will end up eating? We already have the chickens, goats, and Buddy to give scraps to. Now we have cats too?" He devoured his last potato and looked up, sighing as he met Hunter's gaze. "Look, Hunter—I don't hate cats. Believe me, a year ago if Piper asked for a kitten, I'd have considered it, but times have changed. We don't have the luxury of keeping pets."

Hunter knew for a fact that Sean had refused to let Piper have a kitten when she was little, recalling his cousin venting to him about it a few years ago. Her dad hated cats and said they smelled and were useless, but now he was saying he'd be okay with it if the world was back to what it was? Hunter didn't buy it but held his tongue in order to keep the peace. Living in close quarters with his uncle was difficult at times, but they all had to make allowances to get along.

For Sean, they had to ignore his outspokenness. It was just the way he was. At least, that's what his dad had said. Hunter didn't agree—he thought his dad allowed his brother to ramble on because his dad still felt guilty about Trent. It was pointless to feel guilty for something that probably would have happened anyway. The only reason any of them were alive was because of his dad and Elly giving them an extra day's notice and their excellent advice on precautions to take.

When Sean looked as if he was going to try and make another point, Hunter pushed away from the table and quickly soaped and rinsed his plate. "I'm going to see if I can catch a few fish—it won't be such a waste when I can feed the guts to the cats."

Drying his hands, Hunter glanced at Sean to see if he'd noticed his sarcasm, but Sean was slipping a bit of fish to Pumpkin. Hunter hid a grin.

Before he went out on the ice, he checked with Sophie to see if she needed anything, and when she mentioned wanting to make a baby comforter, he ran down to the storage cabin and grabbed some bolts of cloth and other sewing items she'd asked for.

On his way back, he almost ran into Mike as the other man came around the corner of his cabin. Hunter hadn't seen the man except from a distance and worried that neither of them were wearing a mask.

He took a few steps back on the shoveled path, hoping the distance was enough to keep him safe. Instinctively, he held the bolt of cloth cross-wise in front of him, as though it would protect him from contamination. The snow piled on either side of the walkway prevented him from easily stepping aside. Hunter nodded. "Good morning."

Mike smiled. "Thanks. Same. It's Hunter, right? You look different without the mask." He raised his uninjured hand, encased in a thick glove and held it over his nose and mouth. Hunter relaxed. He didn't know if that was sufficient protection, but at least Mike was aware of the danger. "Sorry. I know I'm not supposed to be out but Jenna left her glasses on the table. I thought she might need them." He held up a pair of glasses.

"I think they're just readers, but thanks. I can take them back for you." He reached for the proffered glasses, noting the thick bandage on Mike's other hand.

Following Hunter's gaze, Mike tapped a finger against the back of the bandage. "It feels so much better. I think I might even be able to hold a hammer again."

At Hunter's raised eyebrow, Mike added. "I was a machinist before. I was only supposed to be on the fishing trip for the weekend before starting a big job."

Not knowing exactly what a machinist did, Hunter hadn't connected the hammer comment with his profession. "That's great— about the hammer thing and feeling better." Hunter smiled. It felt good to have some positive news for a change. "Jenna's a fantastic nurse." He remembered how bad his dad's gunshot wound had been and how Jenna had treated it. She'd said the wound wasn't too serious, but Hunter knew better. There had been a lot of blood.

"She's awesome. I owe her a lot. I mean, even before the sickness, things were dangerous, but now? I thought for sure I was a goner. I had a cousin who got blood poisoning once and ended up losing a finger because he didn't see a doctor soon enough. I could have lost my whole hand or worse."

"Glad it worked out," Hunter tipped his chin up towards the house, "but I gotta get back with this stuff before I head out fishing." He hefted the bolt a few inches and tucked it beneath his arm. Mike was friendly, but not over the top so. His behavior didn't set off any warning bells.

"Ice fishing?"

Hunter glanced at the frozen bay. What other kind of fishing was there at this time of year? Before he could reply, Mike shook his head and chuckled. "Duh. Of course. I always ask stupid questions when I'm nervous."

"Nervous? About what?" He shifted the bolt to the other arm.

Mike scratched his beard with his good hand and shrugged. "Just talking. I've never been much for chit-chat before. Give me a fishing pole, or a hunting rifle and point me towards the woods and I'm a happy camper—literally."

"Yeah." Hunter understood where Mike was coming from. School had never been a good fit for him, although he got decent grades. His dad always told him he was smart, just not applying himself but Hunter had always felt as if he never quite fit in with the other smart kids. Grades didn't mean a lot to him. He was good at sports but wasn't especially competitive. He'd rather compete against himself, and that's how he'd excelled in archery. It was just him, the bow, and the target. Hunter started to edge around Mike. "Well, it's great that you're feeling better."

Mike lifted his injured hand. "Oh yeah. Sorry to keep you. I...uh... I just wanted to ask someone if there was something I could do to help out. Just sitting in the cabin is driving me crazy."

Hunter glanced around as he tried to think of a response. What *could* Mike do to help? Joe shuffled from his cabin over to the main house, a little slower than his usual pace, but it was great to see him up and about. Jake was down in the goats' pen feeding them a mix of food scraps. He had another bucket on the ground outside of the pen and Hunter guessed it contained more scraps for the chickens. Nothing was wasted anymore.

Jake didn't need help and Joe, while he was forced to be idle from more difficult work, was tending to the hides they had accumulated since they had begun hunting in the fall. He knew how to treat them and had been teaching Hunter and Jake about it. They planned to work on them later this afternoon, which was why Hunter had to hurry if he wanted to get some fishing in now. Maybe that was something Mike could do. "You want to come fishing with me?"

Another fisherman was always welcome. It seemed they never had enough fish to put aside for later and if they really were leaving the island in the spring, having some set aside for the journey would be necessary.

"I'd love to fish." Mike lifted his bandaged hand. "I better get the okay from Ms. Jenna though."

"Oh yeah. Sure. And you should grab a mask if you have one. If not, ask Jenna. She has one she can give you."

COLE STUDIED the atlas and laid a thin sheet of paper over the map, tracing several routes to Las Vegas. He didn't want to mark up the only real roadmap he had. They might find another—probably could if they explored a library—but no sense in marking up the one he had right in front of him.

When he had the roads traced and labeled, he went through and marked the names and locations of towns along the way. He wanted to know of any places that might hold danger and be ready for it. He rubbed his chin and then leaned his head on his hand, his elbow propped on the desk he'd found at the house with the cats. At the last minute he'd tossed it in the SUV when he and Hunter had left.

It was one of the few items in the house that hadn't reeked of cat urine since it had been sitting in a room that had been closed off to the cats. While the living room was crowded already, he justified the desk because he needed a workspace where he didn't have to evacuate it several times a day in order for someone to cook.

Already he had a stack of books piled on the floor beneath the desk, with several he'd most recently consulted sitting at his elbow. Even with such a high stack, it was a drop in the bucket compared to what they needed. They were sorely lacking in information on how to perform tasks that hadn't been common for a hundred years. They had been lucky to get houses with septic tanks for sewage and the windmill running. Was leaving the island the right thing to do?

What if they left and made it to Las Vegas only to find the dam completely shut down? The weather there was arguably more brutal than a Wisconsin winter. Without irrigation, crops were unlikely to grow and no power meant no air conditioning. It wasn't a complete necessity, but it would make life a lot more bearable. At least here they would have the summer to plant and gather more food.

Cole tossed the pencil down and raked both hands through his hair, resting his head against his palms for a moment. Was having electricity really that important? Sure, it made life easier, but mankind had lived and thrived for most of history without it. Was it worth taking the risk of crossing the country just for the chance to have it?

Communication would still be compromised because telephone companies took a lot more than one person to run and he was pretty certain they weren't self-contained to one city. Perhaps they could get it up and running if they found someone with experience. And that was the root of the problem. Everything was still here. The factories, the utility companies, and the healthcare facilities—there just weren't enough people alive to keep any of it running.

Perhaps if instead of going to Las Vegas, they simply went south? That would solve the winter problem and if they salvaged solar panels along the way or once there, they could generate enough electricity for their own needs.

As their group expanded, which he expected it to do—hoped it would, as long as newcomers were healthy—they could always add more panels. But what about when the panels ran out? Could they manufacture more? He was pretty certain most of the materials were sourced from various locations hundreds if not thousands of miles apart. Hell, some probably shipped from overseas. Back before the virus, sourcing material was just a matter of calling up a company, searching on Google, and placing an order. It then arrived at a loading dock as if by magic.

Manufacturing needed more than a handful of workers too. What if they got there, the electricity still worked, but all they had were lights and air conditioning? Both were important, but how important?

Freezers and refrigeration would be huge for keeping food from spoiling. Jenna would be able to use some of the equipment at the hospital. Computers would work even if the Internet wasn't around. Cole itched to send an email to someone. Instant communication was something he missed almost more than all of the other aspects of modern living.

They had been able to deal with food and shelter, for the most part, but he'd never realized how dependent he'd been on being able to send off an email, text, or call someone at any time. He doubted many of his friends and former colleagues had survived the pandemic so there was nobody to communicate with, but he'd love to be able to establish communication with other survivors. They needed to prioritize getting hand held radios. There should be plenty of them around, but it wasn't something he'd thought of when they'd left in such a hurry.

Cole flipped the page on his notebook and wrote: TRADE across the top. He wanted to revisit the problem after he'd decided how to handle the current problem.

Flipping back to the original page, he wrote everyone's name down and their skill set. Jenna knew how to can fruits and vegetables, was their main medical resource with he and Elly the backup. Both Sean's and Joe's knowledge of building went beyond electrical components as they both were naturally good at working with their hands. Elly had some prepping skills. Joe also knew a lot about the local flora and fauna. He knew where the black walnut, hickory trees, and oak trees groves were in their area and whenever they had gone out to hunt and forage in the fall, they had brought home bags of the nuts. Some had been destroyed in the fire, but they had gathered a bit more before the heavy snows had set in. Joe had shown Piper how to leach the bitterness from the acorns and make flour. Cole was actually starting to prefer the rich, nutty flavor of the bread Piper had made with the acorn flour.

Cole glanced across the room to the bookshelf stuffed with a combination of what they had brought with them, books already at the house when they arrived, and some taken from homes they had entered. They still needed to visit a local library and gather as many books as they could about everything. They may have been plunged into the dark ages, but they weren't destined to remain there if they preserved the knowledge already accumulated.

He finished his list of skills for everyone and noted his own skills were lacking. Only Zoë and Luke had fewer. With a shake of his head, he set the paper aside. The table would be needed soon for cooking preparation.

Thinking of cooking, he wondered if the venison roast would be well-received. He'd seasoned it, doused it with a little olive oil and had let it marinate all morning. With some luck, they'd find some more olive oil but eventually, it would all be gone. Cole sighed. Hacking the roast off the frozen carcass hadn't been easy, and lately they had been using meat more as a side dish, but tonight, he wanted to celebrate.

He had a feeling that survivors would start to emerge from wherever they had hidden once a year had gone by. The virus should have run its course. Once the vectors were gone, the virus would have nowhere else to go. It didn't seem to affect other species—not like the avian flu or the swine flu. That was a plus because it meant there was no reservoir for the virus to hide. If everyone who contracted it had died, and there were no new cases, chances were, the virus would die. If only he could be certain. Cole thought of his years in epidemiology and the reliance he'd had on studies. He didn't have the luxury of others gathering data from across the globe and sending it to him. He could only speculate based on what he knew and observed personally.

There was a brief knock before Elly entered. "What are you doing?"

"Just working out a map to Las Vegas." He sat back, tossing the pencil onto the desk.

Elly crossed the room and stood behind him, leaning over to peer at the map. He tilted his head back to watch her reaction as she studied it.

"Hmmm...that would normally be a two-day drive or so, depending on if you stopped at a motel for the night. How long do you think it would take now?"

Cole rubbed the back of his neck as he calculated. "A week? But that's just a ballpark guess based on what I've seen on the roads around here and what Hunter saw on his trip to the island last summer. He said most main highways were choked with vehicles when the drivers and occupants died."

"But that was months ago, Cole. Do you think the roads are still that bad?"

"You saw Chicago, and Hunter and I have seen some of the main highways around here. They were bad then, and there hasn't been anyone around to clear things."

He felt the slight movement of her abdomen against his back as she sighed. "Do you think it's possible that a lot of people are just hiding out like us? And that we'll be able to return to some semblance of what we used to have?"

"Not here. What we need is electricity to power things and we just don't have the capacity to do that here."

"What about solar panels? Couldn't we install some? And then there's the windmill..." Her hands rested on his shoulders, lightly kneading and he closed his eyes as he answered, "Solar is great and no doubt we could use it small scale here. That's actually an alternative plan I was formulating."

Cole was loathe to sit forward and break contact with Elly's warm fingers and risk interrupting the massage, but her hands followed when he shifted. He rifled through some papers until he found the ones he wanted, tilting them to make it easier for Elly to see the diagrams he'd drawn of the house and the cabins on the island. "If we get some panels and install them on the cabin roofs this summer, along with a separate bank, we could probably get enough power to run the lights, the water pumps, the refrigerator, and especially, the freezers. We're lucky my uncle planned the resort on the southwest end of the island because even in the winter, we get a lot of sun here."

He set the papers down and tapped the rough diagram of solar panels with his finger. "If we could get those working, we would be able to store a lot more food for the winter." They were learning the skills for preserving food and he wanted to keep doing that, but salting and drying were work-intensive and time-consuming.

"Are you sure we need to leave? Why not just move to the mainland in the spring? We should be able to find a good farm to work." Elly moved from behind him, facing him as she leaned back against the right side of the desk.

It was a good question. He looked at his papers as he formulated a reply and finally, drew a deep breath. "Winter, for one. This one was pretty average for this area." Her eyebrows raised and he knew that being from the South, she had considered the weather they'd been enduring as especially harsh. It wasn't. It was a typical Wisconsin winter. "But the big reason is I'd like to find other people."

"But—"

"I know—there's danger from the virus." Cole cut in. "But I think it's worth the risk."

"What makes it worth it? Things here aren't so bad, and if we add the panels like you have right there," she waved to his plans, "then why the need to leave?" Elly crossed her arms as her lips set in a thin line.

He reached for the hand that was tucked beneath her arms, grasping her fingers as she lowered her arms. "I'm sorry I cut you off. I've been meaning to discuss that with you and ask you your opinion on when you think the virus has run its course—but eventually we have to venture off this island. Solar panels only work as long as the sun is shining, and in the winter, days are short and half the time, it's overcast. We would need to install some batteries for storage, and I don't think they're available just anywhere—not that I won't look."

Elly pursed her lips, apparently not quite convinced. He didn't blame her. In some ways, it was less scary to face dangers you knew, even if they were difficult, than something that might be easier, but unknown. "The longer we wait to find out what is still left out there, the harder it'll be to get stuff back up and running. "

"I think we'd be just as well off staying here."

Cole drew a deep breath. He didn't want to argue; not with Elly and not about this. It was true they could continue to exist here, but thrive? No. Not in this environment. "I don't agree."

They locked eyes and Elly was the first to break contact, waving a hand nearly in his face. "It's my turn for laundry. Is yours ready to go?"

Chapter Six

HUNTER GRIPPED the top of the hand auger with one hand and turned the blade using the other hand to grip. It took only a few moments to drill through the ice. It wasn't quite as thick as it had been but at four inches or so, still should be thick enough to fish on. Thinning ice meant spring really was on the way and he couldn't wait. While they had all been busy all winter, they had still all been cooped up mostly in the main house. Joe's cabin was okay too, and he and Sophie had returned to it once Sophie had recovered from her bad flu, but to save fuel, they usually went back to the main house to work on any projects.

He had two tip-up poles to set across the two other holes he'd drilled already, and one jigging rod. If he had just been fishing for fun, he'd have stuck with one or maybe two poles, but fishing to feed people meant he used three at a time. With no other competition, the fishing was usually pretty good. Mostly he'd caught walleye and perch but occasionally he got a nice lake trout. On a good day, he might catch more than a dozen fish. It wasn't much compared to what Elly and Jake brought in when they'd used the boat and nets, but it was enough to keep the group from going hungry some days.

He lifted the auger from the neat hole he'd created and handed it over to Mike. The other man had his own fishing gear from their vehicle, but all he had was one jigging rod.

"When I went on the fishing trip last spring, ice fishing was the furthest thing from my mind," Mike said, as he created his hole. "I only had this in the back from a trip I took last February. It was a fun trip and we caught a few fish, but mostly we sat around in my buddy's ice hut listening to music."

Hunter had made a hut early in the winter and was pretty proud of it, but it was relatively warm today so he'd decided to try some different spots to fish.

He baited a few lines and dropped them in the two holes he'd made. It wasn't long before they each sat on large coolers that did triple duty as fish storage and transport across the ice, and seating. Hunter had retrieved them from the ice hut after he'd drilled the fishing holes.

"So, have you guys been here since the beginning of the epidemic?" Mike sat facing Hunter and with one hand out of commission, Hunter marveled that he'd managed to drill the hole and bait the hook.

"Well, my dad, Sean, Jenna, and my cousins, Piper and Trent came out here first. I was in Colorado at school so I didn't get here for a while."

"Oh wow. Really? How'd you get from Colorado? Fly?"

"Maybe I should have…just worn a mask, but no, it was still very early and things were almost normal. My dad thought I could drive with no problem."

"And…did you?"

One of Hunter's poles twitched and he reached for it, but whatever it was didn't hit the bait again and he relaxed. "Yeah, but things all went to shit pretty quickly. I ended up out of gas in the middle of nowhere and had to camp out near a farm. That's where I found Buddy and the horses. The poor dog was still hanging out by his home but the people who'd lived there were already dead."

Mike shook his head. "That's rough. He's a good dog—at least from what I've seen."

Hunter nodded. "And then I met Sophie." He opened his mouth to tell the story of Sophie's run in with the men who had taken her, but instead, he just shrugged. "We made our way back here. By then, I think most people had died, but I kept my mask on any time I wasn't out in an open field or something. I had Sophie do the same, so that's how we made it without getting sick."

"That's a helluva story. A lot more exciting than mine, for sure. I survived out of pure, dumb, luck. The other guys were planning on spending a week or so up at Steve's cabin to fish, but I was only going for the weekend. I had a job to start Tuesday morning, so I was going to drive home that Monday, only I was so hung-over from the night before, I decided to wait until my headache went away."

"And it never did?" Hunter chuckled. Saved by a hangover.

Mike may have grinned, but he wore the mask Jenna had given him so Hunter couldn't know for sure, but his eyes crinkled. "No, it went away about lunch time, but I wanted to send a message to my boss just in case I was late getting back. The only problem was we barely got cellphone service up there, but surprisingly, the best spot was in the middle of the lake. Since I was out there, I didn't want to pass up the opportunity to fish just one more time."

If Mike had been smiling, it must have faded because his voice dropped low and Hunter had to strain to hear him as he said, "The response I got back was from his wife. My boss had passed away that Sunday evening. While I'd been getting shit-faced drunk, he'd died."

Hunter opened his mouth to offer condolences, but Mike went on, "She told me that things were going crazy and I should stay where I was." He drew a deep breath. "So I stayed and told the others. A couple of guys left anyway, but the rest of us stayed on. Steve had a good amount of supplies because he'd bought staples for most of the summer and I'm grateful that he shared it with us. I wouldn't have survived without him. None of us in our group would have. Late summer, a couple of the guys ventured into town and cleaned out what was left of the store, gas station, and all of the homes nearby. I wasn't with them. I stayed back to protect the cabin. Steve worried someone might come by and try to steal what little we had, but nobody ever did."

There was another tug on Hunter's line but whatever it was had just toyed with the bait. He relaxed and thought about waiting for thieves who never showed because they were all dead. "That's both good news and incredibly depressing at the same time."

"I know, right?" Mike's pole tipped and for a few minutes the only talk related to landing the fish. Hunter had to open the hole a bit wider to accommodate the good-sized walleye. "Mmm...these are good eating."

Hunter agreed.

After the fish was safely tucked away in the cooler Mike sat on, they resumed their conversation. "I was in the Army and did a couple of tours in Iraq. I'm pretty comfortable handling a weapon."

Mike didn't say anything else about either Iraq or guarding the cabin but seemed lost in thought so Hunter concentrated on his fishing. He caught a small perch that in normal times he'd have tossed back, but these days, every fish counted so he tossed it in the cooler.

"How did you cut your hand?"

"Stupid mistake on my part. I—"

One of Hunter's fishing poles jerked and he leapt for it. "Whoa!" The pole bent—the line taut as the fish fought to escape. Hunter played out the line, worried the pole or line would snap. Whatever he'd caught, it was big. Would he even be able to haul it through the six-inch hole he'd made? As the pole jerked again, he put that out of his mind—first he had to get the fish to the hole—then worry about landing it.

"Oh man! You probably got a big salmon on there!" Mike set his pole down and stepped over.

There was no warning crack. Just one second Hunter stood over the hole he'd created fighting to land the fish, and the next, the ice gave way and he plunged into the frigid lake.

Chapter Seven

ELLY LIFTED dirty clothes from the hot soapy water, gripping material in each hand and rubbed the fabric together. As she vented her anger and frustration on the denim and flannel clenched in her fists, she considered the risk of infection from the virus. In the past, pandemics flared up for a few years, then went dormant. This had been much faster moving than any pandemic ever recorded, though, and without a doubt, the most deadly. Would that have any bearing on whether it would continue to circulate? Were there enough people left for the virus to replicate and spread effectively?

She hated doing laundry, had always hated it, and now the hate had reached a new level. What she wouldn't give for a washer and dryer right now. With a toss of her head, she blew a few strands of hair from her eyes.

The only good thing about doing laundry by hand was it allowed her to vent. With a wry chuckle, she tossed the clothes back into the basket of clothing awaiting a return to the huge vat of nearly boiling water simmering outside over a bonfire. They would soak for a bit, then they'd be wrung out via a couple of large mop buckets Cole had found in the kitchen of a restaurant he'd scavenged for food.

After a rinse and a second time in the wringer, they would be hung to dry in the living room. Hooks had been screwed into the walls and a clothesline with loops at each end to fit over the hooks was stretched across the room. There were three sets of hooks, and with so many people, every inch was filled, even though all of them wore clothing more than one day. She thought of all of the times she had worn a shirt for a few hours and then tossed it in the hamper without a thought. Now, she thought nothing of wearing the same jeans all week long. They had plenty of clothing, but washing it was a ton of work, so they got used to clothes that didn't smell daisy fresh.

Not only did the chore take most of the day, it used a lot of wood for the fire for heating the water and afterward to dry the clothes. The house had to be warm for the clothes to dry quickly. On the plus side, there was the benefit of adding moisture to the very dry air.

"Is this basket ready to hang?" Piper came out and pointed to a basket of jeans that had already been through the wringer.

"Yeah. I still have towels and sheets to do, then we're done."

Piper examined her reddened hands. "Thank God. I'm getting chapped."

"Why didn't you wear your rubber gloves?" Elly dropped a sweatshirt of Cole's into the wringer and pulled the handle. There was something satisfying about seeing the dirty water squeezed from the material. She removed the item and tossed it into the rinse water.

"I hate wearing them."

Elly started to chide her, thinking it was youthful vanity to not be caught wearing unstylish thick yellow gloves. After all, Jake always seemed to find a reason to be near the pretty young woman, but Piper shrugged. "I can't help seeing Uncle Cole wearing gloves like them when he went out to where Trent was in isolation, after he..." She bit her lip and didn't finish the sentence.

"Oh, hon. You saw him?" She hadn't arrived on the island yet, but Cole had told her how hard it had been, emotionally, to retrieve his nephew's body and safely remove it for burial.

"I didn't mean to. I just wanted to...I don't know...I guess to just get one last look at my brother. Uncle Cole had said that it wasn't safe to go near the body, but I thought maybe I could see something when he opened the doors. I couldn't see anything, but I saw Cole's reaction and for some reason, the gloves just stuck in my mind."

"I'm sorry. Memories are crazy like that."

COLE GRABBED HIS JACKET. The first whisper of spring warmth beckoned him outside and he couldn't resist the call. With his standoff with Elly weighing on his mind, his concentration was shot anyway. Icicles hung from the eaves and dripped onto the deck. While barely above freezing, it felt warmer due to the bright sunshine and lack of wind. He took a deep breath and spotted Hunter and Mike out on the ice in the bay. Hunter had said he was going fishing to try to bring in something fresh to eat. He wondered if he'd caught anything and decided to join them. He hurried to open the door for Piper as she approached with a full basket of steaming clothes in her hands. "Let me get the door. Need some help?"

"Nope. I'm fine. Elly might need a hand though."

Cole zipped his coat and pulled on his gloves then joined Elly. "I'm sorry about earlier."

Elly shook her head. "You don't have to be. I've been thinking—"

"*Help!*"

The voice carried faintly over the ice, but Cole was already two steps towards the ice before he pinpointed the source of the cry. Only moments before Cole had noticed Hunter and Mike fishing, their forms were dark against the white backdrop, now they were gone and all he could see was a dark lump lying prone on the surface. "*What the hell…*"

Elly was at his side and gave a gasp. "I think someone fell through!"

"*Get Sean and Jake!*" Cole burst into a sprint, his speed hindered by the piles of hard, grainy snow, slick where it had melted on top. As he passed the fish cleaning shed, he remembered rope hanging inside, stored there over the winter. He made a quick detour and grabbed it. The distance of a few hundred yards seemed as vast as the expanse of Antarctica as Cole raced, slipping and sliding over the ice.

It was Mike who lay on the ice and Cole's heart almost stopped. "Where's Hunter?"

"I'm…here…Dad." Hunter answered, his head bobbing in the water as he tread water. Mike lay almost spread-eagled face down on the ice, one hand braced out from his body as the other seemed tangled in Hunter's coat.

Cole's knees almost buckled from relief. There was still time, but only if they moved quickly. While the air was just above freezing, hypothermia would set in within a matter of minutes in water this cold. He circled to the other side of the hole, testing the ice before getting too close. He couldn't rescue his son if he became a victim as well. When he was as close as he dared, he tossed an end of the rope close to Hunter. "Grab the rope!"

Hunter reached for it, but ended up pushing the rope away. If he'd been wearing gloves, they weren't on him now and his movements were clumsy. Cole gathered the rope again, and tossed it even closer. This time, Hunter snagged it.

"Okay, Hunter, wrap your arm up in it good, and I'll bring you to my side. When you get to the edge, try to kick your legs to get horizontal on the edge. Got it?" Hunter said something that sounded like yeah, but his teeth chattered so hard, Cole couldn't be certain.

When Hunter was ready, Cole said, "Mike, you can let go." It was the hardest sentence he'd ever uttered in his life, but circling to bring him over to Mike's side to allow the other man to hang on too could put too much stress on the ice there. He spotted a web of cracks and fissures on that side and worried Mike would also fall in also.

Sean and Jake hollered that they were on the way, although Cole wasn't sure what they could do.

Hunter followed Cole's directions as Cole kept the line taut and moved back. Hunter had his chest up on the ice when that piece broke off too. "*Damn it!*" The sharp tug on the rope bit into his forearm where he'd wrapped it, but he barely noticed.

Mike moved to Hunter's left and, lying flat, he reached out, grabbing Hunter's left arm. "Cole, this time, I'll lift while you pull."

Hunter still kicked as Cole had instructed, but the kicks were weaker. The cold was taking a toll. Cole set his jaw and hauled back just as Sean and Jake reached them. Cole's boots slipped on the ice and he started skidding, with Hunter backsliding. Then Sean's arms locked around Cole's waist and he started pulling him back. Mike lifted and Hunter was on the ice. They continued to move back until he was safely away from the edge. Jake had moved around to Mike's side, and grabbed the man's feet and hauled him away from the edge too. It was then Cole noticed how wet Mike was. His coat had soaked up the water while he'd been on the ice holding Hunter's jacket.

Cole kneeled beside Hunter and unzipped his son's coat. "We have to get you out of these wet clothes."

Hunter sat up, nodding as he tried to shrug the jacket off. Cole unzipped his own coat and put it on his son just as Elly and Jenna reached them, each carrying several blankets.

"Can you walk?" Cole hardly felt the cold as the exertion had him sweating.

Hunter nodded and between Jake and Cole, they had him on his feet, although he shook so hard, he couldn't take a step.

"Stand back a second, Cole." Jenna draped a blanket over Hunter's shoulders, pulling it up to cover his head as well, leaving only his face showing.

Elly had gone to Mike, wrapping him in a blanket as well. "Are you okay?"

Mike nodded, clutching the blanket. "I tried to get him out, but I couldn't grip him tight enough to haul him up onto the ice."

"Oh no. Did you break your stitches?" Jenna moved from Hunter's side to Mike's but he had the hand tucked beneath the blanket. "I'll check it out when we're back at the house.

Sophie is probably going crazy right now. I had her and Piper stay and heat up water. It's a good thing we have a big fire going already for the wash."

Sean helped Mike as Cole and Jake each took one of Hunter's elbows and assisted him back to the island. Halfway there, Cole started shivering hard, the heat from the exertion gone.

"Here you go, Cole."

He turned as a blanket draped over his shoulders. Elly straightened a fold and smiled at him. "Better?"

"Much. Thank you."

JENNA TUCKED a quilt around Hunter and he tried to thank her but his jaw was too tight. It felt frozen in a clench he couldn't relax.

He sat on a recliner his dad had pulled near to the stove before he'd rushed out to get more wood. Hunter huddled into several layers of quilts, a mug of hot chocolate clutched close to his chest, and Buddy sitting with his head resting in Hunter's lap. Every time Hunter looked at him, the dog's tail thumped against the floor and his whole body wriggled. The poor dog had been stuck in the house and had been barking like crazy until Hunter had stumbled in. Buddy hadn't left his side since. Hunter took a careful sip between shivers. The last thing he wanted to do was spill the precious contents of the mug. "Where did you get this?" He thought all they had left to drink was water or a watery coffee, tea, and mint mixture.

Jenna glanced around as if checking for anyone listening, then smiled with a hint of sadness. "I've had a canister of the powdered mix in my room. It was something I grabbed at the last minute when we were leaving our home. The kids, but especially Trent, always loved that stuff. I know it's not real hot chocolate—just the powdered stuff—but your cousin sure did love it."

Hunter nodded. "I remember Trent always asking for it on Christmas Eve."

His aunt bit her lip and busied herself with wiping up a few specks of the powder on the table. She blinked hard a few times before smiling at Hunter. "He sure did. At our house, Santa didn't get milk and cookies. He got hot chocolate and donuts. Trent figured Santa needed something warm, and donuts were a little different than cookies. He always wanted to be a bit different."

His dad entered with yet another armload of wood as the rest of the men followed him, also laden with enough wood to last for days. "Jenna, could you check out Mike's hand?"

Mike, almost as wet as Hunter, had changed clothes at his cabin and had returned sans mask and Hunter looked at his dad and mouthed the word. His dad shook his head. "It's been long enough. Elly and I discussed it and while we were going to wait one more day, that was just out of an abundance of caution. We're as certain as we can be that they're safe now."

Jenna dragged a rocking chair from the living room, shoved it close to the stove, and patted the back of it. "Have a seat, Mike. You can get warm while I look at your hand."

Mike protested. "It's fine. You were gonna take the stitches out tomorrow anyway."

"True, but we might need to throw a little tape on it and butterfly the wound to keep it closed while it finishes healing."

It seemed he was about to protest even that until Jenna pressed a mug into his hands. "Drink this first before I re-dress your hand." Then Mike grinned.

After depositing his wood in the bin, his dad looked at Hunter and sighed. "I guess this means no more fishing until the ice melts completely. It also means it's time to return the vehicles to the mainland. And also get the horses back there before they're stuck here when the ice melts."

Steve had met them coming off the ice and had contributed an armload of wood. He leaned against the kitchen counter, nodding. "I told Mike we should be heading back to the mainland soon. It might harden again, but no guarantees."

"But what about the horses?" Sophie brought another blanket from somewhere in the house and tucked it around Hunter's feet and looked up at him. "Getting warm?"

He nodded. As he warmed, fatigue threatened to overwhelm him but he struggled to keep his eyes opened. He wanted to hear this conversation.

"Good." She planted a kiss on his forehead, her lips searing like a branding iron against his skin—but in the best possible way.

His dad stuck a few more pieces of wood into the stove then brushed his hands against each other, his head cocked. "What do you mean? I just said we'd get them back to the mainland."

Sophie turned from Hunter. "But what about food and water? If the ice is unsafe to cross, how will we keep them fed and watered? Or the garage clean?"

Mike and Steve exchanged a look, with Mike nodding as if they'd come to some agreement. Steve said, "We owe you all for helping us out. We'd be happy to head to the mainland and stay there with the horses until the ice melts and you all can come back by boat."

His dad glanced at Hunter, then back to Steve and Mike. "Mike saved Hunter, so any debt you guys felt you owed is paid in full as far as I'm concerned." He turned his gaze to the rest of the group. "If no one objects..." he paused, allowing anyone to voice dissent, but everyone shook their head or shrugged that they had no objections, and so he continued, "I'd welcome any help you could give us with the horses. I'm not sure what plan they'll play in our future, but we can't leave them here on the island."

Sophie smiled at his dad. "Thanks for thinking of the horses, Cole. They mean a lot to me."

The horses meant a lot to him, too. They had carried Hunter and Sophie safely across a few hundred miles on their journey to the island.

Steve cleared his throat. "I've been meaning to ask you something, Cole."

His dad took a cup of hot tea from Elly. "Thanks." He blew on it before he took a sip. "What's on your mind?"

"Our buddies are dead set on heading to Florida but we're not sure we want to go with them."

Hunter blinked and struggled to straighten in the recliner. He definitely didn't want to miss this.

"No? How come?" His dad sounded cautious but curious. He hid it well as he sipped his tea but Hunter was used to his nuances.

Steve's mouth quirked to the side as he appeared to be searching for words. "Our group is great. Don't get me wrong. Fun bunch of guys. But that's just it. They're acting like this whole thing is a big joke. I went back to check in the other day to see how everyone is doing since it'd been a few days since you'd been there. Do you know they ended up burning down a couple of houses? Just for the fun of it."

Hunter's jaw thawed enough for him to speak. "Was that at the house we went to? It had a nice fireplace but maybe the fire got out of control when they were cooking over it."

Steve shrugged. "That's what I thought, but the way they were talking, it was clear they were just goofing around. Now, I know the houses' occupants are long gone, so it wasn't the loss of the buildings that bothers me, but their...attitude? Since the pandemic first hit, we were all treating it like a great extended fishing trip. We're all a bunch of bachelors since the guys who had families left early." He stopped, clearing his throat. "We never saw them again."

His dad rubbed his chin in thought. "So...what are you saying?"

Mike leaned forward. "What Steve is trying to say is that we're wondering if we could stay with your group." His gaze swept the room. "I know it hasn't been long and we've been isolated this week or so, but you all have a great group. Lots of cooperation. We would rather be with you guys than with them. All they want to do is have fun and destroy stuff just because they can."

After including everyone in their group in a look, his dad said, "We aren't even sure where or what we're doing come spring. Maybe travel west?"

Hunter struggled to stay awake, but the shivering had finally abated and despite his efforts, his eyes slid closed. Distantly he heard his dad say something about traveling west in the spring.

Chapter Eight

HUNTER SLICED through the deer's hide, admiring the size of the buck he'd taken down. It was his third deer, including the one he'd killed in the fall, but this one was, by far, the biggest. He didn't even mind the latest cold snap so much anymore—not when it meant fresh meat for everyone.

The animal had wandered to the island over the ice and he wondered if the howls of a pack of dogs he'd heard earlier in the morning had been the reason for the buck's flight from the mainland.

Hungry and bold, a pack had come up to the house the night before, but Buddy had sounded the alarm before they were too close, and Hunter and his dad had fired a few rounds over the dogs' heads, scaring the pack off. For now.

In the first few months after the pandemic, dogs had wandered around but usually fled when approached. Hunter guessed that people in the final throes of the virus had frightened the animals and now they were shy around humans.

Early on, food had been plentiful for them, what with all of the deceased lying about. Hunter suppressed a shudder as he recalled stumbling upon a scene of a pack of dogs devouring human remains last summer. He didn't think he'd ever look at dogs quite the same way again—except for Buddy, of course, who was still just as sweet and loyal as ever. Most days, Buddy accompanied him, but with the wild dogs so close, Hunter had opted to leave him in the house while he went out checking snares he had set on the far side of the island. He got the idea for snares from a book he'd taken from the library in the fall, and though it had taken a bit of trial and error, he had finally managed to snare a few rabbits, one possum, and a couple of squirrels. All of them ended up in the stew pot.

Today's haul had only been one rabbit, and after resetting the snares, he'd been returning to the house when he spotted the tracks and followed them into a clearing. He'd taken down the buck with a swift arrow right behind the shoulder. The deer had taken one leap forward before collapsing.

After field dressing the deer, he tied the rabbit to his belt with a bit of cord. As he secured it, he marveled at how different his life had become. Last year at this time, he was worrying about preparing for mid-terms. His pockets would have contained a wallet, car keys, and his cellphone. Now, he had none of those on him. Instead, he carried a hunting knife in a sheath on his belt and in addition, a multi-tool pocketknife. No wallet. No car keys. No cellphone.

On his left side, he had a pouch hanging from his belt that held matches, a lighter, fishing line, a few hooks, two needles, a few different weights of thread, cord, and a few plastic garbage bags, and a roll of white medical silk tape.

The tape had several uses. It was strong enough to tape objects together, but could also be used to butterfly a wound together. Jenna had shown them all how to do it. If he had to, he could rip off the bottom of his t-shirt to use as a bandage. After his dad had been shot, Hunter listened to all of Jenna's instruction with far more attention than he had ever paid to his economics instructor.

He drew a deep breath as he looked down at the gutted deer. Now came the hard part. He had to carry the buck back to the house. If it was a straight shot, it was about three quarters of a mile, but a wetland on this side of the island created a bog and he didn't want to risk breaking an ankle on a slippery tuft of slough grass hidden beneath a crusty layer of snow. That meant he either had to go out onto the ice and circle around the way he had come, or head to the interior of the island. He looked at the antlers and envisioned those catching on every bush and sapling so he opted for the ice. It would be colder out there with the wind whipping down from the north and even though the ice looked flat, there were uneven patches hidden beneath the snow. With his dunking a few days ago still fresh in his mind, he swore at his choices. Spring could not arrive soon enough.

He readied the buck for the journey by creating a backpack of sorts of the carcass. It didn't take long to cut partway through the knee joint in each foreleg, leaving a strip of skin and tendon, then slicing through the hind legs between the hamstring and bone just above the hocks. He then sat down, set his bow and arrows aside, and pulled the forelegs over his shoulders then tucked them into the slits he'd cut on the back legs. He turned the legs, locking the joints of front and back legs together. The front legs formed the straps like he'd have on a backpack. He grabbed his bow and arrows, tossed the strap for the quiver over one shoulder and carried his bow in his left hand. The hard part was standing and he grunted as he pushed up, steadied his load, and headed out to the ice.

At a gut level, the set-up made him nervous since he now basically looked like a two legged buck, with the deer's head lolling back, but nobody was around and he'd let everyone know he had gone to check his traps.

He hiked the deer higher and headed for the ice. The buck was heavy, well over one-hundred and fifty pounds, but with the weight distributed over his shoulders, he knew he could get it back to the house even if it took him a little longer. The exertion helped ward off the cold and he worried about sweating through his layers of clothing. He paused when he reached the ice and uncapped his water bottle, taking a swig as he rested for a minute. There was no way he could have been able to do this a year ago. He didn't have the stamina, not to mention he'd have probably been shot by some other hunter.

He couldn't wait to show his dad the buck. The meat was always welcome, and he was proud he'd done it without wasting ammunition. While they still had plenty, it wasn't like they could just run out to the local Dick's Sporting Goods and buy more.

He wondered if Sean and his dad were still fishing. They had left an hour or so before he had set out. Since his fall through the ice, he'd stuck to his snares but felt guilty about it. Why should others take the risk instead of him? It made him work even harder to make his snares the best that he could. If only they had thought to get traps from some place. There had to have been a local store to get them from, but Joe had never trapped before and didn't know any more than the rest of them.

At least the ice was solid once again. The brief thaw that had caused him to fall through had given way to a cold snap, but even so, he didn't like being on the ice any longer than necessary so he stuck as close to the shore as possible. If he hit a thin patch and broke through, he'd be on his own.

The crunch of the snow and ice beneath his feet and his panting as he hiked with his burden filled his ears. The southern tip of the island was close on his left and a few steps more and he'd be within sight of the house and the beach. The thought of a warm stove, a hot drink, and something to eat spurred him on.

Just as he pivoted east, he heard a noise louder than his own breathing and footsteps. It took him a few seconds before he realized what the familiar sound was. He turned and looked north up the lake, scanning the air, not believing his ears at first. It wasn't until he saw it, first a speck in the distance, and then growing larger, that he believed his eyes. *A helicopter—and it was heading right towards the island.*

It was a large helicopter, possibly military, and he started to wave, but then pulled his hand down. Better to watch and see what they did before bringing attention to himself. He dropped to a crouch and hoped he really did look like a deer as he hurried up the beach, yanking at the deer's hind legs to separate them from the front hooves. When he came to the dry dock with the pontoon boat up on blocks, he dumped the deer and shoved it under the pontoon along with his bow and arrows. They were useless against anyone in a helicopter. What he needed was a rifle.

He was out of sight of the helicopter for now, but from the whump of the rotors, it would appear any second now. He raced for the cover of a stand of pines fifty feet from the house, torn between sounding a warning and staying to see where the helicopter went. As he debated, Piper and Sophie opened the door and stepped out on the deck.

Piper spotted him first. "Hunter? Do you hear that?"

"Yeah. I saw it coming from the north." He started to say it looked like a military helicopter, but his words were drowned out by the helicopter as it flew low over the island. Hunter strained to see into the cockpit, but it was impossible from his angle. He waved to Piper and Sophie to return to the house. As he did, Jenna stuck her head out too. They were exposed on the deck.

"Get back!"

They retreated, but they still watched through the screen. As the helicopter moved out over the bay, he called out, "Where's my dad and Sean?"

"Still out on the lake fishing!" Sophie pointed southeast.

The helicopter looked to be turning east. He didn't know if it was returning, but he felt vulnerable and raced to the deck, took the three steps up in one bound and dashed into the house to get a rifle only to find both were gone. Damn. Well, maybe that was a good thing. That meant his dad or Sean probably had them. He still had the semi-automatic rifle. They didn't use it for hunting but they had all been shown how to use the weapon. He grabbed it and the shotgun, along with ammo for each. The handguns were there too, but he couldn't carry it all. Piper, Jake, and Joe could handle those. Jenna could handle the shotgun. He'd take the semi-automatic.

Luke and Zoë peered at him from the kitchen, their eyes huge. Hunter pointed at them. "I need for you guys to get your coats and boots on and hide in the closet by the backdoor. If you hear me yell for you to run, go out the back door and run up to hickory grove. Got it?"

Luke's eye grew huge as he nodded and took Zoë's hand.

Hunter put a hand on Luke's head and dropped to one knee. "It'll be okay. Just hide there until someone comes to get you." He almost let it go at that, but what if something did happen? He added, "I don't think it'll come to this, but if nobody comes, head for the mainland and the little barn." It would keep them warm and there was a little food there. It was the best Hunter could do.

Luke had been to the grove plenty of times and he didn't ask questions, just took Zoë by the hand and helped her get her boots on.

As he handed Piper and Sophie a handgun and ammunition, he asked Jenna to go stay with the kids.

"I'm not going to hide, Hunter. I'm a good shot and I don't want to leave Piper and Sean. Why doesn't Sophie go with them?"

Hunter wanted nothing more than to have Sophie out of possible harm's way, but she was starting to have trouble moving quickly. At about six months along, her balance in the snow was off. The kids needed someone who could get them quickly to safety.

Before Hunter could reply, Sophie did. "You're way faster than me right now, Jenna. If the kids need to run, I'll slow them down."

Piper nodded. "She has a point, Mom." She took a gun, loaded it like she'd been doing it her whole life. "I'm sure we're over-reacting anyway."

Hunter handed her the shotgun. "Take this too." When it looked like she was going to protest, he shook his head. "We have our other weapons. You may need this." He didn't say she was the kids' last line of defense, but when he met her eyes, he knew she'd already come to that realization as she took the shotgun from him.

Jenna had her own handgun but put it in her jacket pocket as she grabbed a few of their homemade granola bars from the pantry, shoving them in her other jacket pocket. It was good thinking. "Okay, we'll be hiding in the hickory groves if we hear you holler, Hunter." Jenna ushered the kids down the hallway as Luke grabbed his and Zoë's jackets from the hooks.

Sophie stayed in the house, but she'd gathered more ammo than Hunter had been able to carry, and grabbed a spare backpack by the door and dumped it in, handing Hunter the bag.

Hunter heard the helicopter returning for another pass. It was possible they were friendly, but until he knew for sure, he wasn't going to let his guard down.

He pointed to the pines and Piper nodded and followed him out. The helicopter looked to be hovering near where his dad and Sean would be fishing. "Where are the other men?"

"Remember they took the SUV to the mainland to search for grain for the animals?"

"Shit. Yeah. I hope they aren't crossing back right now."

"They only left about an hour ago. They should still be on shore. Joe's smart. He'll watch but not let anyone show themselves." Piper bit her lip. "I should run inside and get the binoculars."

"Good idea. They look like they're turning so now's your chance." Hunter kept an anxious eye on the helicopter as it angled in a wide arc. Was it coming back or just heading east over the lake? Maybe they're heading to Michigan?

Piper darted back, two pairs of binoculars in her hands. She gave one to Hunter.

He nodded. "I hate that our dads are out there." Keeping beneath the cover of the broad pines, Hunter worked his way to where he could see past the changing rooms they'd converted into a stable. From there, he had a clear view of the ice southeast of the island. He scanned the ice, spotting what he thought was fishing gear out on the ice.

"Piper, do those dark things on the ice look like poles and gear? They aren't near the ice huts though."

"Yeah, I think so."

The helicopter made a wide arc and headed back towards the island. "It's coming back!"

"Shit! Hunter! What do we do?"

"I'm going down by the changing house. I can cover the ice with the shotgun."

"And do what?"

"Try to keep anyone from coming up to the house. Why don't you go back with your mom, Sophie, and the kids?"

"No. My mom and Sophie will be fine with them. I think we should stay in pairs."

Hunter shrugged. "True. Okay, but can you stay here in case they get by me?" He didn't wait for her to answer, but darted over to the converted stable. Buddy was in the house barking his head off and Hunter knew there was no way they'd be able to pretend that the island was deserted. The smell of wood smoke alone would give them away.

———

COLE PAUSED when he reached the cover of a stand of birch trees along the rocky eastern shore of the island. The trees were bare and only the trunks hid him, but a dozen yards away, maples and pines offered better coverage. "Hurry, Sean!"

His brother had been at a fishing hole a stone's throw farther out on the ice when Cole had spotted the helicopter well north of the island. Where had it come from and where was it going?

There was no reason to think anyone in the helicopter would be hostile—not yet, but he didn't like be caught out on the open ice. Where would everyone else be? Hunter was checking his traps, and Joe, Jake, Steve, and Mike had gone into town. They were looking for grain, but they were also planning on seeing if Mike and Steve's friends were still around.

He and Sean raced as fast as possible on the slippery ice. He thought they may have made it unseen as the helicopter had come up more on the western side of the island. There was a chance they'd been hidden as they angled in, but now the helicopter was past and if they looked north as they turned east, they might spot Sean as he closed the final distance to where Cole stood. He hoped the shadows would hide them. From here, it was only a short hike back to the house.

Cole extended a hand, helping Sean over a boulder slick with snow. They had left everything except their weapons back on the ice, including their catch. It had been a good one too. Damn it. Hopefully they could return and get it once the threat was over.

Catching his breath as he decided the best course of action, Cole listened as the copter neared. The pitch changed and he realized the helicopter was hovering nearby. "Come on, Sean. We have to get back to the house." He didn't like that they'd have to cut through a meadow but it was either that, or take the route along the edge of the beach. Either would leave them fully exposed but there was no help for it.

Sean nodded and darted across the meadow, Cole close on his heels as the helicopter hovered a hundred feet in the air just to his left. Maybe the low hover would keep Sean and him concealed by the top branches of the trees.

It was only a couple of hundred yards to the house, but wearing boots and slogging through thick, heavy snow made the distance seem twice as far. By the time they reached the first cabin, closest to them but farthest from the house, Cole was breathing in great, gulping gasps, drowning out the sound of the helicopter, but he could feel it nearby. The whump of the rotors created a deep, thumping vibration in his chest.

Sean turned and said something to him, but Cole couldn't hear him and shook his head. Then Sean pointed up. The helicopter was landing where the beach would be, if it wasn't covered in snow and ice.

The rotors didn't stop, but a door on the helicopter slid open and two men dressed in military camouflage flight suits jumped out, assault weapons in their hands.

Cole's heart stopped for a half-beat before it zoomed into high gear and adrenaline flooded his veins. His desire to rush forward, shooting the intruders where they stood, warred with his worry about the rest of his family. What if they were all within sight of the intruders?

Sean moved up to Cole's side. "What do we do?"

Casting around for a plan, he spotted the large oil drum they'd turned into a barbecue grill. If he circled around the first three cabins, he could get them in his sights, and still be close enough to talk to them.

"You stay here if you can. Keep them in your line of sight. I'll circle around to the barbecue. I want to see what they're here for, but if they raise their weapons, fire. Got it?"

"Yeah." Sean dropped to one knee, steadying his rifle through the crook of the tree they stood beside.

Cole circled back through the trees and around and behind the barbecue. He kicked himself for leaving the women alone. They were more than competent, but had the kids to think about too, and Sophie's pregnancy wasn't an easy one. She wasn't going to be able to flee if she needed to.

He should have waited to fish until Hunter returned, or had Hunter wait until they returned. But, it wasn't often that all of the men were away at one time and it hadn't occurred to him. From now on, he'd set limits on how many people were away at one time.

After a lifetime lived in relative safety, he'd had to change his whole way of thinking in the last year. He had to get better at looking at situations that could arise—situations he'd never even imagined prior to the last year.

He had factored in the only survivors who were close at hand, but the only ones he knew of for sure were Steve's friends. He hadn't foreseen a damn helicopter.

Keeping a low profile, he watched as the invaders stood wary, their weapons ready. What the hell did they want? They couldn't be looking for supplies. There was a whole world out there ready to be scavenged. Nobody needed the relatively little they had stored on the island.

The rotors slowed and another man disembarked. He wore a flight suit, but his was dark blue. He carried no weapon that Cole could see.

After a moment of looking around, his eyes lingering on the makeshift barn, he and the other men headed towards the house. They didn't need a map to show them which building was the main one—dingy, well-trodden paths led from the house before diverging to different areas. Before they got more than a dozen feet, Cole called out.

"*Stop!*"

The men halted, the armed invaders raising their guns slightly and Cole cringed, anticipating a shot from his brother. He let out a breath when his brother held his fire. For now.

The invader in dark blue stepped out in front of the other two. "We don't mean anyone any harm."

"What are you here for? State your business!"

Pinpointing Cole's location, the man turned towards him, lifting his hands to show they were empty, not that it mattered because his companions were heavily armed. "I'm looking for a man named Cole Evans. Have you heard of him?"

Chapter Nine

STUNNED, Cole didn't reply for a minute. Who the hell would be looking for him? "What do you want with him?"

"It's complicated. Do you know him? Can we talk about this instead of shouting across a hundred feet?"

"*No!* We never heard of this Cole-guy so you can hop your ass back onto that helicopter and take your buddies with you. *Go on. Get out of here!*" Whatever they wanted, Cole wasn't interested in hearing it. The military hadn't been around to help when things had become bad and he and his family didn't need them now.

The man said something quietly to the armed men. There seemed to be some kind of argument before the armed men appeared to grudgingly retreat to the aircraft, but they remained armed and remained a threat.

The other man took a few more steps forward, something in the house catching his attention for a brief instance, before he looked in Cole's direction again. "I understand your reluctance. These are scary times. I only want to talk. I can offer information on what the government is doing to help."

"Government? You mean we still have one? Because we haven't seen evidence of one in almost a year." Cole's finger twitched on the trigger as his anger about the lack of help surged through him.

"Yes, we do, although you're right, it has been hard hit by the virus, the same as everyone else." He gestured to the house. "Can't we talk inside? I really can't leave until I talk to someone."

"Can't leave or *won't* leave?" He didn't care for the implied threat.

The man shook his head. "I'm afraid my orders are to find this Cole Evans."

"He's probably dead. Everyone else is."

"You're not."

Cole froze at the comment. Did he know Cole's identity? Or was he just pointing out that Cole, just some man he was talking to, wasn't dead. His instincts were to get rid of this guy but curiosity about why they wanted him prodded him to respond, "What happens if you find this man?"

"I just want to ask him some questions. I'm not looking to hurt anyone. In fact, our goal is to help everyone."

Cole didn't buy the nice guy act, but if this government agent, or whatever he was, was looking for him, chances are, there was someone higher up who had given the order to find him. Putting this guy off wouldn't put an end to a search. Only drastic measures might do that, and Cole wasn't ready to kill someone in cold blood. But, if he talked to the man and found out what he wanted with him, without letting on that he was Cole Evans, it might set his mind at ease.

He shifted, his legs cramping as he crouched behind the barbecue. Bringing the guy into the main house wasn't a consideration. He glanced at the door of this cabin. It was the one Joe and Jake lived in but neither were on the island right now. The fire in the stove would probably be banked though, and the room would be warm.

Before Cole could do anything, he needed to make sure the others knew what was going on. To do that, he needed to get to the house. He could go behind the houses and in the back door, but he needed to make sure this guy wouldn't pull anything while he updated Elly and the others.

"Give me five minutes. Don't move a muscle." Cole raced around to Sean, gave him the rundown.

"Do you want me out here? Or in with you?"

Cole shook his head. "I need you to keep an eye on those two. I wish we had the radios—"

"I can whistle if they try anything—just before I shoot."

Sean had a good strong whistle he managed without using his hands. Cole had to use two fingers to achieve the same volume. He nodded. "Perfect. I'm going to run and tell Elly what's going on so she doesn't wonder."

Keeping out of sight as much as he could, Cole made his way to the house, going to the back door, only to find it locked.

Before he could knock, Jenna shouted at him to get back or she'd shoot.

"Damn it, Jenna. Open up. It's me!"

She peeked out of the small window before unlocking the door. "Well how was I supposed to know? I have the kids back here ready to escape."

Cole nodded to Sophie, who held a child by each hand. All were bundled with backpacks. "Good thinking. Where's Elly and Piper?"

"Elly's guarding the front door, and Hunter and Piper are out there somewhere. I heard you talking, so I hope they heard too. They should have, if they stayed close."

Cole thought for a second. It wasn't ideal to have them out there, but then again, they were well hidden and having more eyes on the invaders, guarding from the outside, made him feel better. "Okay. I'm going to talk to the guy who seems to be their leader. I'll bring him into Joe's cabin. I'd send him away, but I think it would be good to know why they're looking specifically for me."

Elly shook her head. "I don't like this, Cole. What if they want to kill you?"

"I thought of that, but why me, specifically? I'm no threat to anyone. They didn't need to come all the way out here to kill me. No, they're looking for me for some reason. They went to the trouble of finding out that I own this island. That information was only in a few records that I know of since I only got it the year before the virus hit."

Elly bit her lip, glancing at the helicopter outside. "Yeah, I guess… but dammit, they're scaring me."

"I'm a bit scared too, but I'll be fine and with Hunter, Sean, and Piper out there, and you and Jenna in here, armed and dangerous…" he smiled to try to lighten the mood, but Elly wasn't having it. He sobered quickly and wrapped a hand around the back of her neck, gently pulling her forehead to his lips. "It'll be okay. You'll hear if there's any shooting. Do what you think is best."

"Jenna will run with the kids to the hickory grove. If we have to flee, that's where we'll go first."

"Good plan. The forest is thick there, and there's enough under-growth to build a shelter."

She nodded. "Yeah. And we'll do our best to cover our trail."

He gave her another quick kiss, this time on the lips, then dashed out the back door, stopping only to grab a mask from the store of them they kept in the pantry. He grabbed an extra for the invader. He wasn't sure why he thought of him with that name, but it's what popped into his mind. *Invader*. Their sanctuary was now known, and who knew if the helicopter had been able to transmit by radio to let others know that the island was occupied.

Chapter Ten

BEFORE HE RETURNED to Joe's cabin, he ran past it and around to Sean's spot amongst the trees to let him know that Hunter and Piper were out there somewhere. He didn't want them getting shot accidentally.

By the time he made it back to Joe's cabin, sweat traced a path down the back of his neck into his parka. He saw the leader, huddled and shivering near the helicopter, and smiled. The guy would be thinking about the cold and getting warm for the first few minutes. It would give him a moment to study the other man up close.

Cole stepped out from behind the barbecue grill. He didn't hide his rifle, but he did try to appear non-threatening. "Come on over. We'll talk in here."

The man looked surprised and glanced at the main house. Clearly, he'd thought that's where they would go, but he shrugged and approached.

Donning a mask, Cole handed the man one when he arrived, but the man shook his head. "No thanks."

Cole stood with the mask dangling from his fingers for a few seconds before he shoved it at the man. "Wear it, or leave."

Chuckling, the man shook his head but took the mask, tying it around the back of his head. "Really, there's no need."

Ignoring his comment, Cole motioned to the porch rail. "Put your hands on it, and spread your legs."

The man did as he was told, but fumed, "Really? You're searching me for weapons? What about you? You're carrying openly."

"Yeah, well it's my—" He was about to say 'island' but cut it short just in time. Or he thought he had until the other man finished for him, "...island?"

Not responding and finding the man free of weapons, Cole gestured to the door of the cabin. "After you." He wasn't about to turn his back on this guy to enter the house.

Cole directed the man to sit while he added more wood to the fire. As he'd expected, Joe had left it banked. Crossing his arms, he stood at the end of the table where he could see both his 'guest' and through the window, out to the henchmen standing at attention by the helicopter, seemingly impervious to the cold.

"So, who are you and what are you doing here?" There was no need to beat around the bush and pretend to exchange niceties.

The man's eyes widened briefly before he nodded. "Fine. I'll get to the point. I'm Pete Holland. Several years ago, I was assigned to the bio lab at Aislado Island—maybe you remember me?"

Cole tried to school his face to show no reaction—obviously Pete wasn't fooled by Cole's claims to have never heard of Cole Evans, but he refused to admit anything to this man. Not yet. Pete studied his face, searching for signs of recognition from Cole and apparently not seeing any, shrugged and continued, "There's no real reason you'd remember me although I do recall seeing you around. I also read your report about the work we were doing out there. You were right, you know. We should have destroyed the virus right then, but, anyway, we can't go back in time."

"What does any of this have to do with here and now?" Now wasn't the time to gloat and say, 'I told you so'.

"Bear with me. I am ashamed to admit that at the time of the outbreak, I realized what was going on a day or so before anyone else. My first instinct was to flee, and damn it, I tried like hell to get off the island, but there weren't any seats available." He rubbed a hand along the back of his neck. "That probably saved my life, now that I think about. Those flights would have been hot incubators of the virus and every passenger who got off a vector." He waved a hand. "Whatever. I did the next best thing—I stocked up on food, water, and other supplies, and took off for the opposite side of the island."

Cole remembered that hardly anyone lived on that side. It was arid with very little rainfall compared to the lush, tropical side of the island the base was on. A large, dormant volcano rose up from the middle of the island which disrupted the winds and causing the discrepancy in moisture. He'd driven around the volcano once, but the roads were narrow and twisted with barely any shoulder. It had been a white-knuckle drive and he'd only done it the one time. He supposed, if given a heads up, it would have been a suitable refuge. But that didn't excuse that Pete had fled instead of trying to help stop the pandemic.

His disgust must have shown in his eyes, because Pete said, "I understand your revulsion. Believe me, it's not my proudest moment, but there was nothing I could do by then. Too many people had already spread the virus beyond the island. I did what I could. I had a few other guys from the base, and we managed to survive on our supplies and turtles, crabs, and fish. It was tempting to stay there longer, but we had to know."

"Had to know...?"

Pete rubbed his eyes with the thumb and fingers of his right hand and his voice caught as he went on, "We had to know if anyone else on the island survived." He raised his gaze and shook his head, giving Cole the answer.

"That's rough. We know how you feel, although we have found other survivors in the area. One group was...let's just say, they were bizarre and a bit scary."

Pete drew a deep breath. "Yeah, I found some crazies in D.C. too, when we finally made it there. But, when we came out, I went back to the lab and tried to find anything I could to help me understand what had happened. One of the records I came across listed you as having been ill the year or so before."

Cole blinked. "And...?"

Pete leaned forward. "I think you were patient zero."

Cole knew exactly what that meant. That he had been the first victim of the disease, but that couldn't be because he was just fine and his symptoms when he'd been ill on the island hadn't been the same as those who had Sympatico Syndrome. "I don't buy it. I had a bad strep pneumonia."

"That's what they told you then. What were they going to say?" He made air quotes, adopting a falsetto as he said, "Whoops, we accidentally let our experimental virus escape the lab?"

Cole took a step back, his mind also retreating to that time. He'd been so sick he barely remembered anything about it. He seemed to recall them giving him clotting factor and had assumed he'd developed DIC, a bleeding disorder that sometimes occurred as a side effect of infections.

"To make a long story short, I figured you were the first patient, and from what I can tell, the only survivor of Sympatico Syndrome."

"But my symptoms weren't like everyone else's and you have no proof that's what I had." Elly would know more about what was the current thinking at the time the virus hit, but from what he recalled, there was no definitive test for the disease. There hadn't been time to manufacture one.

Pete leaned forward, his eyes boring into his. "Listen, Cole, *you had it*. The doctors knew about it, but covered it up—but, I figured it out. They even had samples of your blood stored in the lab and were trying to make a vaccine before the shit hit the fan. Unfortunately, they never got a chance to finish."

Cole shook his head, trying to deny what Pete said, but it all made sense and he couldn't think of a reason this guy would make it up. "How did you get here?"

The abrupt change of subject caught Pete off-guard and he blinked a few times before he caught up to what Cole had asked. "The guys who hid with me were—are—pilots. One flies both helicopters and jets, the others are fighter pilots. We had to island hop a bit to change aircraft and find enough that were filled with fuel, but we finally made it to the west coast."

Hope brimmed in Cole. Maybe the disease had been less devastating there. His eyes must have reflected his thoughts because Pete dropped his head, shaking it. "If anything, they were harder hit than here. When we flew to several states and towns between San Diego and New York, down to D.C. and it was the same everywhere. From

the sky, it looks so strange. As if time had stopped. There's no movement—no light."

Cole pulled a chair out and sat heavily. He braced his elbows on
the table and ran his hands through his hair. With next to no communication with the rest of the world, there had always been a drop of
hope that some corner of the country had been spared. Now that drop
had evaporated. "So, you still haven't explained why you're here."

"Look, I'm not going to beat around the bush. I know who you
are. I saw you on Aislado, and I recognize you, so don't even try to
deny it."

He opened his mouth to protest when Holland held a hand up in a
stop gesture. "I'm here to take you to Washington with me."

Caught off guard, Cole pushed back from the table. "Like hell! I'm
not going anywhere with you."

"I need your blood so I can create a cure, and maybe one day, a
vaccine. Only your blood carries the antibodies."

Cole stood, his mind in turmoil. Of course he wanted a cure for
the virus. Sympatico Syndrome had spread like wildfire last
summer and with the warm months approaching, there was always
the threat it could return. But *would it*? It began on an island with
accidental transmission to military personnel. It wasn't a naturally
occurring infection and he wasn't sure if there were still active cases
out in the wild. Viruses often had some kind of reservoir even if
they were dormant. He supposed as fast as it had spread, there had
to be remote villages that had never been reached. At least, he
hoped so. But what if there were still people actively spreading
the virus?

Had his and his family's isolation fooled him into believing that
the threat had passed? There was really no way for him to know for
certain. And if it was still a threat, and if he alone held the key to
survival of the human race, then he had to take whatever measures he
needed to take to unlock the door to a cure.

"I can't leave. I have responsibilities here."

"Your family? I take it they're still alive? How's your son?
Hunter's his name, right? And your brother's family? They're okay?"

Cole clenched his jaw, hiding his surprise at how much Holland
knew about him. But if he found his medical records, it was just one

more step to find out about his family and how Hunter had lived with Sean while Cole was stationed at Aislado Island.

"They can all come. I can't bring them all at once due to lack of room, but in a few days, we can come back and get the rest." Pete smiled as if offering to take them on an all-expenses paid vacation.

"No. That won't work." Even if he was for the idea, which he wasn't, he doubted the others would want to go. Hunter would come with him if asked, and Sophie would go where Hunter went. Elly would come also, he was sure, but the others might not want to leave the island. Sean would probably fight leaving, and if he stayed, so would Jenna and Piper. If Piper stayed, so would Jake. The kids would lose half of their new family too. After they'd so recently lost their own mother, he couldn't do that to them. And Cole couldn't even blame Sean for balking, if it came down to it. He'd throw on the brakes if Sean wanted to drag the whole group to D.C. What kind of life would await them in the capitol? Unless... maybe things were better there. "Is there even a government left in the capitol?" Maybe there would be law and order back East.

Pete gnawed on his lower lip before he replied, "I wish I could say yes, but from what I saw, there were two small factions that were fighting over who would claim leadership. Neither seemed too promising."

"What about the President? Didn't he survive?" His earlier adrenaline had drained away and with heavy steps, he paced between the door and the far wall, stopping to throw a few more sticks in the stove. The drying sweat chilled him.

"I'm not sure. He may have been sequestered away—you know, down in the bunker." Pete spread his hands. "I wish I knew more, but things were chaotic."

"Then why go back there?"

"Because it's the Capitol, there are areas where power is still running for at least a few hours a day. I guess someone at the power company basically kept a skeleton staff locked in, unless they showed any signs of illness, then they were shot dead where they stood."

"Seriously? How do you know this?" It sounded so cold and ruthless, but then again, with no cure and how quickly the virus spread, he understood the drastic solution.

"I don't know for certain, but that was the rumor. They said the government sent the workers supplies—that somebody near the top had enough foresight to at least try to keep services going."

Cole gazed at the men by the helicopter. One stamped his foot, probably starting to feel the effects of the cold and it made him think about Sean, Hunter, and Piper still out there. They'd be feeling the cold too. He should let them know that there was no imminent threat.

"So, they have power, but that still doesn't mean I have to go to D.C. Take my blood here and now. I don't object to that part." He swept his hand out towards the lake. "We have plenty of ice to pack it in."

"But we may need to run a few tests on you as well. And maybe having your family come out would also be a good thing. We could test them as well."

"*Oh, hell no!*" Cole didn't even have to think on his response. It burst out of him like a cork from a bottle. "My family isn't going to be poked and tested by the very same people who destroyed humanity.

"I could make you go." Pete gestured to the helicopter. "We have the firepower."

"I don't think you realize this, but I have snipers stationed right now who have your men in their sights. One false move and they're dead." It was a stretch calling Sean, Hunter, and Piper snipers, but they were out there— hopefully keeping an eye on the men near the copter.

Pete's eyes narrowed as he ripped off his mask, his nostrils flaring. "You're making this harder than it needs to be. If I go, I'll just be back with a lot more back-up. I figured you were dead, even if you hadn't died of the virus, you'd have died of something else, like so many others have."

Cole crossed his arms, his gaze fixed on Pete, who shrugged. "I thought you were a reasonable guy, Cole, and with your background, you'd jump at the chance for a cure or vaccine. I guess I was mistaken."

"Your mistake was in coming here in military helicopters, armed and threatening. I've offered my blood. It's the best I can do right now."

"But we may need to test your family too. They've all survived, which is pretty much unheard of."

Grief at Trent's death tinted Cole's next words, "We haven't been left unscathed. Now, I'm not going to ask you again to leave. I will simply give the signal to my snipers."

Pete's mouth twisted into a snarl. "If you kill us then there will *never* be a cure!"

"So be it. We've survived this long." In the back of his mind, he wondered if he, Elly, and Jenna would be able to create a treatment once they reached the Hoover Dam, if power was still up and running. There were universities there, computers with files and books. They wouldn't be starting from scratch. It wasn't crazy to think they might be able to pull it off. Especially Elly. Her background had more lab work than Cole's own.

As the idea flitted through his mind, Pete strode up to him until they were nearly nose to mask. "Do you *really* want to be the last man on Earth?"

Refusing to back down, Cole leaned close, cocking his head. "It won't come to that, but if it does, I'll be sure to turn the lights off before I die."

Chapter Eleven

"I THINK WE SHOULD STAY PUT." Sean crossed his arms, his bottom lip jutting out as he leaned back against the kitchen counter. "Holland won't be back, Cole. It was an empty threat. And so what if he does come back? We'll be even better prepared this time."

Cole rested his elbows on the table, sliding his hands up through his hair, tempted to pull it out. No matter what he suggested, Sean always took the opposing view. All he wanted was an open mind from everyone. Was that too much to ask? He sighed. It would take an act of Congress to change his brother's mind and, since Congress didn't exist anymore as far as Cole knew, he would get no help from that quarter. "Look, I welcome your opinion. That's why I called this meeting. Everyone gets a chance to speak their mind."

He'd striven to keep his voice calm and neutral but Elly's light tap on his thigh beneath the table warned him that he was close to crossing the line. He reached under the table and gave her hand a gentle squeeze. "Sean...listen...I'm sorry if I made it sound like this was a done deal. It is still very much just an idea I had. I wanted to leave even before Holland showed up, but his threat to return with back-up does have me concerned. Even if we had a whole arsenal at our disposal, I don't want to risk anyone in our group. We might win the battle but at what cost? I think we'd be better off leaving before they can return and try to force us to go to D.C. I'm no dictator—everyone can contribute valuable input before we vote on a decision."

He'd wanted to discuss leaving even before Pete Holland arrived and now wished he had spoken up. The evening Hunter had fallen through the ice had been his initial attempt, but first his son then Mike, had dozed off. Everyone was tired, so they had tabled the discussion. Then the next few days had been taken up by moving the animals and horses back to the mainland. And then Holland had shown up. At least they had some preparations done already. That way, if they decided to leave, they could do so fairly quickly.

Today, they had made several trips back and forth scavenging as many supplies as they could find. The air was warming and open areas farther out in the bay harkened the coming spring. Tomorrow, they'd make their last trip over via car from the north side of the island, where the ice was still thick enough. A narrow channel had opened on the south end, and if tomorrow was warm, he expected it to widen enough to get the boats through.

No matter what their decision, Steve and Mike had agreed to wait until Cole could return by boat to give them an answer as they were taking care of the horses. With the assistance of their plow, Cole had even been able to get to a few farms on the outskirts of town to find some feed and hay for the horses. He'd brought some back for chickens and goats as well.

Cole caught Elly's eye, hoping she recognized that he'd made a conciliatory statement to his brother. She gave a brief nod before she swept the room with her gaze.

Everyone was gathered in the kitchen, either sitting at the table or leaning against a counter.

Elly cleared her throat. "I won't lie—I would love to go somewhere warmer than Wisconsin." She put on an exaggerated Southern accent as she said, "I'm a Georgia gal and I didn't like snow before the virus and I *really* don't like it now." She smiled as everyone chuckled. "But, it's not just a matter of not liking snow, I agree with Cole that if we head south I think we'll have a greater chance of surviving next winter. The growing season is longer, the winters aren't as harsh, and if we get solar panels, going south means more sunshine and less need for energy to heat our homes. If we decide to try for Vegas with the hope that the Hoover Dam is still supplying power out there, then we can either get things running, or help out whomever else is already there."

It was Cole's turn to give her thigh a light touch, but only to convey his appreciation for her words of support. As someone who had grown up in the southern part of the country, she had first-hand experience with what it could be like. "You've made excellent points."

"I could work in the hospital and have real equipment again." Jenna didn't look at Sean as she spoke, and Cole wondered if she was purposefully avoiding her husband's eyes, or if she was just unaware that he'd stiffened as she voiced a differing opinion.

She continued, "Supplies might be hard to come by, but we could adapt; make our own bandages and such. Just having a real hospital would be a huge first step in re-establishing healthcare. If we had power, there's no reason all of the equipment in a hospital wouldn't work. Medical gases might be in short supply, but we could use oxygen concentrators picked up from home care companies."

Cole knew she was losing the others when she started talking details so he cut in, "I agree, Jenna. What happens when someone here gets seriously sick or injured?" He hoped the question would refocus the group on how it might affect them all personally. "We have Sophie due in about two months, right?" He looked to Sophie, raising his eyebrows. Her hand went to her abdomen and she gave a shy smile and a brief nod. She wasn't very big, but Jenna said with it being the young woman's first child, that was normal.

"So we move everyone across the country just because one girl is pregnant?" Sean rolled his eyes. "It's a wonder people managed before electricity. Somehow the human race made it just fine without modern medicine."

Elly squared her shoulders and leveled a look at Sean. "Actually, it shouldn't matter if it's one *woman* or fifty. And people—especially pregnant women—didn't manage just fine before modern medicine. Maternal death rates were about one percent per birth. Let that sink in. So a woman who gave birth five times, which wasn't unusual, had a lifetime risk of between five and ten percent."

Jenna nodded as Elly spoke and added, "Sean, one of the most important things we have to do is protect any new babies and their mothers. What's the point of any surviving if there's nobody left after we die?"

Sean's brow furrowed. "What are you talking about? The point is that *we* keep on living. We have to focus on the here and now, not some distant future."

Glaring, Jenna shook her head and waved a hand dismissively before crossing her arms.

Cole glanced around, noting the squirming and uneasy looks the younger set sent each other. Clearly, they were uncomfortable being in the midst of the couples' disagreement.

He didn't want to add fuel to Jenna's fire, but he had to agree with her. "She's exactly right, Sean." Cole stood and moved to the far end of the kitchen so he could have everyone in his view at the same time. "Elly and I have guessed, based on what we've seen as far as survival rates and extrapolating that to the whole region, the country, and probably the world, that roughly ninety-five to ninety-nine percent of the human population has been wiped out by the virus or secondary effects such as dying in accidents or lack of care. I'm talking about the elderly and children left parentless."

Everyone looked at Zoë and Luke who played in the living room. Over the months they had been here, he and Elly had become surrogate parents to the siblings, but everyone doted on them. They were lucky to have been found and yet, Cole counted himself the lucky one.

He waved vaguely towards the mainland and the highways. "The roads are chock full of accidents and cars full of dead occupants—presumably from the virus. Hunter saw the same on his way here, and Elly and Jake gave us their account of what was left of Chicago. It's not encouraging. Pete Holland confirmed what we'd already feared. He had no reason to lie."

"Yeah, I get that. Millions—I guess billions—have died, but there's nothing we can do about that. We have to worry about what happens today and tomorrow, not ten years or fifty years from now." Sean had a point and Cole hoped to defuse the situation by acknowledging it.

"That's true. We do have to worry, first, about our immediate survival and I think we've done a pretty good job of that so far. Staying here next year, we won't have the same supplies sitting in unoccupied houses. We, or others, will have used them up or they won't be good anymore. Just getting the feed for the animals took most of the day—what with the snow and all of the detouring around blocked roads."

Sean shrugged and looked at his hands. Cole shifted his gaze to encompass everyone. "But, Jenna's correct in that we can't only worry about today, or even next month. We have to give careful thought to what we do in the next few years to assure the best chances of survival— not only ours— but those who come *after* us." Cole swept the group, his gaze lingering on Hunter and Sophie. "I don't know about you, but I don't want my children and grandchildren to live short, harsh, lives, having to scrape every day just to get by and have enough to eat."

"But we're doing fine here." Sean didn't sound as certain as he had only moments before. Then he lifted his chin and shot Cole a look. "And if you're so worried about survival, why didn't you go back to D.C. with Holland by yourself, get the cure going, and then return? Or did you think we couldn't get by without you?"

Sean's pointed question stung. Cole had been second guessing himself since the helicopter took off. "I offered to give a blood sample —which is really all he needed. I don't trust him. I know I'm not indispensable. I think we all make valuable contributions and we can't afford to lose anyone—not just me."

Cole held Sean's gaze until his brother shifted and took a sip from his steaming mug. Clearing his throat, more to clear his mind than his vocal cords, Cole resumed speaking. "And moving on, I fear that usable supplies left in homes and stores in this area are going to be exhausted soon. As few people as there are, we know we aren't the *only* survivors. Between them, the rodents and other scavengers, we're going to be hurting in, at most, a year or so."

Joe hadn't said anything, but he raised his chin in agreement when their eyes met. Cole was glad to have the older man's backing. He was almost certain Joe could have left the group and survived just fine on his own. He was resourceful and competent. The only thing he gained by sticking with Cole's group was companionship and Cole worried that too much strife in the group would drive him away.

"Right now, we can get a few generators running and find gasoline at gas stations. We just need the generators to get the pump running. It was easier before to just siphon what we needed, but fuel left in car tanks is degrading—if we're going to use cars to travel, we need to do it soon. We'll have to tap into what's stored underground at gas stations."

Sean nodded at that, and Cole was relieved that at least his brother agreed on that point. "Right now, we have a brief opportunity—a golden hour, so to speak—to scavenge enough on our way to wherever we decide to go. We need to collect as much food and other supplies to last us several years. It's going to take at least that long to get some semblance of what we had before. We need to go to where the most people lived to find the most supplies. It's also the most dangerous way to go, but we really don't have much choice. Not if we want to do more than just survive. If we want to rebuild society, we'll have to make hard choices and take chances."

There. He was done with the lecture. Cole moved to the stove and poured a cup of hot water from the kettle, grabbing one of the remaining tea bags from an empty coffee can. The bag was already heavily used, but he dropped it in the cup anyway. It would give at little flavor to the hot water. Keeping his back to the group, he sprinkled in some dried wild mint leaves Jenna had found in the fall. She had planted some in small pots that were scattered throughout the house. He thought about plucking a few fresh leaves to add but didn't want to leave the kitchen. The dried leaves gave the tea a good flavor and an even better aroma. He returned to the table and took a sip of the steaming brew as they digested what he'd said.

Hunter caught Cole's eye and looked as if he had something to say. Cole gestured to him as if giving him the floor.

"When I traveled back here, I saw a lot of death even though I did my best to avoid roads and highways. My dad is right. Within days of the virus, stores and gas stations along the highways were trashed. People had been desperate and had cleaned the places out of most of the food. When we went to the supercenter in the fall, most of the food from there was gone too. You all saw what we brought back. That was it. We might find some of it in homes, but we might not ever find where people hid their stash before it spoils. So, I just think the sooner we start scavenging, and I mean, *seriously scavenging*, the better off we'll be. We need time to get tractors running—time to learn how to operate them at all. Has anyone here ever driven a tractor?"

Nobody replied, and Sean looked down, rubbing the back of his neck. Cole felt a spark of pride for Hunter. He was spotting problems and trying to find solutions. "He's right. That's just one thing we'll need to learn. So far we've lived off what we've scavenged, fished, and hunted. We've done okay but we've never had a big reserve and we all learned how devastating one disaster can be. If the fire that destroyed the food shed hadn't been discovered soon enough for us to get at least some of the food out, we would be hurting a lot more right now."

There were nods and murmurs of agreement.

Piper cleared her throat, sending a quick glance at her dad before looking away as she said, "We need more flour and I'm not sure where we'll get it. We need to learn how to grind wheat, I guess. And soon. I'm worried that what we find this year will be spoiled by bugs. I've already had to throw some of it away. I can't imagine flour still sitting on shelves in pantries or stores is going to be bug free."

"Right, so we're going to have to learn not just how to grow wheat, but how to get it from the field and transformed into loaves of bread." Cole gave Piper a brief nod and smile for her contribution. "Most of the advancements in the last century have come with a price —knowledge that was commonly known has been lost. We have had to re-learn basic survival skills, but it would be better if we didn't have to go all the way back to the middle-ages, and instead, could skip ahead a few hundred years."

"Okay, fine—I get that we'll need to start creating stuff from scratch, but why can't we do it right here? I got the windmill going, and I bet we could devise some kind of grindstone using power generated from it."

"That's a good idea, Sean. But one of the things we need to fix as soon as we can is our knowledge deficit."

"What? Are we too stupid?" Sean's reasonable tone had given way to belligerence again.

Cole tried to diffuse it with laughter. "No—everyone here is very intelligent. We have that going for us. I'm talking about knowledge about how to rebuild a civilization. What I hope is that we'll be able to recreate some semblance of what we've lost—not just scratch out a living, barely subsisting on what we can grow on our own. One of my reasons for wanting to travel south is that I think it's where others will go too, and more people means more knowledge and experience we can draw upon. That's what I meant by knowledge deficit. We're all smart, but none of us possess all the knowledge needed to re-create our old world." He hated to say it, but someone had to put the mark of finality on what life had been like before the virus versus what it was going to be afterward. "We will never get back to what we had—not in our lifetimes—but if we start right now, it's possible our grandchildren or great-grandchildren might have it even better."

Sean grunted, then after a long pause, nodded and said, "Yeah. I guess you can count us in."

Jenna threw him a look. "Thanks, but I was already counted in."

His eyes wide, Sean looked at Jenna. "What's that supposed to mean?"

She started to reply, but then clammed up. "We'll discuss it later."

Should he say something? Cole didn't want to get into the middle of a couple's argument, so he changed the subject. "Okay, so…the next thing on the agenda—how do you all feel about Mike and Steve accompanying us? Mike's hand is almost healed, he has a bit of tape on it, but he should be good as new, right?" He raised an eyebrow at Jenna, who confirmed his statement with a nod—"and so they'll either be on their way, or stay with us to head out as soon as the weather turns."

Everyone turned to look at Sean, who spread his arms. "*What?*"

"I guess you've become the devil's advocate in the group," Elly answered Sean's question. "And that's not a bad thing at all, Sean. It's important to look at all sides."

"They seem okay to me. Mike's a machinist. If he'd been here when I was getting the windmill together, I'm sure it would have gone a lot faster. Guys like that are good to have around."

Cole reached beneath the table and found Elly's knee, giving it a squeeze in thanks for her diplomatic response that elicited a well-reasoned reply from his brother. "Good point, Sean. Does anyone else have an opinion?"

Hunter said, "I like Mike. I trust him and I think he should go. I don't know Steve very well."

After draining the last bit of tea from his cup, Cole pushed it away. "Well, no pressure, but Steve told me yesterday that their group got tired of waiting and were leaving this morning. They told Steve that he and Mike could catch up when they were done here. Obviously, they aren't thrilled about being left behind to make their way on their own. They worry about missing the group and never catching up."

"I just want to say that I had nowhere to go until I met up with Elly and if it hadn't been for all of you, I'd probably be dead right now." Jake sent a glance around the room, but his gaze held on Cole's. "I don't really get a say in this I know, being a tag along, but I just wanted all of you to know that I'm so glad you let me stay."

Before Cole could even reply, everyone started speaking at once, letting Jake know that he was very much part of the group and that he had a say in the decision. Cole raised his hand for quiet, holding it up until the comments dwindled. "Clearly, we have consensus here." He grinned then leaned forward, his voice serious as he said, "Make no mistake about it, Jake, you are just as much a part of this group as I am, or Jenna, or Hunter, Piper—in short, all of us." He turned to Sophie. "And you, too. And I'd say that even if you and Hunter weren't about to have my grandchild." His last comment lightened the mood and everyone chuckled.

Jake laughed. "She has an advantage over me." He batted his eyelashes at Hunter in mock adoration.

Hunter shook his head, grinning as he tossed a dishtowel at Jake.

"Okay, so, back to the question. Steve and Mike have some skills we could use, not to mention they are fairly young and healthy. We need people like them to help rebuild. My vote is for them to come along. All in favor, raise your hands." Everyone but Sean raised their hand.

Sean looked around, then slowly put his hand up as a smile spread across his face. "I just like making you all sweat."

Everyone laughed, but then Sean added, "I'm still going to keep my eye on them."

Chapter Twelve

COLE LOOKED over the supplies stacked beside the truck and jotted down the contents of the boxes, baskets, and bags on the clipboard. Every day, he wondered if this would be the day that Holland returned. It had been a week and every second they remained where they were, was another second Holland could be getting closer.

Each vehicle would have an inventory so they would know exactly where everything was. Items they would use while traveling needed to be packed last so they would be within easy reach. Everyone had their own pack—a go-pack— with survival gear in it. If they had to leave sight of the vehicles for any reason, they were to take their packs with them.

Each bag had a supply of food, matches, a lighter, a small fishing kit, a hatchet and a knife, as well as a small tarp and sleeping bag as well as a change of dry clothes, with extra socks. The tarp could be used to make a lean-to shelter. Each bag also had a handgun and ammunition. All of it was packed already, and he'd double checked to make sure each car had the right packs for who was assigned to that vehicle. It wouldn't do Jake much good if he mixed his pack up with Sophie's and had her size clothes in it. He chuckled at the image of the strapping young man trying to squeeze into a women's small sweatshirt.

As he calculated the logistics of packing the growing stack, Hunter set yet another box on the ground, starting a new stack. Cole scratched his cheek. *Damn.* They had acquired a lot stuff over the last week in addition to what they'd already had. He hoped there was enough room for everything. In addition to making space for what they were taking, they had to leave space for items they might find on the journey. While vehicles were easy to find, many didn't have keys in them or had decomposed bodies inside. They were lucky they had a good sized moving truck from when they first fled to the island. He still felt a nagging guilt that he had never returned it, but knew it was ridiculous to feel guilty. The feeling was a remnant from when they had the luxury of not having to make life and death decisions. Besides, even if he had tried to return the truck to the rental franchise the chance of anyone even being there to receive the truck was infinitesimally small.

It had been luck that the truck had been available, but also foresight to attempt to obtain a truck in the first place. It had enabled them to bring enough supplies, and later, gather enough to keep them alive for almost a year.

In the time since making the decision to head west—and in the days since the ice finally melted—they had ventured into almost every home and business within five miles of the shore. Instead of hauling recovered goods back to the island, they stored it in a few garages nearest the truck. Steve and Mike already on the mainland taking care of the horses, had ranged even farther away. They had stripped the library of books that had to do with science, medical, farming, survival skills, Nevada, maps, as well as a good selection of fiction for all ages. Sean and Steve hadn't seen the point of bringing boxes of novels, but Cole and Elly had insisted. If he'd had more room, he'd have brought even more books. Jenna had a few of her own nursing books, and Cole had packed a couple of periodicals about epidemiology—mostly in hopes of coming across something about Sympatico Syndrome—but there had been no information on it. It wasn't a total waste though as there had been several other good articles.

Steve and Mike had collected tools of every kind, spare tires and parts for the truck, along with boxes of nails, screws, washers, bolts and assorted fasteners. Who knew people had kept so much crap in their garages, basements, and closets? An apparent prepper had left a basement stuffed to the gills with canned goods, powdered milk, and several cases of MREs. Best of all, were buckets of wheat, rice, and rolled oats. There was enough to get them through the summer and, hopefully, to a successful harvest.

They had spread the food out over three vehicles and packed it in first. Cole didn't want to have to use any of it on the trip. It was their food supply when they got to their destination.

Sean had grudgingly conceded that maybe Mike and Steve weren't so bad—after all, the men could have taken their find and been long gone before the ice melted. Instead, they were sharing with Cole's group—now their group, too.

Standing flat against the side of the truck were sheets of plywood. Cole didn't know what they'd use it for and had almost left it, thinking if they needed wood, they could always get some from buildings along the way, but Joe had convinced him having a few sheets on hand might be a good idea. These sheets had been stored indoors and weren't warped or damaged.

A second moving truck was on the agenda and they were on the lookout for a rental like the one they already had. Not to rent, of course, but for simplicity. They were big trucks but didn't require knowledge of how to drive a big semi-truck.

Cole had raided a car dealership and taken a couple of high-end SUVs from the showrooms. If he put out of his mind the circumstances, he could admit that it had been kind of fun having his pick of vehicles. Was this how he was going to be from now on? Gleefully taking whatever he could find? He knew it wasn't stealing exactly but it helped tamp down any traces of guilt when he focused on improving the survival odds of his family.

The practicality of choosing the SUVs also played a factor in taking them. Despite their size, they got relatively good gas mileage, according to the stickers in the window. Cole hoped it hadn't been false advertising. They'd had to jumpstart both vehicles since they had been sitting for so long, but once running for a while, the batteries charged right up.

The car lot had been a great place to find gasoline as well. And, as a bonus, it had been cleaner than most that they'd found in the wild, so to speak, since the vehicles had been brand new and barely driven.

"Cole, what about these?" Jake pulled a child's wagon laden with three car batteries.

"Ah, great idea. I can't believe I didn't think of it." He added the batteries on his clipboard. "Just leave them in the wagon. We'll load it up just like it is."

Jake dropped the handle and stretched. "I topped up all of the gas cans earlier. In all, we have about 40 gallons in addition to what we have in the tanks."

Cole's jaw tensed. That wasn't going to come close to getting them to Nevada. "Thanks, Jake." His main worry was fuel, but Steve thought that further out, they might come across a gas station that still had gasoline that they could pump using a generator. He said plenty of stations had generators as back–up when power went out—you just had to know about them. But, for now, they had to make do with what they found and extra they could carry with them.

"Where are we going to store them?"

"Good question." The idea of transporting flammable liquid in the vehicles made him nervous. "Hey, have you seen any of those carts landscapers tow behind their trucks?" If they could find one, it would be perfect. Light enough not to cause much of a change in their gas mileage, but large enough for extra gas and other items like rakes, shovels and other implements that didn't need protection from the elements.

Jake bit his lip as he gazed down the street. "You know, I think there might be one a few blocks over."

"If you need help getting it, let Hunter know. He should be back soon with another load from the island."

"Will do. I'll go see if I can find the house where I saw it." He trotted down the street, his gait easy and relaxed even though he'd been working all morning.

Jake had grown probably another two inches since he'd arrived at the island with Elly, but it was more than his physical appearance that had changed—he still had a fun-loving streak—but now it was tempered by a serious side. In short, Jake had grown up. Cole wondered how well they would have fared without the young man.

Hunter, Piper, and Sophie had all grown up more quickly than they would have in the absence of the global catastrophe. They'd had to. Cole knew he had also grown, in a way. While no stranger to taking command of a situation—his career had trained him in that regard—there had always been a chain of command. There was always someone higher up the chain than he'd been. Now, he had somehow become the de facto leader. He hadn't asked for the position or even wanted it, but he felt everyone's eyes on him when decisions had to be made. Like this one about leaving the island. He drew a deep breath. He hoped like hell he wasn't leading them from the frying pan into the fire.

What if things weren't as bad as they anticipated? What if there were more survivors than he and Elly had predicted? He'd never be more thrilled to be wrong. What if the virus had been stopped, somehow? Holland could have been lying, or he might have just flat out been wrong. After all, he couldn't cover the whole country—not even with aircraft at his disposal.

As he stashed boxes and rearranged gear, his mind wandered. Maybe help just hadn't reached them yet. If there was even a semblance of government in D.C. it was possible they would eventually reach Wisconsin with help.

Cole thought back to the last ten months. Natural disasters often took weeks or even months for everyone to get help and those were in localized areas to some extent. Even hurricanes only affected relatively small portions of the globe at a time. With everyone getting hit by the virus, it would naturally take much longer for the government to respond.

With spring's arrival, he expected whatever help was available to start making its way to cities. That was why they had to leave. He had to know what it was like out there. If they hadn't left as a group, he was certain he would have made his own excursion eventually when he felt his absence wouldn't be missed.

After all, they hadn't had any news outside of their small area since a week or so after the virus hit. News reports back then had shown the disease tearing through cities. He had no doubt that death rates were the same all over. Isolated villages deep in the Amazon, or in Africa or Asia might have been spared, but even they had contact with outsiders fairly often. That was how Ebola had been transmitted, only it went from deep in the jungle to the outside world. This would be the reverse, from outside, in.

Cole expected there were many small bands like theirs, and possibly some lone survivors hiding out in the woods and mountains, but with all communication cut off, there was no way to know how many people there might be.

While Hunter had been in college prior to the pandemic, Cole hadn't thought of him as an adult yet. Technically, he was, but their relationship had been very much one of parent and child, not one of two adults. Now, it was. Only the little kids, Lucas and Zoë, were treated as children, and they too, had chores every day. Nothing difficult, but Cole had been impressed with how helpful two little kids could be.

Elly had been concerned with their education, and so every day, the kids spent time learning math, reading, writing, science and history.

She had even broken into a school and taken books, workbooks, paper, library books and more. Those items were on the priority list of supplies that couldn't be left behind.

He turned at the sound of a boat approaching.

"Dad! Tie me off." Hunter eased the boat along the dock and Cole jogged over to the pier, taking the rope from his son and looping it over a cleat.

The boat rode low in the water and he saw why. Sean had cleaned out all of the tools he had and packed them up, along with parts from the windmill. Jammed in at the front of the boat were the extra stoves, now dismantled to make them fit in the boat. This was the last major load and it meant that they were leaving for good.

"Sean and Elly are coming over in the little boat to help us unload, while Jenna, Piper, and the kids go through the cabins to make sure we didn't miss anything. I'll go back and get them when we're done unloading this."

Sophie emerged from the cabin of the boat, a basket in her hands. "I have lunch for everyone." She moved to step out of the boat, and

Hunter put his hands at her waist to help her, while Cole extended a hand.

"Hey, I can do it." She shook her head, grinning over her shoulder at Hunter. "I'm not that clumsy."

"Hey, I read all about how pregnant women's balance changes."

Cole smiled as even amidst her protests, Sophie put her hand in his and allowed him to steady her as she stepped onto the dock. Her eyes twinkled as she scowled in mock anger at Cole. "Why did you have to give him that *What to Expect* book? He thinks he's my doctor now."

Shrugging, he decided his safest response was to pretend ignorance and change the subject. He took the basket from her. "What do we have in here?" It smelled delicious and he tried to think what it could possibly be.

Their scavenging had turned up more canned food and meals were often eclectic mixes. Yesterday they'd had refried beans, pineapple chunks, and peanut butter and jelly for dinner.

"There's a loaf of sourdough, honey, two cans of peaches, the fish leftover from dinner last night, potatoes baked in the coals, and to drink, Kool-Aid."

"Kool-Aid?" He wondered how that had fit in the basket without spilling.

"Well, there will be once it's mixed. Jake found a canister in a pantry at a daycare. We just need to add water."

When was the last time he's had the sweet drink? Probably not since Hunter had been a little kid.

After lunch and a brief rest, everything was loaded, vehicles were filled with gasoline, and Joe opened his house to the group to spend the night before an early departure the next morning. The only thing left to pack were the animals.

Exhausted, Cole sank onto the pile of blankets Elly had made into a bed on the floor for them. Every room was staked out, with Joe taking one last night in his own room. Elly had claimed a small bedroom upstairs. Sean and Jenna had the third bedroom. Hunter and Sophie had the den because it had a sofa bed that had been too heavy to move, but was still in good shape. In deference to Sophie's more advanced pregnancy, she got the bed. Although dusty, the whole house was surprisingly clean, but that was probably because all the food had long ago been transferred over to the island so rodents had left the home alone. The occasional visits had also been enough to keep it from being too overrun with spiders and the like as well. Furniture had been moved to the island over the course of last summer, so all that was left in Joe's house were a few large dressers, a couple of chairs, and the sofa bed.

Elly snuggled next to him, her head nestled in the hollow of his neck, his arm beneath hers. "How's the mother hen doing?"

"Okay, I guess." He draped his other arm over his eyes and yawned.

"Think any of the eggs will hatch?"

"Probably a long shot, but who knows? We have nothing to lose by trying."

After hearing a rooster crow early one morning while scavenging, Jake and Hunter had headed in the direction of the sound. They hadn't found the rooster, but had caught a couple of feral chickens. It had been a few weeks now and one of the hens had been hiding eggs since caught and Joe said that was a sign she was brooding.

In the last few days, she had been sitting on nine eggs. With Sophie's help—she had a knack for calming all the animals, but especially the chickens—all of the eggs, and then the hen had been carefully moved into the back of one of the new SUVs. They had accomplished the transfer two nights ago in hopes that by the time they got on the road, the hen was comfortable and secure enough not to abandon her nest. Having the hen nest inside was going to make the vehicle stink, but Cole hoped driving with the windows cracked would minimize the stench. Because it was brand new, the SUV had the smoothest ride and the box with the nest had been cushioned with old quilts and blankets beneath it. Cole had checked on the hen this morning, and so far, she seemed content. With any luck, there was still a chance the eggs would hatch. If not, well, they would still get more eggs from her later. If her egg laying days were over, she was bound for the soup pot. His mouth watered at the thought of fresh chicken soup. Soup would have to wait. A batch of chicks would be much better in the long run than one pot of soup. Still, as he drifted off to sleep, his mouth watered as vivid memories of homemade chicken noodle soup flooded his mind.

He rolled over, doing his best to ignore the craving. If the eggs did, by some miracle, hatch, that would be a great start to a real flock. At some point, they would have enough chickens to add soup to their menu. It would be too much to hope that one was a rooster, but he hoped anyway. All they needed was one.

Chapter Thirteen

SEAN RUMMAGED behind the seat of the rental truck as Cole approached and called out, "Hey, Jenna, did you pack my extra boots?"

"Not Jenna." Cole grinned as Sean turned his head, his eyebrows raised in surprise. "I just want to make sure you have your maps and stuff." Dawn hadn't yet broken, but the sky to the east was lightening.

"Oh, sorry." He gestured over the seat to the dashboard. "I have the map right there. I know how to follow a map, Cole." He resumed searching for the boots.

"Of course you do. I'm just double checking with everyone. With how hectic everything has been the last few days, it wouldn't surprise me if things get lost. That's all."

"Yeah, I know." Sean found his boots stashed behind the driver's seat, and apparently satisfied, shut the door and faced Cole. "Look, Cole. I'm sorry. I get why we're leaving. I really do, but that doesn't mean I'm thrilled to go, you know?"

"It's hard to leave. Despite our problems, the island was a pretty good home when we needed one. I'm going to miss it." Cole gazed out over the bay. The island wasn't visible from where they were even if it had been light enough to see, and that saddened him. Would they ever get back here? He chose to believe that they would someday.

Jenna approached, arms laden with last minute items. "I guess this is it."

Cole nodded. "See you guys at lunch." He waved as they finished stashing items and moved down the line. Maps had been scrounged up for every vehicle, with their intended route marked in pencil. Cole didn't know what the actual route would hold and they would adjust accordingly. Besides fuel, his other worry was communication, and he'd asked Sean about CB radios. Was that something that would still work if the power grid was down, and what were the chances of finding any? Steve had offered that he'd driven a truck while in the Army, and had done a short stint as a truck driver after leaving the service. He said that CB radios were still widely used by truckers, so chances of finding them would be good.

His speculation had proven true and now every vehicle had been outfitted with one, and each vehicle also had a hand-held radio—walkie-talkies—as Cole knew them. They had been useful over short distances while scavenging for supplies.

Cole made one last check of every vehicle. Because of the stink from the hen, he drove that vehicle alone while Elly rode with Joe, Luke, and Zoë right behind Cole in the Sean's SUV. It wasn't as new as the others, but it had brought the family to safety last year when the virus hit. His brother hadn't wanted to part with it. Cole couldn't blame him.

Next in line came Hunter and Sophie in the truck they had found on the trek to the island. It already had a hitch but they used a larger horse trailer so they could take the goats as well. It was an added plus that Hunter was used to driving it. Buddy the dog rode with them as well.

Next vehicle in the caravan was an SUV being driven by Jake and Piper. She loved the cats the most so it was natural for them to bring them in their car. Behind their SUV they had a small trailer similar to the kind they were using for the extra gasoline and tools. Theirs held the chickens in a coop Cole had built right into the structure. It would be easiest for traveling. Joe and Mike had jerry-rigged some extra shocks on it to help absorb the bumps they would encounter on the trip and the sides of the trailer protected the chickens from too much wind, while still allowing air to circulate. A few trials around the town had shown that the birds hadn't been too perturbed by the set-up.

Sean and Jenna drove the rental truck filled with more than half of their supplies—the other half had been portioned out to each vehicle. Everyone had at least one rifle or shotgun, and a few handguns and appropriate ammunition.

Steve and Mike brought up the rear in a pick-up with a cap on it. They also pulled the trailer filled with extra gasoline. It made sense for them to bring up the rear so they could be flagged down by anyone who needed gas.

Cole leaned down to peer into Hunter's window. "You guys have your water and snacks?"

"We're all set, Dad." Hunter glanced in the review mirror. "We have plenty of extra water for Buddy as well."

Right now, water was plentiful, but they had to treat any to be used for drinking. Cole worried more about water once they were west of the Mississippi. The highway didn't always pass close to sources of water.

"Good. And don't forget to say if you have to stop to use the bathroom." Between the little ones and Sophie, Cole had factored in frequent breaks even though Sophie had insisted that she didn't need special treatment. That was when Cole used the excuse of the children. They would need breaks and time to stretch their legs.

"Don't worry, Cole. I'll pee every chance I get." Sophie's eyes twinkled and Cole returned her smile. She was finally becoming more relaxed around him. He backed away, giving the roof of the SUV a couple of thumps as he returned to his vehicle.

With a final glance back, he put the car in drive and led the caravan west.

———

"IT'S STILL hard to believe we're leaving the island." Hunter craned his neck to see past Elly's SUV. She had snaked around a nasty pile-up near an entrance ramp. It was a tight squeeze for him to get around the wrecks with the horse trailer, but he went slow and came through without mishap. Those behind him did the same.

"Why is it hard to believe? I'm glad we're leaving." Sophie was keeping busy by cracking black walnuts collected last fall. The meats went into a jar, the shells into a bowl at her feet. Buddy, excited when they had first left, now lay curled on the back seat.

"I just mean the island was a pretty sweet set up." And it was safe. Maybe because not quite a year ago he had traversed the country with the island as his goal, it represented safety and security. "We had everything we needed there."

"Pretty much, but you have to admit, having to transport every-thing over the water was kind of a hassle." He glanced at her as she cracked a nut. After a brief inspection for weevils, she dropped it in the jar with a plunk. "I'm glad we're leaving."

Surprised, Hunter sent her a longer look. Driving was easier for the moment. This stretch of highway was fairly clear and with the only moving vehicles belonging to the caravan, he didn't have to worry about other traffic. "You didn't like the island?"

"Oh, I loved the island. Last fall, especially, it was beautiful. But as much as I love your family, it would be nice to meet other people. I mean, if we stayed on the island forever, who would our baby marry? His or her cousins? There would only be Luke or Zoë in the same age range."

Hunter laughed. "You're already marrying off our child?"

She grinned. "Not quite. I'm just being practical. Besides, the prospect of electricity is so tempting. Can you imagine popping a DVD into a player and sitting down to watch a good movie? It would be almost like the pandemic never happened."

"I'm not sure I'd want to watch a movie."

Now it was her turn to be surprised. "Why not?"

"Because it would be...*depressing*." He thought of his favorite tele-vision shows. Seeing the world as it was would be like pouring salt on a wound. It would be cruel reminder of everything that was gone and they could never get back. Not in their lifetimes, anyway. Maybe in a hundred years mankind would be back to some semblance of what they'd been, but he thought it would take even longer. For the foreseeable future, they would be getting by with scavenged goods and parts. The future of his grandchildren looked bleaker the more he thought about it. By then, everything would be picked over or degraded to the point of not being usable. "I think I want to concentrate on what we have now, and making the best of it."

"The best of it?" Sophie was quiet for several moments. The only sound in the car was the soft snoring of Buddy in the back. "I don't want to keep bringing it up, but for me, I would watch a movie and remember all the times I'd be sitting in my living room with my family, curled up on the sofa next to my mom and watching a favorite movie together. Saturday nights were always movie nights. We took turns choosing—" Her voice broke and Hunter reached for her hand, but she was still busy cracking walnuts. "—and we'd make a big bowl of popcorn." She shrugged. "I miss my family and watching a movie again would make me feel…I don't know…close to them again, I guess."

She blinked hard as she stared into the bowl of shells at her feet. Hunter caught her hand this time, giving it a gentle squeeze as he steered around the remains of a vehicle fire. "First thing we do when we get electricity is find a stash of movies—maybe we could break into one of those boxes outside a store—and stock up on all of your favorites. We'll find some popcorn, cuddle up, just you and me. It'll be like a date night. And you get the first turn at picking the movie."

"Any movie I want?"

"Absolutely."

"My mom and I used to love to watch chick flicks."

Hunter swallowed hard but nodded. What did he know of chick flicks? "Oh…okay. Chick flick it is."

She laughed. "I'm kidding. My mom was a Star Wars fanatic."

He grinned. "*Yes*! We can do a marathon."

Sophie brushed bits of walnut shell off her rounded belly and reclined her chair. "I can't wait. And on that note, I'm going to take a little nap."

After a brief mid-morning break, they resumed their trek. Sophie had offered to drive for a bit, so Hunter leaned his head against the window and closed his eyes. All of the preparations for leaving over the last few weeks had meant days ranging miles from shore to scavenge followed by countless hours of packing and loading vehicles. Last night, as exhausted as he'd been, he couldn't sleep. Nervous excitement for the journey had him tossing and turning. On one hand, he couldn't wait to see what was out there. He couldn't help hoping things had improved since he'd last been beyond their little bubble of relative safety.

He woke up to music filling the vehicle and disoriented, he glanced around. He hadn't heard music for so long, he thought he must be dreaming. Then he glanced at the cord from a cellphone resting in the center console to the dashboard. "Where'd you get that?" He rubbed his eyes. It had started raining at some point and they passed drab brown fields, overgrown and unplowed from last summer. Ragged stalks of unharvested corn lay bent at angles, pressed nearly flat by the snow they'd had.

Sophie tapped her fingers along to the beat, her shoulders swaying as she sang along to the music. During a pause in the lyrics, she said, "Piper let me use her old phone. She's using Trent's."

Hunter picked up the phone and checked out the playlist then made a face. His cousin always had different taste in music than he did. She liked hip-hop and pop while he tended to like rock—mostly new stuff, but also some classic. "Hey, did I ever tell you I used to play in a band?"

Sophie slanted him a look. One eyebrow quirked. "*You*? No way."

He laughed. "It's true. I played lead guitar and sang."

"Were you any good?"

"No. I sucked. But it was fun." Grinning, he scrolled through the list of tunes and found a few he liked. They weren't going to play for a while, but he was just so thrilled for the rare sense of normalcy the music lent the trip, that he settled back and even sang along a little bit, much to Sophie's amusement.

A ballad came on and he grimaced and Sophie, grinning, belted it out. She was pretty good. "You should have been in a band. You have a good voice."

"Why thank you. I sang in choir all through school." She finished singing the refrain, then turned the music down. "Do you ever wonder what's up with your dad and Elly?"

"Wonder? I don't know. I mean, I know they like each other and stuff." He shifted in his seat. His dad and Elly shared the same bed most of the time but he tried not to think about that too much. "Why do you ask?"

"Oh, no reason. I'm just wondering if maybe I'm not the only one who's pregnant." She glanced at him with a coy smile.

Hunter straightened and turned to her. "What? Why do you think that?"

"Because...well, you know our girl products, right?"

"Yeah, I had to get them." His face still burned at the memory of loading the cart.

"Well, some of the supplies you tossed in the cart weren't even sanitary products, but pregnancy tests."

He shrugged. "So?"

"I saw one in the trash. It was positive and it wasn't mine."

Hunter faced forward as he mused. "It could be Jenna." That was the likely scenario.

"Nope. Your aunt had her tubes tied a long time ago. She was telling me how she wishes she hadn't now because of Trent." The amusement that had been in Sophie's voice faded with that observation.

"Oh." He rested an elbow on the armrest and propped his head against his hand. "Piper?"

"That's what I thought, so I was hinting around to her, asking if she and Jake had...*you know*."

"And?"

"Nope. Not yet anyway."

"Oh wow. I thought they liked each other?"

"They do. They just haven't had any privacy over the winter, I guess."

"True. We have been living in each other's laps practically. It's been too cold to leave the house, except for chores, and too many people in the house." Hunter grinned as he said, "And I guess they never went out to collect nuts." That had been his and Sophie's excuse to get away from everyone. It had been warm then. Or warm enough.

"Yep. So that leaves Elly. She and your dad have been pretty tight all winter."

"But my dad is like, forty-two or -three." Physically, he knew it wasn't too old, especially for a man, but that would make his father really old when this possibly hypothetical baby became an adult.

Okay, maybe not that old, but not exactly young. He knew he'd been born while his dad was still in college. In fact, he'd been about the same age Hunter was now.

"So?"

"And Elly...isn't she too old to get pregnant?"

Sophie laughed. "I think she's still in her thirties. Late thirties, but still. And no, that's not too old."

"Well, whatever. That's just weird. My dad will be a new father and a new grandfather in the same year? His baby will be our kid's aunt or uncle?"

"Hey, it happens. And your brother or sister."

"Oh wow." He tried to wrap his mind around the idea of a sibling. He shook his head. "You don't sound at all upset about this."

She looked confused. "Why should I be? And just remember, I don't know for sure it's Elly."

Hunter laughed. "Yes, but that leaves only one other female and that's....ew. I can't even finish that sentence."

"Exactly. Zoë's not a factor so that means it has to be Elly."

Hunter let that sink in for a few moments. "Do you think my dad knows yet?"

"Has he said anything that makes you think he might?"

Shaking his head, he replayed past conversations in his mind. "Not that I can recall, although they were both looking forward to there being a hospital in Las Vegas for you."

She pursed her lips to the side in a manner he knew meant she was doubting herself. "I could be wrong. Maybe it was a false positive?"

"Does that ever happen?" He was surprised at the pang of disappointment he felt at the idea of the test being wrong.

"I don't know. The only test I took was the one for this little guy." She patted her abdomen.

"Or little gal." Hunter leaned over and dropped a kiss on Sophie's shoulder as he covered her hand on her belly.

He turned up the music, singing along, badly, while Sophie tried to sing over him. When a slower tune came on, Sophie said, "Do you think our baby will be okay?"

He wished he could answer with a hundred percent certainty, but how could he? What did he know about babies and pregnancy? He said the only thing he could. "Of course." Then he scooted as close as he could, massaging the back of her neck. "Humans have been having babies since, well, forever, I guess. The baby will be okay, and so will you. I'm positive."

Chapter Fourteen

"YOU SEEM to have remembered how to drive." Joe set a bottle of water in the cup holder for Elly and offered the kids a drink from another.

"I guess it's like riding a bike." She sipped the water and set the bottle back in the holder. The familiar action returned naturally once she was behind the wheel. "It still feels weird to be driving. I keep wanting to reach over to the radio and find a good station, you know?" She glanced at Joe, who nodded as he gazed to his right. She knew he wasn't much of a talker but she hoped he'd be a little chattier within the confines of the car or she'd go nuts. The kids were looking at books and occasionally laughing at something. "I knew the roads would be bad after seeing the streets of Chicago, but I didn't expect this."

Elly stopped suddenly when Cole's brake lights flashed. She rested her hands on the wheel as Cole opened his door and stepped out. He held up a hand and motioned something. She put the SUV in park and exited. "What's wrong?"

"Just some debris ahead. I'm going to clean it up. It'll only take a minute." He waved towards a pile-up of vehicles blocking most of the highway. From where she stood, it appeared that there was enough room on the right to go around it.

"We can't go around?"

He scratched the back of his neck as he threw a glance toward the pile of cars. "Um...not really."

He was withholding something. She tilted her head and tried to read his expression, but he'd turned away and opened the back of his SUV and began rummaging around. He donned latex gloves, grabbed a shovel and a gallon of bleach.

This was no ordinary debris. She started forward, but Hunter and Sophie pulled up, followed by the rest of the caravan.

"Why are we stopping?" Hunter's head popped out of the passenger side window, pulling himself up until he sat on the window ledge. He held the luggage rack with one hand while shading his eyes with the other.

"Your dad says there's debris in the road."

Hunter shrugged and pivoted, popping off the ledge as only a young person can before he jogged past Elly. "I'll give him a hand."

Elly returned to her seat and explained the delay to Joe and the kids.

"Maybe I should go help, too." Joe opened his door when Hunter came back into view, his face ashen. He didn't look at Elly or Joe, but grabbed another shovel from the back of Cole's vehicle and tugged on a pair of gloves.

Gloves, shovels, Cole's evasiveness, and Hunter's suddenly sober demeanor clued Elly in. They must be dealing with a body—but why be secretive? Cole knew it wouldn't be the first time she had dealt with death. As she puzzled out the mystery, both men returned, sans gloves, and doused both shovels with the bleach solution before sticking them back in the SUV.

Elly rolled down her window to ask Hunter about it as he walked back to his car, but head bowed, he passed by as though deep in thought as he returned to his vehicle. She glanced at Joe.

"Well, that was weird."

Joe nodded. "Yep, but I imagine Cole did what he had to do. That's what he does."

She slanted Joe a look. "You know, I really like that Cole faces problems head on, but I really wish he wouldn't try to spare everyone else the details. I've worked out in the field before. I traveled deep into the forest to find villages ravished by Ebola." The scenes would stick in her mind forever. "Mothers died and their babies just lay there, crying and crying but nobody came because everyone else was too sick to take care of the baby." Or too afraid. The fear and revulsion shown to the surviving babies and children had nearly broken her heart. Zoë laughed at something and she was reminded of her own fears when she and Zach, her colleague, had found the children. She couldn't really blame the survivors of Ebola. At the time, the virus was in full-swing.

They drove for several hours before taking a lunch break on a long stretch of road that was one of the few sections they had come across that didn't have countless abandoned vehicles. Cole was following county highways as much as he could, eschewing the major highways due to so many crashed and abandoned vehicles.

By then, Elly was chomping at the bit to get out and stretch her legs. Riding in a car for a long time was something she hadn't done in almost a year. On the island, she had kept busy almost constantly.

The stretch Cole had chosen was in front of a farm that clearly looked uninhabited. A large tree limb had fallen from a big old oak tree and blocked a long, winding drive. Patches of snow still dotted the shaded areas, but most of the ground was covered by a thick mat of brown weeds, but a pasture along the edge of the road showed a few early shoots of grass. The horses, goats and even the chickens were given an hour to graze, and a hand pump on a trough at the far side of the pasture took only a few strong pumps by Jake to get water for the animals and themselves.

"So do you think we'll cross the Mississippi today?" Elly took a sip of water to wash down the last of her lunch. She sat on the lowered tailgate of Sean's truck, her legs swinging.. Cole had the remains of his meal balanced on the tailgate beside her, but he stood, watching the animals in the pasture.

He shook his head. "No. Not even close, I'm afraid. We've barely gone ninety miles east to west. If you factor in the detours we took due to blocked roads, we've gone probably well over a hundred and ten miles, but we're not going as quickly as I'd hoped."

"But look on the bright side—no traffic." She smiled and Cole's mouth turned up as if he was trying to return it, but his eyes were troubled. "What is it?"

"I'm just worried about crossing the river. We have no clue what to expect there."

"What do you mean?" There were dozens of bridges crossing the river. Sure, it was a wide river, but the bridges should be fine. It wasn't as if there had been a natural disaster in the physical sense. Just a lot of cars and trucks to navigate around on the roads. That would probably present a problem on the bridge as well, but they had plenty of strong backs to muscle the vehicles out of the way.

"I'm probably just worried over nothing. Forget I mentioned it. It's not like we can do anything until we reach the river anyway." He sent her a half-hearted smile as he pushed off the truck and headed towards the pasture, whistling for the horses.

It took another quarter hour to get the animals back in their trailers and get everyone settled and ready to go. It was Joe's turn to drive, so Elly settled in for a nap, a blanket pulled up to her shoulders. The kids had fallen asleep within minutes of hitting the road. They had been so excited to leave this morning that they had been racing up and down the line of vehicles as last-minute items were packed, getting in everyone's way. She smiled as she recalled the good-natured way everyone had treated the children's excitement.

While she felt she and Cole had become surrogate parents to the kids, everyone else had also come to love them as well.

The caravan snaked its way across the state in a roundabout way as they detoured when needed, and the massive vehicle pile-ups reminded Elly of Cole's worries. As she drifted to sleep, they crossed a bridge over a small creek and the roiling water surging just feet below the bridge had her wondering if Cole was right to worry after all.

———

THEIR FIRST NIGHT on the road they spent at a dealership lot that had sold recreational vehicles. Most of the stock was gone, no doubt taken by people looking to escape the virus, but several campers at the back of the lot had been left. They were older and used but perfect for what Cole wanted. They had beds and from all appearances, hadn't been touched in over a year. It only took them a few minutes to find the keys in the office. The dealership had been abandoned before anyone had died there, but precautions were still taken. Every surface of the interior of the camper was washed down with a weak bleach solution. If nothing else, it got rid of any mold and dust.

Cole and Elly got a queen sized bed at the back of one while the kids and Jake slept in a loft on the other end. Joe took the bench that converted to a bed when the table was removed.

There was still propane in two of the campers' tanks, and dinner was beans and rice. Piper had been so excited to find real ovens that she had baked four loaves of bread for their breakfast in the morning. She'd burned the first one—a small trial loaf—but she found a pizza stone in one of the campers and it seemed to help even out the heat.

While Elly, Joe, and Piper got the campers aired and cleaned, Cole, Sean, and Hunter had partially unloaded one of the pickup trucks and explored the area for foodstuffs. They could never have enough as far as Cole was concerned. If they had to get another vehicle to transport it, then so be it. Steve, Mike, and Jake took another truck in the other direction. They agreed to meet back at the campers in ninety minutes.

Cole stopped in front of a strip mall, dismissing the convenience store and gas station at the far end. Even from a quarter of a mile away it was easy to see the caved in roof, soot, and twisted wreckage around the gas station. It looked like an explosion had occurred and most of the windows in the stores on that end had been blown out. But, at this end of the mall was a garden center. Tools were always a great find, plus fertilizer, seeds, hoses, and other items.

Cole motioned for Hunter to stay behind him as he entered the store, his flashlight shining the way. Sean was staying with the truck this time. They had brought the handheld radios and checked them before entering the building. If Cole needed help, or Sean saw someone approaching, they could communicate quickly.

He kicked aside a mound of debris from an overturned shelf near the doorway, at first worried the mess heralded what they would find within the rest of the store, but he was happily surprised.

"Come on in, Hunter. It looks as though gardening wasn't foremost in people's minds when the virus hit."

Hunter, gloves and mask in place like Cole's, grabbed a red plastic shopping cart that lay on its side, blocking the aisle. "I don't even smell death in here." Hunter righted the cart and used it to push other debris out of the way.

His son was right. Cole only smelled a dank odor that reminded him of going into a garden shed that had been closed all winter. It was the scent of molding leaves and grass clippings, the acrid scent of various chemicals and fertilizers, and wet wood. Most of the mess was confined to the areas where candy and snacks were usually kept. There was nothing left there, not even a bag of peanuts, but after pausing to listen and not hearing anything, they made their way through the store, stopping to grab items they could use, quickly passing those they didn't.

They collected every package of seeds they could find. Even flower seeds were kept because some varieties were useful for medicinal qualities. Plastic bins to store everything were a great find, and when they found one with wheels and a handle, like a cooler, but for tools and storage, Cole loaded it up like a second cart. A corner of the garden center was set up with animal feed. Most of it was spoiled by rodent droppings, but Hunter found two forty pound bags buried beneath the mess that had been protected by the torn bags of the feed above and beside them.

After loading up their finds, Sean slammed the tailgate and leaned against it. "How about the pub?" He pointed across the parking lot.

Cole looked at the building and joked, "What? You feel like a beer?"

Sean laughed. "Don't you know it. But, I was thinking maybe there's something in there we can use. Even some big industrial sized pots or kettles might be good. We have a big group now."

"Good idea." He glanced at Hunter.

"Sounds fine to me. And maybe we'll find a little booze, too." Hunter grinned.

Cole nodded. "That would be great." It was the one thing they hadn't found much of anywhere. It seemed the world had ended in a drunken party.

With that thought in his mind, he didn't have high hopes for finding any. The front of the pub was exactly how he feared. A putrid stench wafted through the door as soon as they opened it—it wasn't even locked. A quick peek was enough for Cole. Overturned tables, what was left of bodies, broken glass, and enough rodent droppings to make it appear that the floor was a carpet of them.

Cole backed out. "I say we look for a backdoor. I don't want to cross that room."

Hunter agreed with him, and while Sean looked indecisive for a moment, he reluctantly followed Cole around to the back.

The kitchen was nearly empty. Even the cooks must have decided to join the fun—or had fled for their lives. A metal garbage can next to what had been a contraption to roll out pizza dough contained a twenty-pound sack of cornmeal. The cornmeal had probably been used in the pizza pans prior to baking. They took a stack of pizza pans and a huge vat that appeared to have been used to mix up soup or sauces.

In addition to the cornmeal, they found huge cans of tomato sauce and bags of spices used to season the sauce for pizza. "Oh wow, Dad. What I wouldn't give for a hot slice of pizza right now." Hunter carried an armload of the bags of spices out to the truck.

"I hit the motherlode!" Sean's voice boomed from inside a steel walk in cooler. Cole had avoided it because of the stench of rotting produce and whatever else had been inside it when the power had died.

Cole picked through the garbage on the floor to find Sean holding up a case of Jack Daniels. "What the hell? How did that escape the people in the front?"

Hunter came up behind Cole and gave a low whistle.

Sean carefully brought the crate out of the cooler. "Best guess is someone stashed it there intending to come back later. Maybe the owner? He or she had to have seen what was going on out front."

"Probably. Why don't you take that to the truck while Hunter and I will take one more look around?"

Cole found an unopened jar of yeast. He didn't know if it was still good, but he took it while Hunter found bottles of mustard and ketchup. They were still sealed also, so they went in one of the vats.

Sean had a grin from ear to ear on the drive back to the campers. "Wait until I tell Jenna. "

That evening, they broke open a bottle of the whiskey around a bonfire. The campers were comfortable but none of them were large enough for all of them to fit inside at once without feeling like sardines, so they dragged desk chairs from the RV dealer's office, unpacked a few lawn chairs, and sat on the bumpers of the trucks.

"Cheers, Cole." Elly raised a mug to clink against the plastic tumbler Cole used.

"Cheers." He sipped his whiskey, savoring the heat as the liquid slid down his throat. The only people not partaking in the alcohol were Sophie and the kids. It didn't even occur to Cole until after Sean had poured for everyone else that neither Piper nor Jake were old enough to drink if they went by the laws prior to the virus. As far as he was concerned, they did the work of adults so they should be treated like one. He took another sip and put his arm around Elly as she leaned against him.

"Mmm… this is good." She grinned up at him. "But here, have the rest of mine."

"What? You've only had a sip!" He blocked her mug.

"That's all I wanted."

Cole studied her smile. Her eyes danced in the firelight. "Of course you don't have to drink if you don't want to, but I remember once we went out to get drinks before we headed to Africa, and your drink of choice was Jack Daniels and a Coke."

"You remember that?"

"I remember everything about you." He rubbed his hand up and down her back.

"I was waiting for the right time to tell you, and tonight, with the festivities, so to speak, seems like a good time."

His arm stilled halfway to his mouth. "To tell me what?"

"Remember those pregnancy tests you brought back from the first scavenging expedition?"

His mind whirled with images of the devastated store, but her reason for asking the question took up most of his thought processes. "Yes…"

He searched her eyes, hope curling up from his stomach and

burning in his chest. Was she saying what he *thought* she was saying? His face must have shown his question because she grinned and nodded.

The explosion of emotion rendered him speechless.

"Cole? Are you ...okay with it? I know we didn't talk about it—"

The explosion radiated out and he gave her a hug, wishing he had the words to say what he was feeling. "Shhh—of course I'm all right with it. More than all right. I'm..." He gave his head a quick shake, snapping himself out of his shock. "Oh my God, Elly! This is the best news I've had since..." He wracked his mind. "Well, since Brenda told me she was pregnant with Hunter." He pulled her close again, but this time, he dipped his head for a quick kiss, but he was so excited, he felt like he had to see her face and make sure this wasn't some kind of crazy joke. He was in his forties, had a grown son and was about to be a grandfather. And now he was going to be a dad again? It was confusing but in the best possible way.

He smoothed his hand up, smoothing back her hair. "I am...I'm *beyond* thrilled, Elly. I love you and I think I've loved you almost as soon as I met you years ago."

Tears squeezed from the corners of her eyes as she laughed and smiled up at him. "Me too." She raised her face to him, closing her eyes as he leaned in for another kiss. Longer this time. One fitting the occasion.

Nobody had been paying them any attention. The younger group had gathered on the other side of the fire, and Sean was telling some story to the other adults, the alcohol having relaxed him until he was almost jovial. This was the Sean that Cole remembered from before the pandemic. Before Trent died. Cole bent his head. "Can we announce it? Is it too soon?"

"I'm a little more than three months along. I think we should plan on the baby arriving around early fall. And yes, I'd love to announce it. I've been keeping quiet, worried I'd lose him or her. I had a miscarriage a long time ago and the doctor told me then I'd probably never have a baby, so I didn't want to get my hopes up."

Cole drew her against him, burying his face in her hair.

Elly hugged him in return, her hands rubbing his back through his coat.

Sean chose that moment to ask if anyone needed a refill. Cole, one arm holding Elly close, stood, bringing her with him. "I believe I do."

Sean gave him an odd look, but poured a measure of whiskey in his tumbler. Elly covered her mug and shook her head. When everyone had a refill, Cole cleared his throat. "I have an announcement." He turned to Elly and smiled. "I'd like to propose a toast…"

Chapter Fifteen

COLE GRIPPED the railing on the bridge and gazed down at the swollen Mississippi River. They had received plenty of rain but he hadn't expected the river to be this high. The steady drizzle yesterday while they had cleared a path half-way across the bridge hadn't seemed hard enough to cause this large of a rise overnight. He searched up river, noting how the riverbanks on either side were basically non-existent. They were gone yesterday in some places, but the water had been a foot or so below today's levels. Now, the banks were gone and the river spread out like a great flowing lake.

He'd crossed the Mississippi countless times around this area and knew it was wide, but one reason he'd wanted to cross here was because it only grew even wider the farther down the river one went. The only explanation for the flood levels today had to be that there had been a lot of rain north of them in the last few days. For all he knew, there could still be a weather system to the north and the river would continue to rise.

If there was one thing he could bring back from before the virus, not including people, it would be weather forecasts and reports. He had taken them for granted and never realized how big a factor they played even when he didn't have to make life or death decisions. A low curse behind him made him look over his shoulder to see Sean approaching him.

"Shit!" Sean leaned over the railing. "What a mess."

"I know. But, we have to cross today." It wasn't just spring melt and rains that were causing the flooding, but debris. Everywhere he looked loose boats and barges whirled and spun in the muddy brown water. Even as he watched, one slammed into the pile-up around one of the bridge supports. Some had run aground along the river banks and over the last year, other debris had piled up against them. Large branches and even whole trees had become tangled in the boats. In places, the river was nearly dammed. The current eddied and frothed around the obstacles.

Beneath the bridge only a few narrow channels were open, creating a dangerous current that pulled yet more debris towards the center of the bridge. It was only a matter of time before the entire span beneath the bridge was blocked. When that happened, the water had nowhere to go and pressure would build. Some would spill over the various dikes along the banks, but most would continue the southward journey. The bridge would fail.

Cole waved towards a pile-up of debris against one of the bridge supports. "If another one hits that, it could take out the support beam." He wasn't an engineer, but he would bet the support was already weakened. The thought of them being on the bridge if that happened made his stomach clench.

"Maybe we should find another bridge?" Sean raised his hand, shielding his eyes as he squinted downriver.

"You think the next bridge is going to be in better shape than the three before this?" Those had been in worse condition. One was higher above the river, but two overturned semi-trucks made it impassable. One had been hit by a barge and collapsed in the middle. The third was intact, but the river was already lapping across it. They had left it, certain that the next bridge would be better. And it had been—yesterday. *Damn it.*

"Maybe?" Sean didn't sound confident and Cole didn't want to wait. He had a feeling things were only going to get worse the farther downriver they went.

Cole pushed off the rail and shoved his hands into the pockets of his coat. The raw spring air felt even colder when a gust of wind blasted across the bridge. It came from the northwest, and he worried a late spring snowstorm could be headed their way.

"I think the situation is going to be same all up and down the river. With the rain we've had over the last week on top of the snow melt, I don't think that it's even crested yet. When this bridge goes down, it's going to add to the debris and pile up against the next bridge, and so on." He gestured to the dozens of vehicles stranded on the bridge when their drivers either abandoned them or succumbed to the virus mid-crossing. "Every one of these vehicles will add to the problem when they become debris in the river. Besides, the farther south we go, the wider the river becomes and the more vehicles we'd need to clear before we can cross." The last bit was just a guess. He supposed if they were lucky they might come across a nearly empty bridge, but so far, every one they'd seen had been jammed. Everyone had been trying to escape the virus and most hadn't made it.

"Okay, well let's get moving right after breakfast." Sean slapped his hands down on the railing before turning towards their camp on the eastern bank.

Cole cast a glance north, sighing as the muddy brown water swirled around obstacles and crashed against the bridge pilings along the shore. They didn't have much time.

Food was being served buffet-style on a couple of boards laid between the tailgates of Steve's pickup truck and Hunter's truck. Cole went to the end of the line behind Mike. When the meal was over, the boards would slide back into the covered bed of one of the trucks to be used again.

"You want to go ahead of me?" Mike gestured.

Cole shook his head. "No, that's okay. I'll wait." Ever since Mike and Steve had joined up with them, Mike had acted deferential towards Cole and he didn't understand why.

Elly joined Cole in line. "How's it look?"

He shook his head and told her what they'd seen. "It's going to be a long day."

"Better eat up then. You're getting too skinny." She poked his flat abdomen and winked. He gave her a wry smile. They'd all lost weight they couldn't afford to lose—she most of all. "You worry about your own weight. Remember, you're eating for two."

"As if this baby was going to let me forget." She pressed a hand to her stomach. "This is my second time through the line."

"Here, get in front of me." He wanted to make sure she got enough, but she shook her head.

"No, everyone needs to eat—and how would we manage if our fearless leader up and died of starvation?"

Cole grinned. "I think we're all pretty safe from that at the moment." It was the 'at the moment' part that worried him. It was true that they had plenty of food right now, but it wasn't so long ago that he was worried they wouldn't make it through the winter. They had, but they had all felt the pinch of hunger during the worst of it after the fire— except for the children. Everyone made sure they had their fill. Cole knew it wasn't so much the lack of food as it was burning calories. That was something he hadn't factored in to food stores. Before, if he'd consumed as many calories as he now ate daily, he'd have been obese. His daily tasks included hauling and chopping wood, hunting, scavenging and loading or unloading supplies from the trucks. And they were all working just as hard if not harder than he was.

To speed their journey, they were only cooking two meals a day, morning and evening. Lunch consisted of whatever was leftover. He eyed the pile of corncakes, relieved to see there would be plenty for everyone to get a few more later in the day. When people had good food in their stomach with more to look forward to, they worked hard and were less irritable. He took a bite of a cake. After swallowing, he smiled. "These are delicious, Piper."

"Thanks, Cole. Jake's the one you can thank for the maple syrup. He found it at that little store everyone else passed up. He walked back last night to see what they had."

He didn't know if she was giving him a rebuke, or just pointing out that Jake had been the reason for the treat so he simply nodded. Foraging and scavenging had become second nature to all of them, but if they stopped at every store or house along the way, they would never reach Las Vegas.

Jake had spotted the store set back from the road and had mentioned it at dinner last night. They were all exhausted from clearing the bridge, so Cole had only said that he was too beat to check it out and besides, it was his turn to wash dishes. Hunter had opted to stay with Sophie. She was due in a few months, give or take a week, and was the main reason Cole wanted to get to their destination as quickly as possible. It would be difficult enough to care for an infant in this new world, but trying to do so while traveling through what could be desolate and dangerous country, would be even more difficult.

Jake mumbled a response to Piper about how it was no big deal, but Cole didn't agree and let Jake know. "Thanks for literally going the extra mile, Jake. You had to have been exhausted from pushing cars out of the way. I know I was."

Piper beamed and the corners of Jake's mouth lifted. "It's just maple syrup. It's not like we would die without it."

"True, but I really appreciate it." Holding the corn cake, he waved it toward the rest of the group chowing down. "From the looks of it, everyone else appreciates it too." He took a big bite and ambled over to the truck, using the bumper as a seat.

As he balanced his plate on his lap, he felt Lucas watching him, his eyes following the movement of Cole's fork as he brought a bite of fish to his mouth. At first, he was worried the boy hadn't had enough to eat and he was going to share what he had, but there had still been plenty left after he'd gone through the line, and only Mike and Elly had been after him. Then he remembered that Lucas had caught the fish in a small pond bordering the bank while the rest of them had been moving vehicles late yesterday. Joe had helped the boy clean the fish and pack them in snow found in the shade of a small hill.

Cole took another bite and made a show of how tasty it was. Lucas had been eager to learn how to fish and constantly quizzed all of them about how to find food. He'd learned how to gut a deer last month, and was rapidly becoming an expert at cleaning fish. Lucas's months alone with his little sister after their food ran low had affected him deeply. He didn't hoard food, but he never left anything on his plate and when he wasn't asking Cole to show him how to hunt, or Elly how to fish, he was in the kitchen with Piper, learning how to cook.

"Did you cook this, Lucas?"

The little boy nodded. "Jenna helped me, but I caught them all by myself." He had been upset when he'd been told he was too little to help move cars and more to distract him than with any concern of putting food on the table, Cole had given him a fishing pole and pointed him in the direction of the nearby pond. The river was much too dangerous to fish in right now, but the pond was safe enough. He'd been shocked when Lucas had proudly shown him the dozen or so trout on stringers in the pond. Fresh trout was always welcome.

"Man, I don't know when I've had such a good meal. The trout were delicious and the corn cakes are better than anything my grandma made." His grandmother had never made a corncake that he could recall, but that was beside the point.

Cole looked at the gathering. Everyone pulled their weight. Even little Zoë did what she could to help by scraping plates into a bucket and feeding the scraps to the goats and chickens. Now that they were traveling, she also watched the chickens when they were allowed out in the mornings and evenings to forage.

A speck of blueberry clung to his thumb and he sucked it off. The dried blueberries had made the cakes almost like dessert. The dried fruit were thanks to a large bag of them that Hunter had found in some supplies in the trunk of a sedan. The owner of the car, bless her, had packed all of it in heavy plastic storage bins, and it was still good. The woman must have been somewhat of a prepper because she had a good variety of freeze dried food packed in the bin. They would save that for later.

They still had quite a few vehicles to clear at the far end of the bridge. He had thought they could move ahead and then finish the journey when the last obstacle was cleared, but now he decided that only a few of them would venture on to the bridge at a time. That way, if the bridged did go out, at least most of them would survive. It was morbid thinking, but he didn't know how else to do it. If he could, he'd do it all himself and keep the rest safe, but since he wasn't gifted with superhuman strength, at least he could be out there all the time and give the others rest spells.

Some vehicles had keys in the ignition, but the corpses of the owners made it impossible to even attempt to start the vehicles. The stench was horrendous from one car they had opened, intending to try to start it. They never tried again. Even though Cole and Elly both thought the bodies were no longer able to transmit the virus, they were too horrible to deal with after nearly a year of rotting in the cars. Instead, they had to do the back-breaking labor of pushing them out of the way. And that was the easy part. The hard part was forgetting what it was they pushed.

———————

"OKAY, Hunter. My turn now. Go take a break."

"Dad. I know what you're doing." Hunter felt his spine pop as he pulled his hands off the bumper of a car he and Sean had pushed to the far side of the bridge. He winced and bent backward to work out the kink. They had created a path three quarters of the way across the bridge now that was wide enough for the caravan to pass. By the end of the day, it would be clear, but not if his dad kept sending him and the other men off the bridge to take a break every hour or so.

"Doing?" His dad didn't meet Hunter's eyes but looked past him, counting the cars still in their way.

"You're getting me and the others off the bridge as often as you can—yet I don't remember the last break *you* took." He sat heavily on the bumper of the car he'd just moved.

"I've been taking plenty of breaks. You just didn't see me because you were way down here." He pointed to a white pickup truck angled across the road. "I think if we move that one, we can squeeze through without having to move the blue Ford to the left of it."

Hunter nodded but his mind was still on his father's comment about breaks. He looked back to the east side of the bridge where they all retreated to take their breaks from pushing vehicles. The pavement there was on a long approach on the bridge as it crossed over wetlands but wasn't actually out over the river. It was safer than the middle of the bridge and must be why his dad kept sending everyone there whenever he could. It was over a brisk five minute walk away. He supposed his father could be telling the truth, but Hunter was sure he would have remembered his dad passing by either coming or going. "What's going on, Dad?"

"What do you mean?" His father gazed so intently at the white pickup that he appeared to be trying to move it with his mind.

"You seem nervous. Jumpy. I can't understand why you're pushing yourself so much to get over this bridge." Before his dad could reply, Hunter searched his dad's face, looking for the real answer. "Is something wrong with Elly?" Maybe his dad was just worried about the coming baby and focused all that worry on this problem instead. Hunter could definitely relate.

His eyes wide, his dad shook his head. "Elly? No, she's fine." Then he sighed. "Look, son. I'm just worried about crossing the river. That's it. The water's rising and we don't know what's heading our way. With all the snow in the winter and the rain lately…I'm just worried about the flooding getting worse. If we don't get this bridge passable today, we may be stuck on this side until waters recede."

Hunter gazed at the river, nodding. "Yeah, it looks pretty bad, but there's still plenty of clearance below the bridge. I don't think the water would get this high."

"It doesn't need to be higher than the whole bridge—it only needs to cut off either the east or west side. We don't want to get stuck in the middle of it."

Hunter jumped to his feet and shot a look towards each end. His dad was right. While they had been clearing the bridge, the water had crept higher on each bank. When they'd reached the bridge two days ago, the water had seemed safely within the confines of the banks, but now he couldn't even see the river banks in most places, except a few bluffs down the river.

While they were clearing the bridge, Joe and Elly had gone to search for more supplies. Piper and Sophie were cooking and watching the kids. He hoped Sophie wasn't over-doing it. "I may not have seen you, Dad, but I've been hearing you here the whole time. I'm not deaf."

His dad stared at him for a minute, then shook his head and threw up his hands in defeat. "Fine. I'll go get a drink. Be back in a few minutes." He turned to leave, muttering over his shoulder something about raising a bossy son. Hunter grinned and turned to point out the next car to Jake that they needed to move.

Hunter leaned against the last car they'd moved, his muscles quivering with fatigue. It was late afternoon and, finally, they had a lane cleared all the way across the bridge. He just wanted to curl up in his sleeping bag and sleep for about a week, but groaned as he thought of everything they still needed to do today. It would still be hours before he could say hello to his pillow. Tents and supplies needed to be packed and the animals rounded up. Then on the other side, they'd need to unpack it all and set up a new camp.

He looked around for his dad and spotted him heading for the tractor trailer. Dressed in full protective gear, he was going to see if he could get the trailer opened to see if it contained anything they could use. The name of a big box store was emblazoned on the side of the trailer, so they were hopeful, although Hunter wondered where they'd stash more supplies.

Even though they had avoided most vehicle interiors due to the virus, they had checked trunks when they could be opened, finding many useful items and edibles. However, with the tractor trailer, his dad said it appeared the driver had been shot. Bullet holes punctured the driver's door. Whoever had shot him hadn't stuck around to get the cargo the trucker was transporting. The way his dad figured it, victims of the virus hadn't worried about supplies, but were just randomly firing out their car window. In all likelihood the killers were victims in another vehicle traveling in the opposite direction.

The keys weren't in the ignition, but he found them on the floor of the cab beneath the shoe of the deceased trucker.

Sean backed the rental truck up to the tractor trailer and he, Sean, and his dad transferred anything they had room for that would be useful. They found the usual canned foods, but were thrilled to find a case of quinoa in foil pouches. It seemed rodents didn't like either the quinoa or the foil, or maybe they just hadn't discovered it. Another great find was a case of powdered lemonade drink mix that would be good for the sugar already mixed in. It was still edible because the containers were hard plastic and sealed.

Holding up one of the canisters, Sean said, "I can't wait to have a glass of this. All this work makes me feel like having some now, even though it's cold as hell out here."

His dad smiled, swiping an arm across his brow. "Just a little more to do, and we can cross."

Sean scowled. "Why don't we wait until morning instead of packing up only to unpack on the other side?"

They avoided driving at night because they didn't want to get stuck on a blocked road with no access to water or suitable place to camp.

His dad replied, "Because I don't trust this bridge. It might not be here in the morning."

Hunter looked down the length of the bridge. A few cracks showed in the pavement that he didn't recall seeing earlier. Uneasy as one of the cracks ran between his feet, he moved to one side.

Sean held out a hand. "Look. The rain has stopped."

And it had. Hunter dropped the hood of his jacket. The air felt slightly warmer too.

His dad sighed. "Okay. First thing in the morning."

Chapter Sixteen

EARLY THE NEXT MORNING, Cole awoke with a sense of urgency gnawing in his gut and unsettled, he rolled onto his back and stared at the ceiling of the tent. It was barely discernible in the nearly pitch dark. Only the faint glow from the face of his watch lit the tent.

Then he noticed the steady tattoo of rain on the tent. *Shit*. The rain was the probable source of his anxiety. The last thing they needed was *more* rain. The river had already been at flood stage yesterday. He sighed as misgivings over his decision to wait a day caused him to second guess himself. Last night they'd have had to find a place to camp in the dark, but what if they'd missed their chance to cross?

While it was still dark, his watch showed it was almost five a.m. Everything had already been packed except for the tents and bedding. Cole stirred, restless. It would probably be pointless to get up now. What could he do in the dark? But, he wanted to go—*now*—and had to suppress the urge to bolt up from the bedroll.

One of the horses nickered, and he decided he could take care of the animals, at least, and the sooner they were taken care of, the sooner they could cross. It would be one less thing slowing them down. He took a flashlight to set on the hood of a car. He didn't need much light, just enough to get the horses back into the trailer, and he had a feeling they'd go willingly in this rain, even though they had a canopy to shelter under within the circle of vehicles that formed a corral, of sorts.

As eager as he was to get going, he was also loathe to leave the warmth of the sleeping bags. He and Elly had zippered theirs together into one large bag and now she curled against his side. He eased away and unzipped his side enough to get out. Elly stirred and tried to snuggle against him, murmuring, "Where are you going?"

"You keep sleeping. No need to get up just yet. I'm going to see to the horses."

He was glad for the sweatshirt beneath his jacket when he left the tent. The temperature seemed to be only in the low forties, and his breathe billowed into great clouds of vapor.

"Dad? What can I do to help?"

Cole turned as he led Princess to the trailer. "I could use a hand making sure the goats don't get out when I load the horses."

"No problem."

Hunter moved a couple of the goats that they'd put in Princess' slot overnight. In short order, they had both horses loaded and had fed all the animals a little grain. Cole dumped a little extra in the goats' pen since they had been cooped up all night and wouldn't get a chance to graze until later in the day. So far, they had searched and found stores of various types of feed in barns along the way. While much of what they found had been ruined from rodents or bugs, they had found enough to keep the animals happy. The goats gave milk and every day, they had a few chickens that still lay eggs even while traveling.

While Hunter took down the canopy the horses had used as a shelter from the rain, Cole moved to the second canopy they had used while camped as a place to cook and eat. The small pile of wood they'd created over the last few days had dwindled to a few logs and so Cole lit the small camp stove. It would serve them just fine this morning. They had been saving it and the propane to be used for a rainy day and today was, literally, a rainy day.

He poured water from a bucket that had been three-quarters full last night, but now overflowed, into a large pot to boil. Today's breakfast would be oatmeal with some of the maple syrup that Jake had found the other day.

While he waited for the water to boil, he tightened the load strapped to the top of his SUV and moved on to the rest of the vehicles, doing the same for them. When he got back to the stove, the water was boiling and he dumped in the oatmeal and a few pinches of salt.

He found the maple syrup tucked into a box in the back of the SUV they used to keep most of the kitchen supplies. They had backed it up to the edge of the canopy and with the tailgate down it not only made finding ingredients handy, but was a useful work surface as well.

As he stirred the oatmeal, Hunter returned with Sophie. "Hey, just the people I want to see. Can you guys let everyone know that breakfast is ready? I'd like to get across the bridge in the next hour if not sooner."

"Sure thing, Dad." The two split up and within moments, Cole heard the kids waking up as Sophie directed them to the area they'd designated as a latrine. Hunter called out to each tent or knocked on doors of vehicles of those who had chosen to sleep in them.

Cole took a bowl of oatmeal and ate it as he walked towards the bridge. Water lapped at the edges of the road and he knew soon it would be covered. The further he went, the more worried he became. Taking the last bite of oatmeal, he looked down at the raging water mere feet below him. He wore a waterproof poncho over his coat, but water crashed against the bridge supports hard enough to cause him to be drenched down to his skin. He dropped his bowl and spoon and sprinted back to the camp.

"Everyone, let's pack it up. *Now*. I have a feeling we only have minutes to cross the bridge. Get loaded up and get your radios on. We're leaving in five minutes."

Sean, spoon poised in front of his mouth, stared at Cole. "What do you mean?"

"The river has almost swamped the bridge. We have to hurry."

His brother scowled and looked as if he was going to say something, but Jenna said something in a low voice to him, and whatever it was, it succeeded in getting Sean to down the last bite of his meal.

In five minutes flat, everyone was in their vehicle, including Cole. He keyed the mic on his radio and called out for everyone to check in.

When he'd heard from all of the drivers that they were ready, he pressed the button to speak. "I'm going over first. You all wait here until I give the word it's safe."

Immediately, his radio started squawking as Elly, Sean, and even Hunter protested that he shouldn't go first. Cole shook his head.

"Whoa, guys. Listen, somebody has to and it might as well be me. I'm already first in line. If I have to, I can jump out of the car and walk back. Since it's just me, I'll only have myself to worry about. It would be stupid and dangerous for all of us to get stuck out there. There's no way we'd all be able to turn around."

"Keep us updated, Cole." Elly's voice cracked, and the mic clicked before she spoke again. "And be careful."

"Always. It'll just be a few minutes. Hang tight."

He set the radio down and checked his rearview mirror to make sure nobody followed him before he drove ahead.

The path they'd cleared was awash in a few inches of water, but still drivable. His windshield wipers thumped furiously back and forth as he strained to see through the torrential rain and the water crashing over the railings.

He navigated around a wrecked semi-truck they had been unable to move, but instead had cleared the opposite lane. With no other traffic, he could take whatever lane was clear and so he weaved his way over the bridge. In the middle, the river splashing over the railings had lessened and he breathed a sigh of relief. Just a little farther.

"*Shit!*" The western bank had flooded more and that end of the bridge was under a good eight inches of water. He was able to cross it, but water lapped at the undercarriage of his SUV. A few more inches and the bridge would be swamped. He drove all the way off the bridge, down the exit ramp they'd cleared as well. The rendezvous point was a gas station just to the left of the ramp.

Luckily, where the ramp crossed the riverbank, or what was the edge of the flooding river now, it was still a few feet above the water. The banks must be higher on this side of the river. That explained why the flooding was worse on the lower eastern bank. Unfortunately, that was also the reason for the higher water at this side of the bridge. It had nowhere to go but up.

He keyed the radio. "Okay, we can cross, but the western end of the bridge is flooding fast. Drive quickly, but carefully. Oh, and watch out for the semi-truck about halfway over. It was hard to see in fog and rain. You'll have to go left of it."

Everyone checked in when they began moving forward.

Cole drove back up the bridge from the ramp and did a three point turn, parking his vehicle perpendicular to the bridge with his headlights cutting across the lane the others would be in. From this vantage point, he would easily be able to make sure they all made it across and take up the rear of the caravan for the final quarter mile until they were safely on solid ground.

His headlights highlighted a crack in the pavement. Had it always been there? It was impossible to know unless someone had been on the bridge prior to the virus. He didn't see any weeds growing out of it, which would indicate that it was new.

Whenever it occurred, he just hoped it would hold for a bit longer. Cole dragged his eyes from the defect and found a spot on the opposite wall that was a few inches above the water line. That was approximately how deep the water would have to be before the road was unpassable. He gnawed on the edge of his thumb, worrying a callous as he waited, his eyes fixed on the water creeping up the opposite wall. Soon, it would surpass the mark but headlights came into view and he breathed a little easier.

Elly, Joe, and the kids drove by, Elly's knuckles white against the dark steering wheel as they passed in front of him. He lifted the radio and said, "Elly, don't forget to head to the gas station. The road is clear of standing water from what I could see."

"Got it." The reply came from Joe, which Cole had expected with Elly driving.

Next came Hunter, Sophie, Buddy, and the trailer with the animals. They hit the crack a little hard, the trailer jolting, but they moved past without any difficulties. Was the crack wider than it had been just a few minutes ago? With water swirling on the pavement, it was difficult to tell.

Piper, with Jake in the passenger seat, were next in the caravan She looked relaxed and even waved as she passed Cole. He grinned and waved back but then held his breath as he watched them get to the end where the water was deepest. The small trailer with the chicken coop looked dangerously close to floating...or sinking. *Dammit.* They should have left the chickens. A few eggs weren't worth the risk. What if the trailer pulled their car against the side of the bridge? The thoughts flew through his brain in an instant, but he blew out the breath as they made it to the other side.

Sean and Jenna passed without event, and Cole rolled his shoulders, not realizing how tense he'd been.

Only Steve and Mike were left. Just as they came up to the fissure in the road, a jolt shook the bridge. Cole's first instinct was that he'd been hit by another car, but that wasn't possible.

It took him a second to process what he saw in front of him. Steve's quad-cab pickup lurched nose down in the widening crevice.

Cole picked up the radio as he flung the door open. *"Steve! Mike! Get out!"* The bridge lurched under Cole's feet as he raced to the truck. Mike jumped the crevice just as it split even wider. He landed on Cole's side, but fell hard and lay motionless. Steve remained in the truck and from the sound of the engine, he was attempting to reverse out of the fissure. Cole shouted again. "Leave the truck!"

They could replace everything in it. Cole knelt beside Mike, relieved when the man moaned and rolled onto his back, but his eyes were closed. Cole grabbed him under the arms and dragged him towards his own vehicle. He set him down to open the passenger door when Steve shouted. Cole turned to look and swore. Steve's truck canted at a precarious angle, the back wheels almost off the ground. Steve leaped off the running board as the bridge shivered hard. Cole crouched, feeling like he was in an earthquake. Something must have hit a support beam. Asphalt broke away from beneath the truck and the vehicle lurched deeper into the hole.

Steve took a few steps back and jumped the now six foot gap. His front foot hit, but only the edge of the gap, and slipped off. Arms flailing, he stopped his fall abruptly, his arms braced on the road as his lower body dangled over the raging river.

Cole dashed to Steve, grabbed his arms, and tried to haul him up and onto the road.

"My leg's caught on something! It's stabbing my left leg!"

"Hang on. I have to look!" Cole hated to release the other man's arms so he grabbed Steve's coat collar in his right hand, twisting to wrap the fabric around his fist for a good grip. With the bridge rocking, Cole carefully dropped to his knees and left hand, craning his head to look down into the hole.

The sky was growing lighter, but it was still too dark to see anything clearly. Lying flat on his stomach, he reached for whatever Steve was caught up on.

"I'm slipping!"

"I got you!" Cole found a piece of rebar tangled in the fabric of Steve's jeans along the outer edge of his thigh. He tore at the hole, making it bigger as he struggled to see.

Rain and river water drenched him and he dipped his head against his shoulder in a futile attempt to clear the water from his eyes. Blinking hard, he assessed the situation.

The rebar had impaled Steve's leg, but only the outer edge. There was no exit, so cringing, Cole followed the rebar with his hand to see if he could reach the end of it—to see how deeply embedded it was in Steve's thigh. He tuned out the stream of swearing and groans that spewed from Steve. He'd do the same if their places were reversed. The hard, blunt end of the bar entered the muscle, but it didn't seem to be in too deeply. Cole thought he could disengage it if Steve cooperated. Less than a half inch, by what he could feel.

"Steve, listen to me! I'm going to push your leg back. Work with me, buddy. When I push it back, it's gonna hurt like hell, but it'll be okay. You have to bring your leg next to your other one, then I can pull you up."

"Yeah...okay," Steve gasped.

"One, two...*three*!" Cole wedged his fingers between the end of the bar and Steve's thigh, then twisted his hand so the bar pressed against the back of his hand, and with his palm flat, he pushed Steve's leg away from the rebar, ignoring the pain as the bar gouged the back of his hand.

Steve grunted, but followed Cole's direction. His leg swung free of the rebar.

Grabbing Steve's left arm, Cole inched back, trying to bring the other man up onto the deck of the bridge.

The other side of the hole buckled more and the truck teetered. If it fell, Steve was sure to be taken down with it. Then Steve's arms started slipping and Cole gripped them tighter, horrified as he felt Steve's arms sliding out of the jacket. Pushing with his elbows, he lunged to get a better grip, and Steve's hand shot out, grasping Cole's forearm. But, Cole was too close to the hole and his own arms dragged over the edge. He needed something to hook his feet over to gain leverage.

Hands clamped onto his ankles as though he'd willed them there.

"Hang on, Cole."

Sean. Relief washed over him, giving him extra strength. He tightened his fingers and hollered over his shoulder. "Pull me back!"

A second set of hands gripped the waistband of Cole's jeans and tugged on his coat.

Before he could process who it was, the truck's front bumper scraped against Cole's edge of the hole as the front tires disappeared beneath the bridge.

"Pull!" The command was meant for Sean and whoever had him. The cab of the truck loomed only a few feet over Steve.

Cole contracted his arms, bringing them close to his chest as he strove to drag Steve out of the hole, but at the same time, the truck toppled and the driver's side mirror crashed into Steve's back.

One second Cole was holding two hundred pounds of man in his grasp, and the next, the bridge shook from the impact of the truck and he clutched only a balled up winter jacket. At the same time, he was hauled back about five feet as Sean pulled Cole's ankles. The sudden loss of weight sent Sean stumbling back with a yell as he lost his grip, but he'd already pulled Cole to relative safety. The other set of hands tried to lift him but, stunned at the loss of Steve, Cole could only stare at the spot where Steve's head had been then down at the empty jacket.

Then with a shout, Cole jumped to his feet, shaking off the restraining hands. He rushed to the edge. *"Steve!"*

Sean gripped Cole by the shoulders. "He's gone, Cole."

"No...I almost had him..." In vain, Cole ran to crevice searching for some sign of Steve. The truck lay on its side along the fissure. It wouldn't take much to dislodge it and send the vehicle down into the water rushing by only a few feet below. He'd hoped to see Steve still hanging on to something, but the man was gone. Truly gone.

"Dad..." Hunter took Cole's right arm. *"We gotta go, Dad.* Before the bridge collapses."

Cole looked at his son, hearing the words but having a hard time processing them. His mind felt thick and fuzzy. There was something else he needed to do. Something important. "Mike...oh my god, where is he?" Had he lost that man, too?

"He's okay, Dad. I got him in your car. Come on." Hunter tugged, but Cole felt as though his feet were bolted to the bridge.

Sean's arm draped over Cole's shoulders. "Let's go. The rest of them need us alive. Elly needs you. That new baby needs you."

Cole nodded forcing his feet into action as he trudged back to his vehicle, but when he went to slip behind the wheel, Sean nudged him to the rear driver's side door. "I'll drive."

Hunter climbed in from the other side and Cole wanted to ask him where his car was, but he couldn't force the words through his constricted throat. Still clutching the soaking wet jacket, Cole shivered hard. They all shivered, soaked to the bone, but Cole didn't feel the cold. He felt numb.

Chapter Seventeen

ELLY WATCHED Jenna tend a deep scrape Cole had sustained on his left side. His left hand sported a new bandage too. Everyone was stunned and saddened when they learned what had happened to Steve, but Cole hadn't said more than two words since Sean, Hunter, and Mike had come off the bridge. "I'll be right back, Cole."

He sat on the edge of the rental truck passenger seat, his feet planted on the ground. Without meeting her eyes, he simply nodded.

Mike had already had a minor head wound treated and he was resting on the passenger seat of Piper and Jake's SUV. It was the roomiest for the big man and he liked the cats.

Mike's eyes were closed but maybe he sensed her shadow on his face because he opened his eyes and rolled the window down. "Is Cole okay?"

Nodding, Elly gestured to the rental truck. "Yeah. Jenna's patching him up now. How are you?"

"I'm okay. A little headache, but that's all."

A big bruise on his temple showed it was probably more than a little headache, but Elly nodded. "I'm so sorry about Steve. He was a good man."

Mike drew a deep breath and opened his mouth as if he was going to confess something. That was Elly's impression, which she pushed aside immediately because it didn't fit the conversation. In the next instant, the expression on Mike's face changed to sorrow and he tipped his chin to her. "Thank you. Yeah, Steve always tried to be a good guy. He wasn't perfect...but he was good. "

One of the cats Cole and Hunter had found leaped onto the back of Mike's seat, eliciting a soft chuckle from the man. He reached up and scratched the kitty behind the ears, then patted his chest. The cat accepted the invitation and promptly curled up and closed her eyes.

"Well, you get some rest."

"Thanks, Elly. And, tell Cole that I appreciate everything he did. Sean told me how Cole tried to rescue Steve."

"I will."

She returned to Jenna's side, helping her treat a cut on Cole's arm. Cole hadn't mentioned it earlier and she raised an eyebrow at him but he didn't notice her look. He wasn't paying any attention to her or even what Jenna did as she closed the wound with tape applied in a butterfly pattern before she put a dressing over it.

"Do your best to keep this dry, Cole." Jenna packed up her first aid kit as Cole stood. He'd already changed into dry clothes, and for the moment, the rain had stopped.

"Do we keep going today...or what?" Sean scrubbed his head with a towel as he sat in his vehicle and turned to look at his brother.

Cole glanced at him and shrugged. "Whatever."

Elly bit her lip then said, "I say we keep going. The farther we get from this river, the better I'll feel. Tonight, we should have a special meal in honor of Steve and maybe Mike will say a few words." They had to acknowledge Steve's death and remember the man. It was the right thing to do, out of respect and in order to get closure. She wished they could do more, but under the circumstances this was the best they could do.

When Cole moved to enter the driver's side of his car, Elly rushed forward. "I'll drive. Joe will drive with the kids today."

For the first time since Cole had come off the bridge, he seemed to see her, but his eyes narrowed. "I can drive my own damn car, Elly."

"I know you can, but I thought you might want some company today." She squared her shoulders, not intimidated by his glare. He was hurting and she could deal with his anger. He wasn't angry with her. Not really.

Then she felt a hand on her shoulder. "I've got this, Elly."

She looked up from the hand to find Sean at her side.

"Come on, Cole. I'll drive. It'll give me a break. Jenna's missing all the women talk."

Elly wanted to hug Sean. "Yeah, Joe's a nice guy and all, but I think he could also use a little peace and quiet. You know how I can chat your ear off, Cole."

Cole looked from her to Sean then threw his hands up like he didn't care either way and sulked to the passenger side of his SUV. "Just don't bitch about the heat. The eggs need it."

"You got it, brother. I am looking forward to being toasty warm."

Elly rounded to Cole's side, catching the door before he closed it. "See you later." She took his face between her hands and searched his eyes. For just a moment, she saw a flicker of anguish before he averted his gaze. It was enough. She gave him a quick kiss, relieved when he returned it. She backed out and shut the door, giving him a wave. He nodded.

HUNTER DRUMMED his fingers on the steering wheel as he waited for Joe to move in behind his dad and Sean, and for Sophie to come back to the SUV. Buddy had whined to go out just as they were ready to leave so since she was close to grassy area on her side of the vehicle, she took him.

He'd seen and heard what his dad had said to Elly. He hoped she understood that his dad wasn't angry at her. Elly was astute though. She would know he was upset about Steve, and when she gave Hunter a small wave as she climbed into Jenna's car, he nodded back, relieved that she was okay. Or, as good as any of them could be after what happened.

At least his dad had her to get him through this. She was so good for him. He hoped his dad was good for her too. The first few times he'd seen his dad hold her hand or whisper something in her ear, he'd felt uncomfortable. It was new to him. His dad had gone out on a handful of dates in the fifteen years since Hunter' mom had died, but nothing serious. Out of all the horrible things that had happened in the last year, he was happy his dad had found a little happiness.

It would have been better if his dad would have let Elly ride with him, though. She had a calming effect and in the last two months, Hunter had become so used to little displays of affection between Elly and his dad that he'd barely noticed them anymore. And his dad needed a little TLC about now.

The scene on the bridge replayed in his mind and he ran a dozen different scenarios where he had reacted in a way that could have saved Steve, but every scenario met with the same outcome. It was a freak accident. It could have been any of them, but Steve was the unlucky one. Even though Steve and Mike weren't blood-related to any of them and had only been with them a month or so, in the close confines of the island, it hadn't taken long for everyone to feel like family.

Mike had fit right in. He was easy to talk to and after he'd saved Hunter, everyone had completely accepted him. Steve, however, was more like a distant cousin or something. The man had been talkative, but hadn't offered much information about himself. Hunter didn't even know if he had ever been married. Why hadn't he ever asked Steve about himself? It felt so rude and selfish now to just assume that Steve's life wasn't worth asking about. And now he would never have a chance to ask the man anything ever again. How many stories had he listened to at dinner time where everyone would bring up funny incidents from their childhood when no one asked Steve about his stories? He must have had some. Everyone did.

"Everyone ready to go?" It was Sean's voice on the handheld radio.

Hunter looked and saw Sophie returning. "Give us a minute. Buddy had to use a bush."

The dog took a moment to shake his fur, spraying Sophie. She opened the door to let the dog in the back seat, and said, "Let me change into a different sweatshirt. This one is soaked now."

Hunter nodded even as he continued to dwell on Steve's death. What did he know about the guy? He didn't have to think too hard about the first thing that came to his mind about Steve. And that was that he had been generous with his supplies; never seeming to be upset about sharing what he'd had. He'd seen Steve slip the kids candy. At first, he'd been suspicious of the offerings and made a point of never leaving them alone with the man. And then Steve had given Buddy a large chunk of fish from his own plate a few times, and Hunter even caught him down at the stables feeding Red a piece of candy cane. The man had looked embarrassed to be seen, as if his secret was out. Hunter had grinned and said it was okay. Red and Princess loved sweets. Steve had smiled and shrugged. It was apparent that the man just liked giving treats—be it to kids or animals.

"...Hunter? They're moving."

He shook his head and glanced at Sophie. "I'm sorry. You said something?"

"I said you might want to get going so we don't get too far behind." Sophie rubbed his shoulder. "Do you want to talk?"

The last thing he wanted to do was talk. "Not really."

"Okay. But whenever you want to, if you do, I'm right here."

He glanced at her, wrapped in a blanket, her face peeking out over it, eyes wide. "Thanks. I know."

He wasn't sure Uncle Sean was the right person to offer comfort to his dad. He wasn't certain who would be the right one because how do you comfort someone who had a man's hand slip from their grip and that man was swept to their death?

He blinked hard and coughed to cover the sniffle and swore under his breath. His dad would be okay. He was strong. But, he thought of how his father had taken Trent's death and hoped he wouldn't blame himself to this one too. It wasn't his fault any more than the virus was.

To take his mind off Steve's death, he filled it with thoughts of the baby's birth. Even jitters about being a dad didn't dampen the joy he felt every time he thought of the baby. Jenna had put his mind at ease about the birth. Yes, there were dangers, but it wasn't quite the same as delivering before modern medicine just because they didn't have electricity. Even if the Hoover Dam no longer provided power, Jenna had antibiotics for both Sophie and the baby if needed, and had other medications at her disposal.

"Hey, Soph. Have you given any more thoughts to names?" The

next hour passed with them tossing names back and forth, debating whether middle names were still needed, and the merits of the baby taking Hunter's last name when they weren't legally married. And then she worried about a birth certificate and went on to worry about immunizations and how the baby would ever get them.

Hunter couldn't give her an answer and they worried together until Sophie said, "Well, if we look at this way, there aren't going to be many other kids to pass their bugs onto the baby, right? If there are only a couple of babies around, and nobody travels much, diseases won't spread either."

"You have a point. I'll ask my dad about that."

"Or Elly."

Hunter grinned. "Or Elly."

"I'm so excited she's having a baby too. It means my little peanut will have a playmate."

"I can't believe the playmate is going to be his or her uncle or aunt!" Hunter chuckled.

COLE WATCHED the drenched landscape pass by, hardly noticing the overgrown lawns, wrecked cars, or burned out buildings on the outskirts of some town. They'd passed a lot of burned out buildings since leaving the island. It made him wonder how the fires had started. Some were obvious when the burned out remains of a vehicle stuck out from the charred remains of some building near a road. But, other fires were a mystery. Perhaps lightning had started a few of them and spread, or chemicals had spilled and ignited. Whatever the cause, the destruction of whole blocks wasn't uncommon.

"I can't believe Steve's gone."

Cole turned to look at Sean. Was there an accusatory note in his voice? Sean stared straight ahead, his expression open, and somber. He didn't look at Cole and it was possible he didn't know Cole was watching him, but his brother spoke again. "I should have been nicer to him. I wasn't big on him or Mike hanging out with us. You know me. I was being my usual 'friendly' self around both of them." He slanted Cole what he must have thought was a smile. It was more of a sad grimace.

"You were okay with them—you are, still, to Mike, I mean." Cole sighed, his sentiment getting lost as he mixed the past tense that was Steve with the present that was Mike. "What I'm saying is you were welcoming to Steve. Remember when you guys talked hunting strategies a few weeks ago?"

Sean gave a real smile that time. "More like hilarious hunting stories. It felt almost like old times, shooting the breeze with the guys down at O'Malley's Pub."

Cole had always been a little envious of Sean having guys to hang out with at the corner bar. His brother wasn't a barfly, but once a week he'd buy his employees a round and go watch football on Sundays. Jenna claimed it gave her Sundays to watch what she wanted, and she had her own circle of friends she'd go out with once or twice a month. Cole, well, he'd gone a few times to watch a ballgame, but he didn't have the history with the guys like Sean did, and always felt out of place.

Sean cleared his throat. "You were right. We should have crossed last night. If we had…"

"We had no way of knowing the bridge would fail right as Steve's truck crossed it. I don't have a crystal ball."

"But you wanted to go last night. I talked you into staying one more night and crossing today."

"And you had good points. By the time we had everything packed and over, it would have been dark. Finding a place to spend the night in the dark, driving on unfamiliar roads that could be blocked or flooded wouldn't have been safe either."

They rode in silence, each lost in their thoughts, but the silence was comfortable. Cole closed his eyes as the heater blasted through the cold that had seeped down to his bones. As he relaxed, his mind wandered to his own interactions with Steve. The first night he'd been at the island and offered brown bread from a can. If he was ever fortunate enough to eat that again, he'd think of Steve and how the kids had raved about the bread for days afterward, begging Piper to learn how to make it.

Chapter Eighteen

COLE ROUNDED a sharp curve and slammed on the brakes. *"What the hell?"* After a glance in the rearview mirror to make sure there were no chain reaction accidents behind him due to his sudden stop, he returned his focus to the road.

A boy, hunched into a red jacket, had been in the middle of it a second before, but where had he gone? He scanned the area until a flash of red caught his eye and watched as the boy scuttled behind a bush on the side of the road.

The sky was a deep purple behind them and a brilliant pink and orange straight ahead, but they were at a bend that curved north between two hills and cast the road in dark shadows. They had less than an hour of daylight and Cole had planned to stop a few miles down the road at a campground so they could get settled before it was fully dark. Since Steve's death a few days ago, they had made decent time, although they had been forced to take alternate routes several times when they found roads blocked. Gas had been an issue yesterday and they'd spent time searching out usable gasoline.

Tonight, they had a campground circled on a map. It was their destination. He wondered if the kid had come from there and if he had, did that mean other survivors were nearby as well?

Cole started when his radio blasted.

"Is there a problem, Cole?" Joe sounded calm, but his voice held a hint of concern.

"There was a kid in the road. *A live one*," he amended. They had seen plenty of dead children along the way, or what was left of them. He'd learned to look away from small bundles of bones wearing tattered clothes. "A boy, I think. I'm going to see if he needs help."

"Be careful." Elly must have taken the radio from Joe.

Cole opened his door slowly and stood half out of the car, his hands up and open, worried more about scaring the kid than any danger from the child. "Hey, I'm getting out. I'm not going to hurt you. I'm just wondering if you're okay?"

There was no reply and so Cole scanned the area and felt to make sure his gun was still in its holster beneath his arm. He had a bad habit of removing it when driving, but he was relieved to feel the solid weight of it right where it should be. He stepped away from the safety of the vehicle but left the door open for quick re-entry if needed.

He saw a patch of red through the bush and took a few steps in that direction. "My name's Cole and we're passing through on our way west. We're mostly family. How about you? Have a name?"

The bush rattled a little, and he thought he saw a shoulder.

"Are you hungry? We have plenty of food. I can leave some for you if you want. Or you could join us for dinner. We're heading your way—just up to a campground a few miles up the road."

"Best not."

The words were so low and quiet, Cole wasn't even sure if he heard them. "Excuse me?" He took a few steps closer. "I didn't quite get that."

The voice grew louder. "I said y'all best not go to the campground."

"Oh? Why not?"

"It's where *they* live now."

Cole perked up. "More survivors? Are they your family?"

"Ain't no family of mine. Don't have a family anymore."

"I...I'm sorry to hear that." Cole took a few more steps until he glimpsed the top of the boy's head. Matted dark hair nearly blended into the bush. "If we shouldn't stay at the campground, do you know of another place we can camp for the night? Like I said, we're just passing through and don't want any trouble with anyone."

Maybe it was Cole's question—asking for help—or maybe it was his non-threatening demeanor, but the boy rose slowly from behind the bush. His dark skin stretched taut over sharp cheekbones. He had scrawny shoulders and a neck so skinny it looked as if it could barely hold his head, but his eyes were large and clear and when he spoke, his teeth gleamed. "I'd just keep on going, mister."

Cole studied the boy looking for any signs of the virus but saw only a child who looked frightened, hungry, and yet resolute. "Are they sick there?"

The boy shook his head. "No. They're too mean to be sick. They've been shooting anyone who comes near and stealing their stuff. I saw them kill four or five folks who was just passing by.""

His answer eased Cole's worry about the virus but ignited a worry about other survivors. This kid seemed to know a thing or two and it wasn't just luck that he was still alive. Cole took in the gaunt cheeks and the way the clothes hung on the kid. He may have been lucky to survive so far, but he wasn't thriving. Softening his tone, Cole said, "I meant it when I said we have food. Are you hungry?"

The kid stared at Cole for a long moment, then his eyes flicked to the line of cars stretched out behind Cole's SUV. An expression of wariness tinged with hope flashed over his face before he nodded, licking his lips.

Cole did a mental check of what kind of food he had stored in his car. Most of their provisions were with Piper since she did the majority of the cooking, but every car had an emergency stash, plus there was his Go bag, but he couldn't touch any of that. It was only for emergencies.

He had a few cakes of their own pemmican made from the last deer they had shot. It was easy to eat and nutritious but he wasn't sure the boy would recognize it as food. While their meals were filling, they had to be cooked. Ready to eat food was harder to come by and he had already eaten some of today's supply to tide him over until dinner. The MREs they had found in the prepper's house were packed away for a rainy day. He thought he might have a few sticks of beef jerky in his center console left from a few days ago when they'd scavenged from a remote gas station. He'd stuffed them in the console and had forgotten about them.

He backed to his vehicle. "I'm just going to get some food I have in here."

Opening the console, he dug around until he found the sticks. The pemmican was in a bag there too, and he took one out to offer if the boy didn't want to travel with them. Just because the kid was alone now didn't mean he might not have friends somewhere.

The sticks were wrapped in the heavy plastic from when they had been commercially packaged and could have stood up to being tossed to the ground near the boy, but Cole held them out in front of him and took a few steps closer to the bush. "Here."

The boy eyed the caravan once again before narrowing his eyes at Cole. "How do I know you don't have the sickness?"

Cole pulled a mask out of his pocket but didn't put it on, intending to get more information first. "You're smart to be asking that question, and I can't promise for certain, but I can say that we haven't been around anyone who has had it since last summer. Have you?" Even though he was almost positive the kid was healthy, he wanted to hear what he had to say.

"Nope. Almost everyone around here died before winter. The ones who are left took most of the food into their camp." He tilted his head indicating down the road where Cole had intended to camp.

"How come you're not with them?"

"They don't want me." His head dipped as he scuffed a toe in the gravel on the side of the road but he didn't offer any more details.

Why would someone not want a kid around? Especially now, when every life was precious. "Do you have friends around here?" Cole almost added 'still', but didn't. It sounded too cold phrased that way.

The boy blinked hard a few times then just shook his head, unable or unwilling to voice his answer.

"I'm sorry to hear it." Cole sighed. *Poor kid.* He was all alone in the world.

The boy shrugged then bit his lip as his gaze slid to the beef sticks. Cole gave himself a mental shake. The kid was starving and here he was asking questions when the child needed food. "Here."

When the boy hesitated, Cole wiggled the beef jerky. "It's okay. Take them."

He finally moved toward Cole, snatched the food and retreated to the bush as though it offered some sort of protection. He tore the first stick open with his teeth and devoured half of it in the space of a few breaths.

Concerned, Cole lifted a hand and took a couple of steps closer. "Whoa. Slow down. You might choke."

The boy shrank back, but continued to wolf the food down.

There was the creak of a car door opening behind Cole, and the boy backpedaled until he was almost hidden in the bushes again.

Elly approached Cole and whispered, "Is he okay?"

"I'm almost certain he doesn't have the virus, if that's what you're talking about. If he did, he'd be running to us instead of hiding, but he's half-starved. It appears that he's been on his own for a while. Probably since the fall. He said almost everyone around here had died of the virus by then."

Her eyes softened as she glanced towards the bush. He knew that look. It was the same one she got when she spoke about Luke and Zoë. "Do you think he'd come with us?"

The idea had already entered Cole's mind. "I don't know, but he seems like a smart kid and he's got survivor instincts. In fact, he warned us away from the campground. Something about survivors being there. Mean survivors, according to him."

Elly inched closer to the bush. "Hey there. My name is Elly."

His cheek bulging, the boy stared at her.

With a quick glance at Cole, who nodded encouragement, she turned back to the boy. "What's your name?"

He swallowed. "Travis."

"Nice to meet you, Travis. Like I said, I'm Elly, and this is Cole."

"I know. He told me his name. Is he your husband?"

Cole grinned. He couldn't help it. He stepped alongside Elly. "Officially, no, but only because there are no officials." He put an arm around Elly's shoulders. "My son, Hunter, is a few cars back. We have a few kids with us who were orphaned by the sickness. We're their family now."

A look of naked longing darted through Travis's eyes, but he didn't say anything. Cole had hoped he'd ask to come with them, but then he saw the boy square his shoulders as he tucked the last beef stick into his back pocket. "I gotta get going. I have to be settled before dark."

Cole had an idea. "Hey, do you think you could do me a favor? I'll trade a hot dinner in exchange."

Suspicious, Travis said, "What do I gotta do?"

"Just show us a safe place to camp for the night. We're from Wisconsin and don't know this area like you do. We definitely don't want to mess with the folks at the campground."

Travis thought for a minute, then nodded. "Yeah, I can do that."

"Awesome." Cole waved to the caravan to let everyone know things were fine, then gestured to his vehicle. "If you can stand the smell of chickens, you can ride with me to show me where to go."

"You got chickens in there?" Travis's voice was equal parts curiosity and revulsion.

"Sure do!"

After settling in, laughing as Travis waved his hand in front of his face a few times, Cole let the others know via radio of the change of plans and that they had a guest. Then he turned to Travis. "Point the way."

Chapter Nineteen

TRAVIS DIRECTED Cole to get off the highway at the next exit. "The guys at the camp cleared this road before the first snow but now they use another road most of the time. I think we can get through."

Cole wasn't sure he liked the sound of that, and sent a message to the others to be ready for visitors. That was the word they had decided upon when encountering others. It could mean someone friendly as well as hostile, but caution was implied in both cases.

"How come they don't come this way anymore?"

Travis shrugged. "The town is on the other side of the camp-ground. There's not much out here but more highway. They already cleaned out all the houses and stores this way."

It made sense. Cole followed directions to turn off another road, this one turned back west. It was a half mile south, but roughly seemed to run parallel to the highway, so they weren't getting too far off track.

After driving for about a mile, Travis had Cole make one more turn, and this time, the road was gravel and ended at a small lake. Perfect. Water wouldn't be an issue. "And the people at the camp-ground don't come here?" Cole looked around the small beach and a couple of swing sets, but no homes. It looked like a park.

"No, there's a bigger lake at the camp and cabins and stuff. There's nothing here but some toilets and a water pump." He pointed to a small building. "That used to have a concession stand. It's where I sleep now. I lock myself in the storeroom."

"Aren't you worried someone might come looking for the food?"

"Naw. They cleaned it out before winter."

"What have you been living on?"

"I find stuff now and then in cars and offices. You just have to avoid the dead people. I once found a whole vending machine full of chips in a back hallway of an office building. I think it was forgotten."

His matter-of-fact advice to avoid the bodies sounded so wrong coming from one so young, but he was right. "You're resourceful, that's for sure."

"What's that mean?"

Cole smiled. "It means you're smart."

After the rest of the cars pulled in, everyone crowded around to meet the guest, unintentionally overwhelming Travis. He edged towards the concession stand, looking ready to flee.

The kid had shown them his home, and it occurred to Cole that he was now having second thoughts. Cole waved everyone back. "Listen up, guys. Travis is understandably a bit nervous to be around a bunch of strangers. Let's give him a little room. Everyone get to setting up camp. I promised Travis a good meal in exchange for leading us to this fantastic camping site."

The adults all began their duties and Cole checked on the chickens and the eggs. They were almost ready to hatch. Travis stood beside him, offering suggestions and asking a few questions. He quieted when Luke and Zoë approached. Luke started talking about the chickens and Travis lost his shyness, showing he knew a lot about them, mentioning something about his grandma having chickens in her backyard.

Cole excused himself saying he needed to check on something else and let the kids talk. If anyone could get Travis to trust them, it would be Luke. He'd been in Travis's shoes not long ago. Cole didn't want to let the kids out of his sight though. He didn't think Travis would do anything, but he wasn't ready to trust him around the younger kids just yet.

After he had unloaded and was setting it up his tent, Luke ran up to him. "Cole, can I show Travis how to fish?"

Cole glanced at the sky. It was almost completely dark outside the glow of the two fires they had going already. While warm during the day, the nights were still cold. The lake was only a few steps away though, so Cole got the poles out and handed them, plus a can of worms, to Luke. "Stay right there on the beach where I can see you. Zoë, you stay here."

The little girl jutted out her lip, crestfallen, but only for a moment because Elly came up and asked her to help her spread the sleeping bags out. The little girl loved how they puffed up, and would pounce on them, squeezing the air out.

A little while later, Luke raced up to Cole, shouting that Travis had caught a fish. Travis trailed behind, a nice sized fish hanging from a stringer. He acted like it was no big deal, but Cole felt his eyes watching him intently as Cole inspected the small mouth bass. "This has to be almost two pounds. Nice catch, Travis."

Then he saw it. A smile. The first he'd seen from the boy. He shrugged as the corner of his mouth turned up. "I never fished before."

"No way! You must be a natural like Luke here." Cole rested a hand on Luke's head, tousling his hair. "I think this kid must have been born with a fishing pole in his hand."

"Maybe I can catch dinner for myself now and then—if I can find a pole."

Cole didn't say anything then, not until he'd had a chance to talk to the others. He was hoping Travis would stay with them tonight, at least. "Travis, I know you have a nice set-up in the store room over there, but I was wondering if you'd want to bunk with Luke tonight? It's been a long time since he had a kid near his age to hang out with."

Before the words were even out of his mouth, Luke was jumping to his feet. "Yes! Let's go get your sleeping bag, Travis!"

Travis was less enthusiastic. "I…uh…my sleeping bag is kind of a mess right now." He bent his head and avoided looking at Cole. Was he embarrassed?

To put him at ease, Cole said, "Travis, we have extra bedding. You can use what we have tonight, if you want."

His head shot up, his eyes wide. "Really?"

"Of course." Cole pointed to Luke. "Get the green sleeping bag out of the backseat of my car."

About an hour later after a hot meal that featured Travis's fish, another that Luke had caught, a hearty potato soup and sourdough biscuits, the kids were all sleeping. Cole looked around the fire. Everyone had gathered, except Sophie, who had gone to bed already. Cole worried about her. This pregnancy seemed to be taking a toll on the young woman. Elly, on the other hand, seemed to be thriving, but she was just beginning her second trimester while Sophie was in her third.

Pushing his worries for Sophie aside for now, Cole cleared his throat to get everyone's attention, then asked, "So, what do you guys think of Travis?"

Elly leaned against Cole, letting her head rest on his shoulder. "I'm already half in love with him. He's so quiet but he seems kind. He helped Zoë after she scraped her knee earlier. Got her smiling in no time."

Hunter joined in with, "He seemed pretty proud of his fish, but like he didn't want anyone to know he was proud of it. He also showed us where the best firewood was. That's pretty generous. He could have saved it for himself."

"Good point, Hunter."

Cole did a double take at Sean's comment. He'd be kidding himself if he hadn't expected an argument against inviting Travis to stay with them. Sean was the cantankerous one; the person who was always the voice of dissent. He noticed the surprise on Cole's face and shrugged. "I like the kid. He…well, he doesn't really remind me of Trent…I mean, because he's a lot quieter, but it was nice having another kid around and there's something about him."

"There's hope for you yet, Sean." Cole grinned.

Jenna wrapped her arms around her husband and repeated Cole's words. "There's hope, Sean. You're not a completely lost cause."

"Jeez, guys. You're making me sound like an ogre."

Everyone laughed, throwing out comments. Cole rubbed a hand up and down Elly's arm, bending to whisper, "Looks like we have another member of the family."

Elly snuggled closer. "If he agrees, that is."

Cole nodded, but then wondered. What if Travis didn't want them? They couldn't force the boy to join them, but he sure hoped he would.

In the morning, after a meal of pancakes, eggs made with a combination of what the chickens had laid and powdered egg picked up in a school cafeteria, they loaded up their gear to head out.

Travis sat on a log, watching the activity as he traced lines in the dirt with a long stick. When Cole had his car packed, he sat on the log beside Travis.

"First, I want to thank you again for sharing your home with us."

Travis nodded, drawing wobbly Xs in the dirt as the stick stuttered over the ground.

"And I have a question for you."

The end of the stick hovered a few inches in the air.

"We talked it over last night and wondered if you would like to join us?" Before Travis replied, Cole added, "We really like you, and I'm not sure I would feel good leaving you here, always wondering how you did."

The stick dropped and instead of Xs, started tracing crescents. "Where y'all headed?" He sounded casual, but Cole wasn't fooled. The boy was definitely interested.

"West…Las Vegas area, most likely. It's too cold in Wisconsin in the winter. Plus, we think there might be electricity still in Vegas."

Travis's eyes shot to Cole's. "Really?"

"It's a theory. We have no proof. But even if not, it'll be warmer. Maybe we'll find other survivors."

Pushing up from the log, Travis jabbed the stick into the dead ashes from last night's fire and shook his head. "I don't want to meet other survivors." He stared at the stick as it quivered.

Cole watched Travis and how his hands curled into fists, his shoulders stiff. After a few moments, he stood beside the boy. "I'm a little nervous about meeting others too. Who wouldn't be?"

Arms crossed, eyebrow raised, Travis asked, "*You're* nervous?"

"Absolutely. Like you, we've run into some not so nice people. People who feel that they can take what they want."

Travis nodded and swiped a hand across his eyes. Cole pretended not to notice as he went on, "I don't agree with that, but on the other hand, someone has to stand up to them. We can't let people like that take over the world."

"But they have guns and control the food." He paused. "They chase me sometimes and holler that they'll throw me in the stew pot." He took a deep breath then turned to face Cole. "Do you think they'd do that?"

Anger, red and hot, surged through Cole. Anger at what this kid had gone through and anger that he'd had to face it alone. It was more than anyone should ever have to deal with, let alone a kid. *If he ever met those monsters…*

He let his head drop back and drew in a long slow breath before blowing it to the sky. He didn't want to scare the kid and Travis's shoulders were already shaking. It was all he could do not to throw his arm around the boy, but he sensed that would be the worst move.

"Travis, just remember, *we're* survivors too. You, me, Luke—all of us. While we expect everyone to pitch in and do their part, we don't chase anyone and we certainly don't *eat* people."

Travis sniffed but slanted a look at Cole. "Better not. I'm too tough for any stewpot." A trace of a smile flashed across his face.

"I'm sure you are. We'd have to fatten you up a bit first. Probably wouldn't even be worth it." Cole, fingertips angled in his front pockets, toed a stone, working it free from the dirt as he shot a quick smile at the boy.

There was no mistaking the glint of amusement in Travis's eyes. "Nope. Not worth it at all." Then he grew serious. "I'm a hard worker. I promise."

Cole stuck out a hand. "We'd be honored to have you come with us. I already know you're a hard worker. You must be to have survived this long all alone."

Travis nodded as he shook Cole's hand. "Yes, sir."

Chapter Twenty

ELLY HELPED Travis gather up his possessions from the concessions stand he'd turned into his home. She was surprised at how much he'd managed to accumulate. They packed up several rifles, a couple of handguns with boxes of ammunition for all of it, as well as pans, knives, and surprisingly, a lot of medication.

"Where'd you get all this stuff?" she asked, not intending to come off as accusatory, but Travis's spine stiffened.

"I only took it from houses where people were all dead. I never stole from nobody."

She nodded. "I'm sure you didn't. We've also had to find things in people's homes. I just meant that I'm amazed at what you've got in here." There were a few rabbit and squirrel skins, but Travis hadn't dried them properly and they were rotting—there was no way to turn them into useable skins. She lifted one with a stick. "I'll show you how to treat these so they'll last. We didn't know either. Joe had to teach us." She pointed to Joe, who was helping herd the goats back into their trailer. "He's the man to ask if you have any questions about hunting and fishing."

Travis looked at Joe, then back to Elly. "He knows more than Cole?"

Elly threw back her head and laughed. "Oh, god, yes! And Cole will be the first to tell you that."

Not looking convinced, Travis shoved sweatshirts and jeans into a backpack. "If you say so."

Clearly, Cole had impressed the kid. "It's okay that he doesn't know everything—he's smart enough to recognize everyone's skills. You know what he told me about you after you agreed to come with us?"

Travis stilled, one hand on the zipper of the backpack. "What?"

"He said, 'We're lucky to have Travis coming along. He knows what it takes to survive. He's got skills we can use.'"

The boy bit his lip as though trying to hide a grin, then shrugged as if Cole's words hadn't meant much, but he carried himself straighter when he shouldered the pack and gathered his weapons. "I'm ready to go."

Elly thought for a moment. "Do you want to ride with Luke? He's in my car."

Travis shook his head. "I'd like to ride with Cole, if that's okay."

"His car is kind of stinky from the chicken. She's brooding some eggs. We're hoping they'll hatch."

"I don't mind. I can help. My grandma had chickens and she used to let me help with them sometimes."

"Oh? Well, see, Cole was right about you." Elly shrugged. "I'm sure Cole will be fine with you riding with him. I think he's been getting a little lonely driving all by himself."

"Who's getting lonely?" Cole popped his head into the room.

"Not you, that's for sure." Elly handed Cole a garbage bag full of over the counter pain relievers, bottles of allergy pills, allergy nasal sprays, and eye drops.

Cole did a double take as he glanced in the bag, looking at Travis. "Do you have an allergy problem we should know about?"

Travis laughed. "No, sir. I found boxes of those in the backroom of a drug store. Everything else was gone, but those were under a box of old people diapers. I guess nobody noticed them. I thought I could trade them for food sometime."

"Good thinking." Cole caught Elly's eye. "Hey, could I talk to you for a minute?"

"Sure." She took a couple of the least ratty looking blankets, shook them out, then folded them. "Here, Travis, put these in Cole's car. He'll be there in a minute."

Once Travis was gone, Cole moved up, wrapping his arms around Elly's waist. "How are you feeling?"

Elly cocked her head. "I'm fine. Why?"

"I'm just asking. I'm worried about you and the baby." He put a hand on her abdomen before leaning in to nuzzle her neck. "I wish we were settled. For you and for Sophie. This traveling isn't good for either of you. All the time in the car, setting up camps—just everything."

"But we'll be there soon, right?"

"We'll skirt around Denver. I'm hoping to avoid what I think will be blocked highways, and also hoping we'll find a gas station where we can pump some gasoline with the generator. That worked well the last time."

"So, another couple of days?"

"Probably. Depends."

Elly draped her arms over Cole's shoulders, tilting her head and laughing as his mouth tickled along the spot between her neck and shoulder. "Depends on what?"

Cole drew back, his playful mood gone in an instant. "It depends on so many things. I'm worried about the nice folks Travis told us about. The people who threatened him. I want you to be ready with weapons loaded."

"In the car? I don't know, Cole. We have the handguns and the rifles are packed, but not loaded. What if one of the kids messes around with one?"

"Look, we've made sure they understand how to use these and when to use them. Even Zoë knows the basics."

"I know…okay. But other than Travis, we haven't seen a soul, so I don't know who you're afraid of."

"Travis told me about a group of survivors living where we were going to camp. They aren't very friendly. I just want to be ready in case we run into them."

Travis's story about the group of survivors who had threatened him worried her also but how would the group even know they were around? Helicopters? The thought made her shudder as she thought of Holland. If he'd had his way, Cole would be little more than a test rat in some secret lab. That's who she was afraid of, but the country was huge and finding them would be like searching for a diamond in the Sahara. Granted, the people Travis had spoken of lived nearby, but they could take another route now that Travis had warned them.

Elly finally nodded. "Okay. We'll be ready. And Cole, you made quite the impression on Travis. He wants to ride with you."

"I did?" His face lit up. "Well, the admiration is mutual. Thanks to him, I've mapped out an alternate route that I hope will take us south of where he said those survivors were camped." He dug in his pocket and pulled out a stack of folded sheets of notebook paper. "I tried to draw a map, but I wrote it out as well."

She took the map and studied it. "Will we be able to connect back onto the main highway down the road?" From what she recalled from the map, this route would take them north before turning south again.

"I know it's a bit of a detour, but I'd rather avoid coming into contact with anyone. Especially if we already know they're hostile."

THE ALTERNATE ROUTE took them through several small towns instead of bypassing them on the highway. When they came across a herd of deer grazing in the center square of the town, they stopped, and Cole shot a large buck. They would have liked to have killed more, but they didn't want to stick around long enough to process the meat. As it was, they stopped for the day a few hours early to butcher the deer.

Unhappy about the lost opportunity, Jake looked at the meat they wouldn't have room to pack, and scowled. "I bet I could smoke it by morning."

"The roast is going to take an hour or so to cook, so if you think you could get something rigged up in that time, have at it." Cole built the coals up around the cast iron pot they had sitting on a grate right in the fire. He turned the roast a smidgen and sprinkled a pinch of salt over it.

"I bet one of these houses has a smoker in the backyard." Jake surveyed the homes bordering the south side of the town square. "I think I'm going to go check them out. Hunter, want to come with me?"

His son shrugged and set down the box that contained plates and eating utensils.

The graceful Victorian style homes had probably belonged to the town's elite. Even with a years' worth of weeds and debris, Cole could picture what they must have looked like exactly a year ago. The homes would have had thick, lush grass, an emerald hue rivaled only by the neighbors' lawn on each side.

Piper brought over a bowl of quartered potatoes.

"Make sure there's nobody around before you go into any back-yards—and take your radios!"

Piper handed Cole the bowl. "Go where?"

"We're going to look for something to smoke the meat so we don't waste so much of it."

"Oh! I'll go! I need to stretch my legs after the long drive today."

While Cole tended the roast, he kept an eye on Luke, Travis, and Zoë, who played a game of tag. Travis purposefully fell down a few times, flailing around as though he was trying his best to escape Zoë's tag. Cole smiled. Luke laughed and teased Travis for getting caught, but then he followed the other boy's lead and did the same thing. Zoë squealed in delight.

"I'm glad we saw the deer when we did. I think we all needed this." Elly unfolded a lawn chair and sat beside him. "The kids haven't had much opportunity for play, and fresh meat will definitely be welcome."

Cole nodded and took her hand. "So, how did the check-up go?" Jenna had taken the opportunity offered by the early stop and had done a quick maternal check-up on both Elly and Sophie.

"Looking good. My blood pressure is fine but I gained a few pounds—which Jenna tells me is absolutely a good thing." She chuckled and rubbed her rounded stomach. "I'm not so sure though. This little one even kicked a bit for Aunt Jenna's exam. Thumped right up against the stethoscope, I guess."

Grinning, Cole leaned over and gave her stomach a light rub, speaking directly to the bump. "Behave in there!"

A few minutes later, the young people returned sans smoker, but with grates from grills and a few wrought iron planter stands. It seemed they'd decided that they could put the stands over the fire and set the racks on them to smoke the meat. Cole had heard of that technique before but was impressed that they had thought of it on their own.

Piper had a basket in her hands and a secretive smile on her face.

Sean joined them, having gone to clean up in a stream that created the northern edge of the square. It's where they had replenished their water bottles and large water jugs. The water had come down from the mountains to their west and was the best tasting they'd come across since leaving the island.

"Brr... that was cold, but man, do I feel better!"

"Maybe we should heat up a big pot and let everyone get good and cleaned up tonight?"

Cole nodded. "I can get started on hauling water, but I'm going to wash up first. If Sean can take the cold water, so can I." He slanted his brother a teasing grin, feeling closer to him than he had in a long time. Since Steve's death, Sean had driven with Cole a few times and each time, their conversations became easier. They reminisced about growing up, shared anecdotes about their parents and kids, and even told raunchy jokes they couldn't share in mixed company, and since the virus, they were almost always in mixed company.

"I'll go too." Hunter grabbed a bucket and soon, all the guys, even Luke and Travis, had buckets and towels and raced to the stream. Jake won, with Hunter a close second. Cole hung back to watch out for Travis and Luke. They had seen no signs of human life, and plenty of death as they'd driven in, but Cole knew better than to let down his guard. He was glad Sean had stayed back at the camp. With him and Buddy standing guard, he was free to wash up and even make sure Luke actually used soap and didn't horse around too much.

On the way back, their hair all stood up in wet spikes, except for Travis's, whose hair sparkled with trapped drops of water.

Hunter spotted a stack of kiddie pools leaning up against the front wall of a hardware store on the far side of the square and trotted over to get one, returning with it upside down on his head. One hand steadied it while the other carried his pail of water to contribute to filling the pool. The boys laughed and darted around him, spilling half of their own water as they asked if they could swim.

"You guys just got done swimming, you goofs. This is so the women can take warm baths." Cole reached out and tousled Luke's wet hair.

"Why do they get warm baths?"

"Because they work hard doing all kinds of things for us, so I want to do something for them."

"But you shot the deer and helped gut it."

"Yes, I did, and while I did that, the women were setting up the tents and spreading out the bedding so everyone would have a nice warm place to sleep tonight."

"Oh. Yeah. I guess."

The atmosphere was almost festive an hour later. Cole designated the feast as a celebration of Travis having joined the family. Piper had surprised them all with fresh asparagus she'd found growing in the remains of a garden. This early, that's all there was, but everyone—even the kids—devoured the fresh vegetable. It was the first they'd had in months.

After dinner, Jake lit another fire, and when the coals had died down in both of them, he set up the planter stands with the grates on top of them, and laid the deer over them to smoke. The planter stands kept the meat from actually cooking, but kept it close enough to be swallowed in the white plumes of smoke.

"I'll stay up tonight and keep an eye on it. I think I can do about four batches. Maybe more. This wood is perfect for it."

It was well seasoned from sitting for over a year. Good hardwood that would give the meat a rich, smoky flavor. And they would all be able to add it to their emergency Go-bags.

That reminded him that Travis didn't have a Go-bag yet, so Cole spent the last hour creating one for the boy. He rummaged through supplies, finding one of their extra backpacks, a good water bottle that would keep a day's worth cold, plus water purification tablets, and then pulled some fishing gear from his tackle box. He made a small kit with hooks, weights, bobbers and string. A good hunting knife, a small hatchet, two ground cloths—one could turn into a tent, added a first aid kit with tape, bandages and disinfectant. He found resealable bags and filled one with matches and added a lighter. He dumped a bottle of aspirin into another baggie, and took the bottle and stuffed it with cotton balls soaked in alcohol. He closed up the bottle and added the aspirin to the first aid kit. Next he found a lighter and a change of clothes with extra socks. He wasn't sure of Travis's size, but Piper said she had an extra pair of hiking boots that she thought would fit him and generously offered them. The last thing he packed was a handgun. It was one Travis himself had scavenged, along with ammunition for it.

By morning, the meat was dry, Jake was dead tired, and Travis was thrilled when Cole presented him with his official go-bag. "Remember, this is only for emergencies. I've stocked it with some non-perishable food, including the dried venison Jake was so kind to provide, and other basic supplies. It's everyone's job to make sure their water bottles are filled every morning. One for the bag and one for drinking throughout the day. I've done it for you today, but after this, you'll be doing it on your own."

"Yes, sir." Travis took the bag, his eyes glowing with pride, and climbed into his vehicle as soon as everything was packed and breakfast of leftover roast and potatoes were eaten. A good portion of the deer meat that hadn't been dried was packed into coolers powered by the cars. It would stay good in there for a few days.

Chapter Twenty-One

COLE CHECKED HIS FUEL GAUGE. *A quarter tank.* According to the last road sign, they should make it in before he needed to get gas. As he wove around yet another pile-up, he added a few miles to the distance. It wouldn't be a straight shot, not if he had to wind around the more and more frequent pile-ups and he fully expected that to be the case.

They had managed to avoid traveling close to any large cities, knowing they would have a greater likelihood of encountering blocked freeways, but even a dozen miles out, they were reduced to a speed of not more than thirty miles per hour and in some places, they had to go even more slowly.

He rubbed his eyes, wincing at the gritty feel behind his lids. The sun, low on the horizon, would soon be hidden by the hills and mountains. His plan to arrive no later than mid-afternoon so they could scope the area out for other survivors before camping, was out of the question now since he hadn't factored in having to take detours when confronted with obstacles where there wasn't even room to navigate around them. Still, he couldn't resist the final push to reach the city. He had to know if the power was still on. What if they had come all this way and were no better off than they had been on the island? Possibly even worse since at least they knew the area around the island. Here, other than a few vacations, nobody was familiar with the city. They all had favorite casinos, shows, or hotels, but none of that knowledge would help them now.

In fact, Cole had no interest in exploring the tourist areas. None of that would be any use except to check out the kitchens for canned goods. If the virus had spread with the same speed here as it had in Wisconsin, he had an inkling that it would have had even a greater impact here. The tourists were already primed to be out and about and the virus would have spread faster than a juicy rumor in high school. Even the areas not around the touristy spots would probably have an increased rate of spread of the disease because so many people were employed in hotels, shows, casinos, or restaurants. The virus probably thought it hit the host motherlode.

He glanced in his rearview mirror automatically noting everyone in the caravan. At least he never had to worry about losing anyone in traffic.

Over the ten day trip, they'd witnessed firsthand the miles and miles of highways devoid of human life and the ghost towns that were frozen in time. Sales signs in store windows still touted Memorial Day sales from last year and upcoming Father's Day promotions. In the middle of Nebraska, they had come across a town that had been nearly leveled by a tornado. A clear path of destruction and denuded trees told the story. The lack of any sort of cleanup efforts or rebuilding indicated that the tornado had occurred sometime after the virus had wiped out the population.

More numerous than the huge pile-ups when they had to clear a path, were the cars parked on the road, some neatly along the edge, but others appeared as if the driver had simply lost interest in driving and decided to halt. It was eerie—like vehicular ghost towns.

When they stopped for breaks, Cole sent or joined a detail to check the vehicles in search of supplies. Of special importance were tools since theirs had gone down with Steve back at the Mississippi River.

More often than not, they found human remains in the cars—sometimes what must have been whole families, but occasionally, vehicles were empty. Where the occupants had gone was anyone's guess. Perhaps they were the origin of the remains that dotted the shoulders of the roads.

Cole figured those people had abandoned their cars due to the obstructions, or out of confusion wrought by the victims of the virus. Either they succumbed to the Sympatico Syndrome, injuries from accidents, or died of thirst. Out here, it wouldn't be unheard of.

The sun hit him square in the eyes and Cole squinted as he flipped the visor down. Travis dozed in the passenger seat and Cole smiled at how he still clutched a book in one hand. The kid had devoured books almost as fast as the food set before him. The book currently in his lap dealt with raising chickens. It was part of the mini library they had brought with them.

The eggs hatched and the chicks needed frequent attention and Travis had taken to caring for them like a mother hen.

He made sure they had clean water at every break, and kept the pen clean. One of the little chicks had died, but the others seemed healthy. Cole had rigged up a heater by using a couple of jump starters and inverters to power a small heat lamp and red light for the chicks. They rotated the jump starters to keep one charging at all times so they could swap it with the depleted battery at regular intervals.

Then he'd hung a thick blanket between the backseat and the storage area in the back of the SUV, more to keep the heat out of the rest of the vehicle so they didn't roast to death. He still tried to keep the air conditioning low though, but he was pretty damn proud of rigging a mobile chick nursery if he did say so himself. Now, if only he could do something about the smell but the blanket helped keep it confined somewhat.

Travis made sure the chicks stayed warm, but not too warm. If they survived, they would more than double their flock. Cole had worried Lucas would be upset that Travis had taken over the care of first the eggs, and then the chicks, but Lucas was happy to concentrate on the goats, making sure they got time to graze during every stop, and with Buddy's help, kept them from running off while they grazed. As a result of the careful attention, the two who gave milk still had an abundant supply. Cole had been certain the stress of the trip would be too much for them.

All in all, the animals had come through the trip with flying colors. If only all of the people had too.

He swallowed hard as he thought of Steve but did his best to put it out of his mind for now. He couldn't dwell on the loss—not when they still had so much to deal with in the coming days. If they were successful in establishing a new home here, there would be plenty of time for guilt and anguish later.

Yawning, he reached over and gave Travis's shoulder a shake. "Hey, we're almost there." The words sounded good to his ears.

Travis blinked, then straightened and leaned forward to see the hills they were traveling through. "It sure looks different from where I grew up."

Cole had been to Vegas before, but he had never lived there and he agreed with the kid. "I might miss the green of Wisconsin, but I won't miss the snow, that's for sure."

Travis grinned at him. "We probably didn't get as much snow as you all, but we got some. And lots of storms. You ever seen a tornado?"

"I did, but just a small one that didn't do much damage. And a few water spouts over Lake Michigan too."

"Wow! That sounds so cool!"

Cole chuckled. "Yes, it was." For all Travis had been through, he still held a note of wonder in his voice and a determination to learn as much as he could—hence, all the reading.

"So, did you learn anything new about raising chicks?" Travis had been proud of knowing a little bit about the chickens from helping his grandma, but like the rest of them, didn't know a lot about taking care of chicks.

Travis turned over the book in his hand, noted where he was and folded the corner over before wedging it between the seat and center console. "You really think there's gonna be electricity in Las Vegas?"

Cole used his thumb and fingers to reach under his sunglasses and rub his eyes. Resettling the glasses, he sighed. "I guess we'll find out soon enough."

———

HUNTER SWITCHED songs on the MP3 player, singing under his breath as he followed Elly. It was in moments like this when he could almost pretend the virus had never happened. A hundred miles back, the highway had been nearly devoid of stalled cars. The few he'd seen, at a distance, looked like normal traffic and he'd found himself lulled into daydreaming about the past. He daydreamed of going through his favorite burger drive-thru, jamming to his stereo, and hearing the ping of his notifications on his cellphone.

He propped his arm on the edge of the door, resting it against the cool window. There really wasn't much he missed now that he thought about it. He'd lost the craving for fast food months ago, and the notifications had only been a lure to draw him to his phone; a dangerous lure and one that he had fallen for more than he should have. It was pure luck that he'd never had an accident while texting and driving, but he'd come close a few times. Ironically, he could probably text without compromising safety now—if only phones still worked and there was anyone to text outside of his family.

He yawned, scrubbing his hand down his face. Driving in the caravan seemed like it should be easy. With no other traffic, he only had to watch out for Elly driving the car ahead of him. She followed his dad, and he'd learned to leave enough room to stop suddenly if his dad had to swerve around an obstacle—which caused a chain-reaction.

The problem was driving now was beyond boring. When there had been other cars on the road, simple cruising on a highway required him to be semi-alert. Even Now, he found himself scanning the highway and checking his mirrors, but for what? There were only a few vehicles behind him and he knew them. They weren't going to drive erratically or speed past him. He chuckled at the thought of Jake or Piper getting road rage and passing him while flipping him the bird.

While keeping one eye on the cars ahead, he had more time to look around while he drove. What he saw was both depressing and beautiful. The mountains and desert were just as stunning as he remembered them from a trip he'd taken a few years ago with a friend's family, but, as always now, signs of death were everywhere. It niggled at his conscience that he was pretty much numb to it now. Heaps of bleached bones and clothing on the side of the road garnered no more notice than a dead skunk would have a few years ago.

He glanced at Sophia, and she lifted her head from the word search booklet they'd found at a gas station, her eyes questioning. "Something wrong, Hun?"

He loved when she abbreviated his name like it was an endearment. "Nope. Just bored. How's the game going?"

She shrugged and shifted in her seat. "Okay but I'll be glad when we stop. Do you think there's really going to be electricity in Las Vegas? I'd *kill* for a hot shower."

"It's kind of freaking me out that we made this whole trip because I happened to have seen that show about the Earth without people. I mean, I think everyone was speculating. How could they know for certain?"

Sophie reached out and rubbed his shoulder. "No matter what, we needed to leave Wisconsin. Remember how hungry we were some nights in the winter? Before your dad went hunting and got that deer?"

It was true. They had gone hungry a few times. Getting the deer had probably stopped them from having to kill and eat one of their animals. Once there was a break in the weather, they had been able to find more deer and the day after the helicopter, Jake had found a cow. The poor cow had been skinny and probably would have died soon anyway, but she had been pregnant, and between her and her unborn calf, had provided enough meat to keep them from having to take the more drastic measures.

"But what if we're trading cold weather for drought?"

"I guess we can head someplace that's warmer in the winter and gets plenty of rain, like Seattle. This is just the first place we're going. It may not be the last."

"Seattle could be nice. They don't get very cold, do they?" He'd never been there before.

"Nope. Not compared to Wisconsin, anyway. And plenty of rain. Jenna's garden would thrive." She circled a word, then crossed it off the list. Apparently it was the last one for that puzzle because she turned the page in the book.

"Hey, it seems like you and Jenna are getting along better now."

"Yeah. We are. I don't know what I'd have done without her these last few months—just giving me advice and stuff." Sophie flipped through her word search book then tossed it aside. Her profile as she looked out her window was softer, less angular than it had been when he met her last summer, but she was still too thin. It made her belly seem bigger than it was. He followed the movement of her hand as she absently rubbed it.

"Is he kicking?"

"*He*? What if it's a *she*?"

"He, she…I don't care."

She smiled and nodded. "Yeah, she's kicking."

He laughed, and making sure he had enough space between him and Elly's car ahead, reached over to see if he could feel the baby's movement. It amazed him how firm Sophie's stomach felt. It wasn't squishy like fat. It was taut. Suddenly, he felt a tiny thump against his palm. He grinned. "I felt a kick."

"Isn't it awesome?"

He didn't answer as another series of thumps came in quick succession, then stopped. He waited a few more seconds before reluctantly withdrawing his hand. "I guess she decided to take a nap."

Sophie smiled and rubbed the spot where his hand had been. "I'm going to have to stop to go pee sometime soon."

Hunter nodded. "Okay. I'll call and let everyone know. It's been a few hours since our last stop."

As he turned to get the radio from her, a movement in her side mirror caught his eye. He squinted, certain his eyes were playing tricks on him. A cloud of dust billowed a mile or so behind them. Was it a large dust devil? For an instant, the dust curtain parted, and Hunter started. Were those vehicles moving?

He ground the heel of one hand against first one eye and then the other. That couldn't be it. They hadn't seen another car moving since they left the island.

Hunter glanced in his own side mirror, confirming that his eyes hadn't played tricks on him. Three vehicles raced up behind them, weaving around wrecks with speed their own group hadn't dared to take, not knowing what was on the other side of the piles of wreckage.

The cars were still well back, hazy in the waning sunlight. The gap between the approaching cars and their group was closing fast. Hunter grabbed his radio. "Uh, Dad… we have three vehicles moving up behind us. What should we do?"

Chapter Twenty-Two

COLE ANGLED his mirrors so he could see past the other vehicles. The cars were coming up fast, weaving in and around the pile-ups at a breakneck speed. That signaled two possibilities to Cole—either they were daredevils, possibly infected with the virus—or they were very familiar with this road and the wreckage. He wouldn't discount the first, but would put his money on the second. Or he would if money mattered anymore.

His first instinct was to form a circle with their cars like an old time circling of the wagons, but there was nowhere to do it. He felt Travis's gaze on him and saw fear in the boy's eyes. "We're going to be fine, Travis. It's okay. They're probably just excited to see survivors."

Travis shook his head. "The people I saw in my town weren't happy. They didn't like folks coming around."

Cole didn't have time to answer as he scanned the road ahead looking for a safe place to pull over and either let the other cars go by, or confront them. He feared the boy was right though. While it wasn't quite Mad Max, it wasn't a welcome party either.

"Dad...?"

Cole picked up the radio. "I heard you." He spotted a gas station off the next exit. It was on a slight hill. It wasn't much of an advantage, but if they could get there and turn, facing down, they'd have a good defensive position. There looked to be an exit on the far side of the gas station as well so they had an escape route if needed and the other group would have to pass their caravan. "Everyone, next exit on the right is a gas station. Get there fast, turn around facing out, get your weapons loaded and ready."

He tucked the radio alongside his thigh and pressed his foot to the gas. "Travis, I need you to climb in the back there and get the rifles and shotgun ready. They're already loaded, so be careful. I want you to stay back there and stay down.

Travis nodded and dove into the backseat. The guns were close at hand and Cole was glad for that. "You want the handgun, too?"

Cole almost said yes, but changed his mind. "No, you keep that one for yourself." If something happened to him, the kid needed a way to defend himself.

After a brief pause, Travis replied, his tone somber but with a note of confidence. "Yes, sir."

"Buckle up back there. This is going to get rough." The click of the seatbelt came only a few seconds before Cole was forced to scrape past a car that was on the shoulder edge of a huge wreck that blocked the rest of the ramp. The car sat perpendicular to the road with only inches of clearance on either side. If he took it slowly, he could probably get by without touching the other car, but there wasn't time for careful driving. The truck Sean was driving would need to fit through here too, and so with that in mind, Cole aimed for a location that would turn the car so it would almost be facing the wrong way.

"Hang on!"

The impact jarred the SUV, but he succeeded in moving the other car and not having his air bags go off. He'd worried about that and had slowed at the last second. Not far past that was another car, but this one was stopped still facing forward, as though it had stalled there. Maybe it ran out of gas just short of its goal, not that he cared why it was there. It just was and it was another obstacle. "Shit." He glanced in the mirror to see if the cars were still coming towards them, but for the moment, the big truck blocked his view of the road behind him as he was on an incline.

He slowed until he was nearly stopped, hoping Elly wouldn't slam into the bumper of his own car, but there wasn't time to tell everyone his plan. His front fender made contact with the rear of the stalled vehicle and, pressing steadily on the gas, his SUV moved the other car forward. He pressed harder on the gas, praying the other vehicle wouldn't turn towards the shoulder but would instead turn towards the center of the road.

His prayers were answered as the car angled ever so slightly to the left. Giving his car a little more gas, he disengaged when the car's wheels hit something and turned at a sharper angle and rolled out of the way.

Gunning the SUV, Cole shot ahead, grateful there were no more cars between them and the gas station. He just wished he could block the road off from the pursuers. The next stopped police car he saw, or the next police station they passed, he vowed to check for the strips that he saw used in police chases. The strips that police officers would place on the road which would puncture tires of any pursuers.

He raced into the gas station, cranking the steering wheel hard to the right as he performed a U-turn. Stopping just inside the entrance from the top of the ramp, he angled the car so there was just enough room for the others to enter, but was ready to do his best to block access from the pursuers. It also gave him an angle to use the rifle.

Cole shoved the gearshift into park and snatched the rifle Travis handed him along with a pouch full of shells. "I need you to stay down. Slide the boxes over to my side of the car and hunker down behind them." Cole grabbed Travis's and his own insulated water bottles and tossed them in the back. "If things don't go well, take the water, and run. Put your backpack on."

"Yes, sir."

There came rustling and clanking and Cole breathed easier, able to focus on the approaching cars as Sean entered the station. He was the last in their caravan, and the others had parked at angles just a little behind Cole, bringing their weapons to bear on the cars racing up the ramp.

Cole grabbed the radio. "Everybody hold your fire."

"Until we see the whites of their eyes?"

While he appreciated Sean's attempt at levity, Cole didn't have time to comment on it. "Let's just find out what they want first."

A series of quick replies confirmed he'd been heard. Sean simply said, 'Okay'.

He studied the approaching cars, now merely a quarter of a mile away. Were they slowing? It was hard to determine. If only he could communicate with them and decipher their intentions. What he wouldn't give for a loudspeaker right about now. Cursing his lack of foresight for not obtaining a megaphone from somewhere, Cole drew a deep breath and gripped the steering wheel.

He tried to tell himself that these were people just like them but he wasn't sure he believed it. Everyone seemed to react to the worst case scenario differently. Had his own reaction been wrong? There hadn't been much time to plan and then the focus had been on immediate survival, not keeping humans from going extinct. Now, it was foremost in his mind but that didn't mean others felt the same way.

It would have been easy to slip into and remain in short-term survival mode, living in the moment. They had been plunged into a free for all lifestyle with survival of the fittest the only law, but Cole refused to lose his conscience—his humanity. And now, he could only pray that the approaching car contained survivors who felt the same.

How times had changed. How many thousands of people had he sped past in his lifetime without giving a second thought? Or parked near and walked into a store. It was crazy to think that now the prospect of meeting strangers sent his heart thumping so hard he could feel it all the way up into his throat.

A trickle of sweat slid down his neck and he reached over and turned the air conditioning to max. Hadn't the helicopter been enough of a challenge? All they wanted to do was find a new home in a mostly empty land. He wasn't at all eager to engage with more strangers.

The strangers were definitely slowing, and came to a stop a long stone's throw away. That was something, anyway. Despite chasing them to the gas station, they didn't seem to be in a hurry to charge at them. Then again, that could be due to the rifle barrels poking out of the windows of the cars in Cole's caravan.

There wasn't enough room for them to stop three abreast. The best they could do was stagger their vehicles so none blocked the other completely. Cole hoped that was a good thing for them. He glanced at the vehicles in his group. All but the children were armed and ready. Hunter's SUV was on his left, and he noted with approval that his son not only had his rifle ready, but the top part of his bow and arrow were visible, resting upright against the seat.

The strangers remained facing them and Cole tried to count heads but with the shadows deepening it was difficult. At least that worked both ways. Plus, it had to be a good sign that nobody was shooting yet. After about thirty minutes of silence, Cole took a deep breath. Maybe the strangers were waiting for them to run out of gas as they idled.

Cole looked at Hunter and Elly, on either side of him, glad to see they were focusing forward, but Sophie, in the passenger seat of Hunter's car, looked to be in some distress. He didn't know what it was and when he mouthed the question asking if she was okay, she nodded, flashing him a strained smile.

That did it. They couldn't just sit here all night. He had to find out what these people wanted. He handed Travis the radio. "If something happens, jump in Elly's car, okay?" Elly was on the passenger side, and with the driver's side rear door barricaded with boxes for protection, it would be the quickest escape for Travis.

Wide-eyed, Travis nodded.

Reluctantly, he left his rifle in the car. He was glad when Travis reached over the seat and steadied it. He'd be able to grab it quickly if he had to. He left the door open, slight protection if they decided to shoot, but it made him feel safer. He spread his arms, hands wide to show he was unarmed. The trickle of sweat turned into a stream and a few drops ran down from his brow and stung his eyes. He blinked, not daring to rub them.

The cars opposite him were covered in dust, their colors impossible to discern. If he had to guess, he'd say the front car, a crossover vehicle, was a deep red. The next one was a quad cab pickup with a cap on the back. It was probably black beneath the reddish dust. The last one, on his right, Cole easily identified because of the round headlights and build of a Jeep.

Each second seemed to last a year as he remained with arms outstretched and his shoulder muscles burned, but he ignored it just as he ignored Elly's harsh whisper asking him what he was doing. He didn't have an answer for her. He just knew the only way to end the standoff was to do something. This was preferable to opening fire, and since he hadn't been shot immediately, his confidence grew. Whoever they were, they weren't impulsive.

A movement from the Jeep caused Cole's breath to quicken. Maybe he'd given them too much credit too soon. Cole rested his right hand on the roof of the car and his left on the doorframe. They could still see his hands, but if he needed to, he could dive back in the car.

The door on the passenger side of the Jeep eased open and a woman stepped out. She wore sunglasses, as he did, so he wasn't able to see her eyes. Like him, she held her arms wide, and seeing as she faced almost a dozen weapons aimed at her, he had to give her credit for guts if nothing else. After a moment, as if giving them time to judge if she was a threat, she folded her arms on the top of the door frame. She was probably only a few inches shorter than his own six foot two inches. She wore her dark hair pulled back from her face, and when she turned to say something to her driver, he saw it lay in a flat braid down her back.

She turned back to face them, and her head cocked. After a moment, she said, "Hey, Cheesehead, what are you doing so far from home?"

Her comment caught him off guard and he laughed. The corners of her mouth turned up for an instant, but then flattened. Cole sobered. He shouldn't have laughed—not when inappropriate laughter was one sign of Sympatico Syndrome. He raised his hands once again. "Sorry. I just wasn't expecting you to call me a *cheesehead*. I'm guessing you noticed our license plates."

From the slight shake of her head, he imagined she was rolling her eyes at him. He'd forgotten that the plates would identify them as outsiders right off the bat. They should have removed them, but he hadn't given it a thought. There were so many things to think about when an apocalypse hit

"Nothing gets by you, does it?" Her attitude screamed confidence, but he saw her head turn a fraction towards Sean's truck, behind and to the right of Cole, parked at an angle due to its length and the gas pumps. His brother sat a bit higher than the rest of them and his weapon was a semi-automatic. The distinctive barrel poked out of his window. Jenna sat with her body through the window; her weapon steadied on the roof of the cab.

"So, you didn't answer me. Nevada is a long way from Wisconsin. Why are you here?"

Cole tilted his head, scanned the opposing vehicles for signs of movement, noting the glint of metal jutting from the windows. He'd expected them to be armed, so it didn't come as a surprise. With a tiny shrug, not wanting them to take it for more than it was and shoot him, he said, "It's a free country." At least, he hoped it still was. Wanting to get the upper hand and not comfortable being on the receiving end of questioning, he threw one back at her. "Why do you care?"

"This is *our* land. You don't belong here. Go on back to Wisconsin."

"*Your* land?" He made a show of looking around at the barren landscape. "You own all of this?"

"Pretty much. Me and my family."

Cole gave a tight smile. "Really? You must have a helluva big family to need this much land to yourselves."

From this distance, it was difficult to tell, but he could have sworn she flinched at his comment. Taking a different tact, sensing she wasn't as tough as she tried to appear, he stepped out from behind the door, lowering his arms to his side after making sure that it was obvious he was unarmed. "I'm going to come a little closer."

After letting his comment sink in, he took about eight deliberate steps forward, making sure he was still far enough back that he wouldn't be in any of his own people's line of fire. It made him uneasy that he couldn't see her face clearly enough to read her expressions and the shouting made it almost impossible to detect nuances in the other's voice. And right now, he wanted nuance—he needed it if he was to read the situation correctly.

She straightened, her back ramrod straight before she turned to her driver and spoke something he couldn't make out, but her tone sounded scolding. Then she, too, came around her door, her arms held out momentarily before she eased them to her sides.

With the gas station in deep shadow, he took another chance, and removed his sunglasses. Not only did it allow him to see her better, but he also wanted them to see him.

It took steeling every nerve in his body to stand unprotected with who knew how many guns pointed at him, but he remained still, forcing his shoulders to relax.

She studied him so long that Cole had to stifle the urge to squirm. He felt naked. Vulnerable. He wasn't wearing a mask, not having anticipated leaving the safety of his car. *Dammit*. On the bright side, it was apparent he wasn't hiding anything, not even his expressions, but he had to think about the virus. It was another reason he wanted a closer look, though. To see if she, or any of them, displayed symptoms.

Removing her glasses, her gaze swept over the vehicles behind Cole, pausing briefly on Sean's, as she raised her hands wiggling her fingers. "I'm coming out there. My mom always said that shouting isn't ladylike."

Cole couldn't stop the smile that cracked his face and she caught it, flashing one of her own before dipping her head slightly, as if embarrassed. His smile widened. As she moved closer, he realized she was younger than he'd thought. Probably mid-twenties at the most.

She halted about a dozen feet from him which he reasoned was a safe buffer from the virus since they were out in the open. Plus, the wind had picked up a little and came out of the west and blew their breath away from them.

When she didn't speak right away, Cole crossed his arms and decided to be direct. "Look, we're here and we're not leaving on your say so. It's been a long trip and we're not turning around now. We don't want trouble, but we're ready for it if it comes our way."

"So you say." She crossed her arms as well.

"*Excuse me?*"

She waved an arm wide, causing Cole to tense but her gesture was just to emphasize her words. "Your group isn't the first to come here. I bet you're hoping the power is on, aren't you?"

Cole schooled his expression to remain neutral and didn't reply.

"Yeah...I thought so. Everyone thinks the Hoover Dam is still supplying us with electricity, but—"

"It's not?" He cut to the chase.

Eyes narrowing, she said, "It is but probably not for long. The intake pipes are clogging. So, while it's working, we get first dibs. It's ours. My family and a few others grew up here, and now people are wandering in from all over, thinking they can force the rest of us out."

Cole shook his head. "Hold on. We have no intention of trying to force anyone out. If anything, even more of a draw than the possibility of electricity was the hope that other survivors would also arrive. The only way we can get some kind of civilization up and running again is with old-fashioned manpower."

Amanda's stiff posture eased slightly, but her mouth was still set in a firm line before she said, "Well, that's not how others see it. I sometimes wish we could blow up the damn...dam." For one brief moment, her expression softened as she seemed to fight a smile at her word choice.

"Listen, I get that having strangers flood the area has to be frustrating, but if you have electricity, it would be in everyone's best interest to keep it running and to get basic services back in place."

Her arms tightened, her lips compressing again. "It would be great if the people coming to use the electricity wanted to share it with us, but all there's been is fighting. We tried to stay out of it and just take care of our livestock and farm."

"Do you have anything up and running? Water? Fuel? What about a hospital?"

Her eyes slid away and she shrugged. "We don't have anyone to work at the hospital. They mostly died right away, I guess. Got a veterinarian though."

"So, let me get this straight—you don't have enough people to staff even a clinic, but you're chasing people from the area? Where's the logic in that?"

She blinked. "Um...well...we don't need or want anyone else to come around here, spreading the virus and who knows what all."

Ah, so that was it. Her group was understandably worried about getting sick. "I get it. We isolated our group since the virus hit and all winter long. We haven't seen anyone with it since last summer. But, if you're so worried about it, why are you here talking to me without any protection at all?"

She bit her lip. "I'm not supposed to …but…"

"But…what?"

After a long moment when she remained silent, Cole said, "If it makes you feel any better, I was an epidemiologist and another person in our party was as well. Diseases and transmission of them was our *thing*. We think, at least for now, the virus has gone dormant."

He didn't mention that he might carry the cure right in his own veins. Electricity meant computers would work. He and Elly had access to whatever was stored on hard drives. He was certain with their science backgrounds they could try to come up with some kind of treatment. He'd loved microbiology and had taken more hard science classes than his degree had required.

But that was a goal down the road. Right now, he'd settle for a working hospital so Sophie and Elly and their babies would be able to get care. With any luck, he might find some childhood vaccines still in a working fridge somewhere.

It was as if his words lifted a weight from her shoulders as she blew out a deep breath, visibly relaxing. "I want to believe you. Really, I do. But the last time we trusted some newcomers, we lost our farm to them. Now, we're trying to start over on a new farm, but irrigation there isn't as good. And we lost most of our livestock."

He didn't know who 'them' was but he could guess. He also had no answers for her, just a gut instinct that if they knew each other, they could help each other. "Listen, my name is Cole Evans. Most of the people in the cars behind me are family. My son, his wife, my brother, and his family. Plus a few folks we met along the way. Every single newcomer has been a valuable addition to our group. I don't know if we could have survived without them."

It was the truth. Even the children had supplied much needed joy and laughter. It would have been a long winter without them to light up the house.

Scuffing a booted toe along the dusty pavement, she squinted at him, the lights from his car becoming brighter in the deepening dusk. "I'm Amanda Glenn. The people in the cars behind me are my family, too."

She didn't elaborate and Cole didn't push. "Nice to meet you, Amanda."

He surveyed the cars behind her. It was impossible to tell how many of her family members filled them. She looked beyond him at the vehicles facing her as well. Cole took a small step forward and offered, "So, here's what I propose…you and your family let us out of here and we go on the way we were."

"See, here's the thing, Cole, like I've said, we've heard this spiel before, or one like it. We won't fall for it again." She bit her lip then she cocked her head. "I hear Flagstaff is doing okay. Maybe y'all could go there?"

Cole stared at her. Maybe his gut instinct was wrong. "Let's get one thing straight. Where we go is our business. I don't need your permission nor am I seeking it. I know that we will be an *asset* to whatever community we decide to join." He ticked off his group's talents and professions. "We have a nurse, an electrician, a machinist, hunters, scientists, and more. If you don't want us here, you'll have to fight us." He paused, holding her gaze. "Now, you can try fighting us, but I don't advise it."

Her chin lifted. "I didn't hear soldier in any of your group's specialties. We have a couple of guys from Nellis."

"The Air Force Base? Well, that's great. I'm glad some military survived."

It wasn't the response she expected and she looked indecisive for a second before her expression hardened again. His gaze never wavered. Hers did.

He didn't take her for a killer and could only hope the rest of her family was like her, but he knew if pushed, he would do whatever it took to keep his family safe. He assumed she would respond in kind. "Now, you have two choices— you can get your cars out of the way and so we can pass, or we can fight this out. We're prepared either way."

She took a step back. "Ah, well, I gotta go talk to my family."

"You do that, and while you're talking, let them know that if we combined our groups, we would be a lot stronger than we are individually."

She nodded and crossed the gap back to her vehicle faster than she'd approached. Cole didn't feel good about scaring her, and in reality, knew they didn't have nearly the fire power they probably needed. They had armed themselves for deer, not humans. The few assault weapons they had were a drop in the bucket compared to what other groups probably possessed.

Cole waited until her door shut, then turned and, forcing a leisurely pace, returned to his car.

The second he shut the door, Elly's voice came over the radio. "So, what's going on?"

Taking a long sip of his water, he wiped his mouth with the back of his hand before replying, knowing his answer would be heard by everyone.

"I guess we'll see. I think they're just a small family group. She tried to be tough, but I think she's scared."

"How many are there? Can we take them?"

Cole sighed. "I didn't ask because I'm assuming she wouldn't have told me. However, I doubt there are more than a dozen of them judging by the size of their vehicles."

"But you don't know if there are more of them hiding somewhere?"

"You're right, I don't, Sean. I didn't ask for numbers, just as I didn't give any. I wanted to play up our strengths and how we could benefit any community because that's what I want. Our goal should be to join a community so we can rebuild."

"Do you think we'll have to shoot them, Cole?" Travis leaned over the front seat, peering out the windshield.

Cole didn't know whether to laugh or cry at the matter of fact question. Laughter was his first inclination, but he stifled it, saddened that Travis at only eleven years old or so, already had learned the law of the wild, so to speak. Kill or be killed.

"I don't think it'll come to that." He prayed it wouldn't—especially now that he'd met Amanda. He wasn't eager to pull the trigger on her, or anyone in her family. Of course, if he had to, he'd defend his own, but it would be senseless killing.

It seemed like hours had passed, but when he glanced at the dashboard clock, it had been only fifteen minutes since Amanda had retreated to discuss matters. Now, she emerged, arms outstretched.

"Okay, Travis, hunker down back there again."

The boy groaned. "I could go out there and watch your back."

"You can do that just fine from in here." Cole drew a deep breath and opened his door, showing his empty hands before he stepped out.

Amanda walked towards him, apparently comfortable that she wouldn't be shot as she didn't even glance at the other vehicles. She seemed deep in thought.

Cole only went as far as a few feet in front of his SUV. Let her come to him. He waited, his stance wide, arms crossed.

She stopped a few feet away. "Okay, so here's the deal...we'll let you all out...and even lead you to a good place to stay tonight if you'll do something for us."

Chapter Twenty-Three

HUNTER GLANCED AT SOPHIE, who bit her lip, her brow furrowed. "Are you okay, Soph?"

She grimaced, one hand on her belly. "This is embarrassing, but I *really* have to pee."

"Oh, shit. I forgot. Um…okay, well you have to go, you have to go."

"I'm not peeing my pants, Hunter."

"No, I wasn't saying that you should. I'll just step out; tell them what we're doing so nobody shoots."

"You're just going to announce to everyone that I have to go to the bathroom?"

Exasperated, Hunter shrugged. "You got a better idea?"

Practically panting now, her legs clenched together, she shook her head. "I guess not—but I don't want you getting shot!"

"I won't. They didn't shoot my dad and look, they're talking now. Just hang on a few more seconds." Hunter set his gun down and opened his door, mimicking his father as he showed his hands.

"Hello? We have a little situation here." A glint of metal in one of opposing vehicles made him freeze. "Don't shoot!"

His dad turned to look at him. "What the hell are you doing, Hunter?"

"Sophie's gotta pee, Dad. Really bad."

The woman talking to his dad smirked as his father gave his head a little shake. Hunter defended Sophie. "She's pregnant, okay? Her bladder is about the size of an acorn these days. And right now, the baby is tap dancing on it."

The smirk disappeared and the woman took a few steps closer, her eyes wide as a genuine smile stretched across her face. "She's going to have a baby?"

"Yeah." He let the smart remark about how pregnancy generally meant someone was going to have a baby die on his lips as she moved to within dozen yards.

"Okay, let me tell my group to give her a few minutes." She turned and motioned to her group.

"Thanks!" He ducked back into the truck. "Okay, I'll go with you."

"Where am I going to go?"

Hunter glanced around. "Behind Sean's truck." He jumped out and ran around to Sophie's side, helping her get out of the vehicle. Even just a few weeks ago when they'd started out, she hadn't had trouble getting in and out of the raised truck, but now, Hunter felt the need to help her. Since they'd left the island, her stomach had really grown. She was so thin everywhere else, he worried about her.

She tried to wave him away. "I don't need help."

He took her hand anyway. "Humor me." They retreated to behind Sean's truck, after explaining to his uncle and aunt what was going on. His uncle chuckled and Jenna asked if Sophie was okay.

"I'm fine, Jenna. Just embarrassed." Sophie broke from Hunter's grasp and practically ran, or her version of running while nearly eight months pregnant. By the time Hunter got to the corner of the truck to stand guard, Sophie was sighing in relief behind him.

"You know what really sucks, Hunter? I'll have to go again before I even pull my pants up."

He laughed, but didn't turn to look at her. She was sensitive about this stuff even though while traveling they'd all had to relax their privacy standards. When she was finished, she walked back to the truck, her head held high even as her cheeks turned pink.

Hunter waited until Sophie was back in the vehicle, then approached his dad and the woman. He put his hand out. "I'm Hunter."

"Amanda. A pleasure to meet you." She nodded, her smile appearing genuine.

Hunter glanced at his dad and raised his eyebrows in question. "So...what's going on, Dad? We're going to have to find a place to spend the night before long."

"I was just telling your father that I had an idea. We have a small ranch a few miles from here. You could stay there tonight, if you want."

His dad drew a deep breath. "What do you want in return?"

Hunter bit back an apology to Amanda at his dad's hard tone, but Amanda didn't seem to notice. She said, "I'll be honest. We need help getting my father back. Then, I want the ranch back. We have a different place we're staying at now. There's a barn the men can stay in, and the women and any kids, can stay in the guest house. There should be room."

"Why can't you get back in," Hunter asked.

"A group of men came along a few days ago and forced us out. We weren't ready—we hadn't seen anyone out by our farm. We knew there were some survivors because of the Dam, but most stay up in Las Vegas where the lights are still on at a lot of the casinos."

Hunter recalled a couple of detours they had taken due to power lines across the road. It was almost certain the lines they encountered weren't live, but he filed away that lines around here could very well be live.

Amanda shrugged. "I don't know why they want to go there. I went once and it's horrible. Bodies, bones, rats, roaches." She shuddered. "I guess there are supplies if you want to wade through all that mess, but no thanks. I doubt there's much food anyway. Tourists cleaned out most of it before they died."

With the sun almost set, the desert was turning cool and Amanda rubbed her hands up her arms. "We tried to get around behind them, but they shot my dad." She stopped and looked away, blinking hard. "They forced us off the farm at gunpoint. I thought you were with them until I saw your license plates. We were going to drive them away, if we could. But, the guys who stole our farm had Arizona plates."

"What makes you think we won't take your ranch from you once we make the other men leave?"

Shocked at his dad's question, he opened his mouth to protest, but snapped it closed. His dad would never do something like that. He must have a reason for asking such a crazy question.

Amanda looked taken aback, retreating a step but when she glanced at Hunter's face, she saw something on it that must have reassured her. Maybe he hadn't hid his shock as well as he'd thought he had.

With a defiant chin jut, she said, "You can try, Cheesehead."

Expecting a retort, Hunter was dumbfounded when his dad snorted in response, the corners of his eyes crinkling.

With a wave of her hand, Amanda dismissed Hunter's shock. "It's an inside joke."

Inside joke? His dad had known this woman for all of twenty minutes. When he glanced over, his father just shrugged agreement with her.

She beamed.

Her posture elicited a slow smile from his dad. "Yes, I suppose we could try to drive you away too, but then we wouldn't have you as an ally. I'd much rather have you and your family with us than against us."

Hunter reached out and caught his dad's sleeve, tugging him back several feet. "Can I talk to you a second?"

"Sure. Excuse us, Amanda."

It was as if they were at a backyard barbecue instead of discussing life and death. "What the hell is going on, Dad? Do you two know each other somehow?"

"No, we've never met before, but I just have a feeling about her. She's out here representing her family. That takes a lot of guts. I'd like to help her, but I'm not sure if we can."

He took a few steps back to Amanda, with Hunter trailing a pace behind, digesting what his dad had said. He was right. If Amanda had the courage to stand out here facing two men, alone, she was probably someone who would be good to have as friends, not enemies.

"Here's the thing. I want to help, but…" His dad paused, staring over Amanda's shoulder, but Hunter knew that look. He was thinking through a plan.

After a glance at him that must have shown something on his face, his dad seemed to come to a decision. "We have a couple of pregnant women. They and the kids are my first priority, but, tomorrow, I promise to consider helping. "

Hunter nodded. "Me too."

———

"YOU PROMISED TO HELP THEM?" Elly stood beside Cole as they waited for the other group of cars to circle around the gas station and head back down the road so they could follow.

"I promised I'd consider it. There's a difference. I won't do anything to jeopardize our own group, but Amanda is local. Her family is local. We need people on our side who know the area."

"Our side? Since when did we have a side? What *is* our side?"

"You know what I mean. Good people. These guys who took over their farm shot her dad."

Elly swore. "That's terrible. Did he die?" She felt bad for the other group but that didn't mean they should fight for them.

Cole blinked. "I'm not actually sure. She didn't say. I guess I can ask her later. We can all stay with them tonight. They are on a little farm not too far from here."

"I thought they lost the farm?" She was so confused.

"They lost their own farm, but managed to find another one, but it's smaller and not as good."

Sean's door slammed shut and he sauntered over to their group. Cole had given everyone a quick rundown on the radio, but talking face to face was better.

"I'm confused, Cole. We're following these guys back to their farm? Why would they let us do that?"

"He says they need our help and in return, we can stay there tonight."

"Whoa. I didn't agree to help anyone."

"Like I said, I told them I'd *consider* helping. I didn't volunteer anyone else. Just me. And then Hunter also volunteered. They have water." Cole swept a hand out. "Water is all important out here. Granted, we can find a lake on the map, but we won't know if other survivors are there already."

Elly pulled back, barely hearing the part about the water. Her mind had caught on that he had volunteered himself. "You're going to risk your life for complete strangers? What if something happens to you? You have a new baby on the way." She threw an uneasy glance in Sean's direction, uncomfortable voicing her fears in front of him, but she was too scared for Cole to hold back.

Cole's jaw clenched and she knew she'd hit a nerve. She realized the last thing he wanted to do was fight in front of Sean, but what did he expect of her? If the shoe had been on the other foot, he'd have put that foot down on the idea and squashed it like a roach under his heel.

"We'll talk later, okay? We have to get going before we lose Amanda's group."

"What? In all the traffic?" Sean laughed at his own joke before returning to the truck.

Cole climbed in his SUV and sat staring forward. She reached in through the open window and stroked a hand down his cheek. "Listen, Cole. I want to help too. I can't help it I'm a little scared, okay? But we'll talk it over after we settle in and see what's up."

His expression softened and he caught her hand, pressing it to his lips for a brief kiss. "I would never risk you or the baby. Not if I can help it."

"I know you wouldn't." She returned to her car, worry still lingering but she had decided for herself that if Cole felt these new people warranted their help, then she would do whatever he asked. He had earned her complete trust over the last year.

Following Amanda's group over a highway that looked to have been cleared enough to get through at a reasonable speed, Elly explained the situation to Joe. "I trust Cole's judgement, but damn it, I wish he didn't feel like it was his responsibility to save everyone on the planet."

Joe chuckled. "He does seem to have a hero complex. But he has a point about needing locals. They know this area while we mostly only know about Las Vegas or the Hoover Dam, and what we know of that is just surface stuff. What we really need to know is how to grow anything in this desert."

The statement was the longest speech Elly had ever heard from Joe. "That's true. Jenna's a great gardener but I don't think she's ever tried to make a garden thrive in a desert environment."

———

ELLY ALTERNATELY FUMED and worried as she unpacked just the items she'd need for one night, setting the bag on the ground, grabbing her go-bag too. She wasn't about to leave it, not trusting their safety here.

Zoë and Luke came around the back of the SUV. "Kids, get your go-bags."

Joe ambled around to the back, scanning their surroundings. A light on the barn flooded the farmyard. He gave his head a shake. "I don't know if it's smart to have the light on or not, but it sure is nice to not have to stumble around in the dark."

Elly glanced at the flood light. "Doesn't seem smart to me. It'll pinpoint this place as being a place with people." She shook out the mask she'd stashed in her pocket They were running low on masks and this stop forced them to use up precious stock. Making sure the kids had theirs secured once they returned with their packs, she headed towards Cole and Travis, glad to see that Cole had at least worn his mask and had made Travis do the same.

Car doors slammed as the others in their group exited their vehicles. The local group had already parked, circling around so all of the cars faced out, they stood near them, but appeared to be unarmed. She knew they had weapons, but they had the grace to not carry them openly while meeting with them.

Elly looked at them. She picked out the one Cole had spoken to, Amanda. The woman was gathering her people close, talking to the group, presumably about them.

She took the moment to study the locals. What struck her was that other than a few much older women, and an older gentleman wearing gray coveralls like a mechanic would wear, the rest were very young. The woman speaking to them wasn't old by any definition, but she looked to be the oldest of the younger group.

Elly counted six other young women who ranged in age from about fifteen to twenty-two or so. A couple of teenage boys stood glowering at Elly's group, their stares directed at someone behind her. She turned to see who they were focusing on, and saw it was Jake.

Surprised, it took her a second to realize that Piper stood near Jake and he had his hand on the small of her back. That was a new behavior. She knew the two had a thing for each other, but she had never seen Jake tense. If the stakes hadn't been so high, it might have been amusing to watch the interaction. Hiding her amusement, she stepped up to Cole. "So now what?"

"Amanda is just briefing her family on what's going on."

"Her family? All of those people are her family?"

Cole shrugged and she could tell he was still a bit miffed about her outburst at the standoff. Well, she wasn't going to apologize. She caught a sidewise look from him, his gaze roving her face. Then he extended his left hand to her. She accepted his peace offering, giving his hand a light squeeze.

As the rest of their group gathered around them, Cole stepped forward, still holding Elly's hand, so she moved with him.

WITH ELLY'S hand folded into his own, Cole felt a surge of protectiveness. He hoped he'd read Amanda correctly and that her group wasn't so different from theirs. He rubbed his thumb on Elly's palm, not sure if he was trying to soothe her or himself.

What if he was wrong? Amanda could have an ambush set-up. The fact that there were only three men in the group facing them should have put him at ease, but it made him even more apprehensive. Where were the other men?

He cast a look around, but in the now full dark, it was impossible to see beyond the perimeter of the floodlight attached to the barn. The hairs on the back of his neck prickled. There could be snipers up in the hayloft aiming at them right now.

Only the proximity of Amanda's group gave him a sense of safety. Anyone firing from a distance would have to worry about hitting one of their own since the barn was to their right and slightly behind them. In fact, at this angle, Amanda's family would be in even greater danger since at least Cole's group had their vehicles between themselves and the barn.

Amanda turned from her group. "Sorry, I was just clarifying some things with my family." She didn't smile, but she nodded at Elly and held her arms wide in a welcoming gesture. "As you may know, Cole and I agreed to have you all as our guests tonight, and in the morning, we'll talk about a situation we—my family—find ourselves in. We've only just moved onto this ranch a few days ago, so we haven't checked it all out, but we did clean out remains and wipe up the place. Luckily, whoever lived here before seems to have not been home when they were overtaken by the virus. The only bodies we found belonged to a poor dog trapped in the house, and a few chickens that seemed to have been killed in the henhouse. All that was left of the chickens were a handful of feathers, so I'm guessing a fox or something got to them."

Cole lifted a hand. "Speaking of henhouses, we have a few chickens. Would it be okay to let them into the henhouse for the night?

Amanda shrugged. "Be our guest. The barn has an office with bunkbeds, probably used by some cowhands at some point, but it looks like it hasn't been used in a while. It's a bit dusty. We have a broom you all can use to sweep it. And, the main house has plenty of room for the rest of you. The people who built it must have had a huge family. Six bedrooms! And the basement has an office with a pull-out sofa. Our boys here," she gestured to the sullen teens, "have agreed to bunk out in the old camper beside the house."

Cole looked to where she swept her hand out and saw the front end of an RV. He caught one of the boys' eyes and nodded. "Much appreciated."

The boy's sullen expression melted away and he shrugged. "No problem."

Elly released Cole's hand. "Hello, Amanda. I'm Elly. Thank you for your hospitality and I would really love to talk with all of you, but the kids are getting hungry, and we're all tired."

"Of course. There's just one more thing. We have been setting up a couple of sentries at night. I know you're all tired, but if a couple of you could take a turn with ours, it would really help us out. We do three hour shifts with two people each shift. With how it works out for us, it allows everyone to get an undisturbed night's rest every other night."

Cole nodded. "Absolutely. I'll take one of them and ask for a couple of volunteers for the other two slots."

"And we have an electric stove, so you can use that to cook and there's a grill out on the deck out back."

"An electric stove? That'll be a nice treat." Elly bit her lip for a second before asking, "Won't we be in the way?"

"No, we've already eaten dinner." Amanda turned away. "Sandy, why don't you show the women where they can put their stuff, and Derek, please show the guys where they can bunk."

"If you don't mind, while I won't be bunking inside, I would like to take a quick look around first."

Amanda's eyes widened in surprise. "Oh wow. Yeah. I wasn't thinking. Of course you'd want to make sure everything is okay. Be my guest."

Cole followed Sandy, who didn't appear to be older than sixteen. Her name fit her, with her long, blonde hair and golden complexion.

The house was an old farmhouse on the outside, but it had been renovated not long ago, judging from the granite countertops in the kitchen and bathrooms, and the stainless steel appliances. One of the younger girls opened the fridge and took out a pitcher of water. Cole stopped to look at the lighted interior for the brief instant it had been opened. If someone had asked him if he would miss that welcoming little light that came on every time the refrigerator opened, he'd have laughed. And yet, here he was getting a longing in his gut for a stupid refrigerator light. He shook his head and trailed Sandy through a spacious living room with a stone fireplace, a large screen TV anchored on the wall above the mantle. A black leather sofa and love seat sat a comfortable distance in front of it.

Cole stopped dead and Elly ran into his back. A movie played on the television—a DVD no doubt—but it was surreal to see the overly bright lights flashing in the darkened room.

"It's like going back in time," Elly said in a hushed voice.

"I know."

"Um, excuse me, but the bathroom is this way, and there are two bedrooms at the end of the hall. You might have to double or triple, in the case of the kids, on the beds, but feel free to grab towels or blankets."

Cole dragged his eyes from the TV screen. It wasn't that he missed any specific show, but he missed not worrying about survival, and just being able to kick back in the evening and click on a favorite show or movie. In short, he longed for the security he'd felt his whole life—that all of them had felt and not even known they'd had.

Chapter Twenty-Four

COLE RODE with Amanda the next morning so she could take them by their family farm.

Her family's ranch was several miles away by road, but this road had not been completely cleared. At times, they were forced to go off road to avoid obstacles.

Cole sat in the passenger seat gazing at the mountains in the near distance. "So, how have things been out here? What's survival been like?"

She bit her lip, her expression pensive. "Hard. We lost several family members, including my mom and my uncles and two cousins. They all worked in the city and got trapped there. Roads became impassable as everyone tried to escape to the country."

She paused and drew a deep, shaky breath and Cole wished he hadn't asked his question. He hadn't meant to bring up her own personal losses, just a general sense of how things were. "You don't have to talk about it."

Amanda shook her head. "I know, but I'm sure you're no stranger to what's happened. We all have similar stories. This is mine."

Cole nodded.

She continued, "So, we got a string of really bizarre texts from my mom, and my aunt got a strange phone call from her husband—my uncle Lyle. We never heard from the others. When nobody ever arrived home, we realized they'd died."

Cole nodded. "I'm sorry."

Amanda tipped her head, indicating she'd heard him, but she remained quiet for a few minutes, seeming to concentrate on driving. With a half-shrug, she finally said, "It's been almost a year but I still miss my mom every single day. There's so much I don't know. Every year, we'd can veggies from the garden, but we always did it together. If I had a question, I could always ask her, you know?"

He nodded along, even knowing it was rhetorical. Amanda sniffed, a tear tracking down her cheek that she didn't wipe away. "Now, I have a million questions, but she's not here. And my younger brothers, Derek and Tyler, have had a really hard year. Teen years are already hard on boys, but going through this as a sixteen year old?"

"They're twins?"

She nodded. "Yep. Not identical though. Anyway, we managed on what we already had on the ranch. We had about fifty head of cattle and the boys rounded up four steers that had wandered away from their own ranches. A ranch hand who did most of the care for the cattle died though, and I don't know how many cattle we have left. We knew the brands and checked on the owners, but they didn't make it." She cleared her throat. "They were good neighbors."

"I'm sorry." There was nothing left to say about the losses. Every person left alive had probably lost many loved ones and good friends.

"We butchered two steers—one had gone lame and had to be put down anyway. Along with what we had in the garden, we're doing okay as far as food goes, but we're running out of other items like medicines, coffee, flour, sugar—staples. "

"Can I ask how you all avoided catching the virus?" He hoped that didn't come out as skeptical or accusatory. His goal was to know everything he could about the virus, from an epidemiology point of view.

"Well, that's the crazy thing. We only survived because the twins got a nasty stomach bug. And then my little sister got it. I had taken a vacation from my work—I was a hostess at a casino—and had plans to be in my college roommate's wedding. Maid of honor. But the day before I was to fly out I felt a little queasy and thought for sure I'd caught the stomach bug too. I didn't want to get the whole wedding party sick so I rebooked my flight for two days later. Luckily, I'd planned to go out early so I had wiggle room in my plans. I don't even know if they ever had the wedding, but I doubt it." Her voice became soft and wistful.

With a shake of her head, she continued, "That's a long explanation to say that I was home taking care of everyone. My mom didn't want to go to work, but she was a lab tech at the hospital and they were swamped."

Cole nodded. "You didn't come in contact with anyone because you all already had a different illness." They had self-isolated due to a run of the mill stomach bug putting them out of commission for the two or so days between when the virus still seemed like a distant threat—just before it tore through the country.

"Yep. And the others at the farm came over later, during the winter. They had run out of food and were looking for some. What could we do but take them in?"

"That's generous of you."

"Not really. Everyone makes contributions and works around the ranch. It's a win-win. I have to admit it was scary being around other people at first, but nobody has shown signs of the virus."

"It could have gone dormant. We can only hope it's gone for good, but I wouldn't count on it." He wished he could give assurance, but there had never been a virus that just disappeared completely without a vaccine being the reason it disappeared in the wild.

Amanda sighed. "I was afraid of that." She maneuvered around an overturned semi-truck, her moves practiced. It was obvious she'd driven this stretch more than a few times since the truck had overturned. Throwing him a grin, she said, "You want to hear something funny?"

"Sure." A laugh was always welcome in this grim new world.

"My friend, Tina, was so busy binge-watching a bunch of DVDs of her favorite 90s television shows that she didn't even know the world was ending until four days had passed. She was feeling nostalgic, I guess, and didn't notice when streaming services stopped working since our power didn't go out. It flickered a bit, but someone must have hit the right switches before they died, or maybe they're still hard at work at the power company."

Cole smiled at the story, but his thoughts went to what Holland had said, about how power had been kept on in D.C. and wondered if something similar was at work here. He wanted to ask more questions, but Amanda stopped at the end of a long, winding drive. Set well back from the road, protected by a set of closed gates, he saw a large home, several buildings that might have been barns or housed equipment, and pens. The pens contained several horses and a dog lolled in a patch of grass beneath a tree.

"We're here." She scowled, peering through the front window. "They chained the gate. *Assholes*."

"It's beautiful." Cole didn't know what he'd expected—maybe something closer to the red or white barns common in Wisconsin, with fieldstone foundations surrounded by cornfields and cows grazing in a green pastures. The house was large and modern with a green lawn protected by a few trees, but beyond that, the landscape, dotted with scrub and clumps of dark grass, spread out flat and far, fading to various shades of brown— from the palest tan to deep rust. Mountains in the distance provided a backdrop he'd never find in Wisconsin.

Several horses ambled around an enclosure that looked like a long shed that had been chopped in half length-wise. He guessed that was a stable and on the side away from him would be stall doors. Beyond that was another larger building with various gates and fences around it.

"At least it looks like they're caring for the horses. I hope the cattle are okay."

"Are there a lot of cattle around here that survived?"

"Sure, if they had access to water."

If her assessment was accurate, they could begin building a society that had a secure food source. Despite the arid climate, if the power was running, irrigation could keep the farms that were already established productive. Everything they needed was right here. But how to convince everyone that it was in everyone's best interest to share and cooperate?

As two armed men approached the gate, Cole drew a deep breath.

This was going to be his first—and he hoped not his last—attempt at getting people to work together for their mutual benefit.

Amanda's mouth twisted. "Here they come." She reached for her rifle.

"Wait!" Cole put his hand on the barrel. "I don't blame you, but I'd like to try talking to them first."

Her eyes narrowed but she finally nodded. "We just want what is ours."

"I know." And now he needed to find out why these men chose to take this ranch when there were likely many that were unoccupied.

Cole eased his door open, repeating his tactic of showing his hands before fully exiting the vehicle. He doubted the Jeep door would provide much protection if the men decided to fire their rifles at him, but it gave him the illusion of protection.

At first, the men looked identical to Cole. Both wore jeans, light colored shirts and brown cowboy hats. Dark scruff covered their jaws, but as they came closer, he noted the one on the left was taller, his boots well-worn, and he walked as though he owned the ranch. "This is private property!"

Cole refused to argue the point. Not yet. "Good afternoon. My name's Cole Evans and we stopped by to invite you to a survivor meeting."

He was making this up on the fly, but it occurred to him that if survivors could gather some place neutral, they could collaborate to help distribute resources, share information, and help each other.

"A survivor meeting? What the hell for? So we can risk getting sick? No thanks." The taller man shook his head. "Not interested."

"Let me explain… " Cole moved a fraction to bring his arms down, freezing when the rifles leveled on him. "Look, I'm unarmed here, but I'm not going to keep shouting with my hands up, so I'm going to take a couple of steps closer and put my hands down." He lowered his arms, bracing for the impact of a bullet, but the men held their fire, their expressions nearly carbon copies of wariness and hostility.

"Let's be honest…I know this isn't your ranch—not really—but times are crazy and I can understand that you saw this working ranch with all of its resources and decided to claim it for your own. Obviously, you two are strong young men." Behind the first two men were several other guys back near the stable, rifles angled across their bodies as though eager to be put to use. Cole ignored them, focusing on the taller of the two in front of him.

"Amanda told me how you came and forced them out and killed her dad—"

The taller man interjected, "We didn't kill anyone!"

Cole shot a look at Amanda, who had left the Jeep and stood on the other side of the hood. She shrugged. "I said they shot him. I didn't say he died. They made him stay."

"He's a prisoner?"

The taller man protested again, "No—he's only here because they didn't bother to take him with when they fled. Damn cowards! *We* took care of him. We're not barbarians." The shorter man moved up alongside the taller. Cole wondered if he'd read their body language wrong. Maybe the shorter guy was in charge.

"We're not cowards! I had to get my younger siblings to safety after you all started shooting! It's what my dad wanted me to do!" Amanda strode up next to Cole, her fists clenched, her face red.

Cole didn't debate the issue. "So, is Amanda's father okay now?" He wanted to keep using Amanda's name so the men would become familiar with it, thinking it would make it harder for the men to do her harm if she wasn't just a nameless young woman they'd forced from her home.

The men exchanged a look but then the shorter one shrugged. The taller one said, "Yeah. He's okay for now. He's even helping us—"

"Helping you? As in, he's up and about?" Cole cut in, hoping the good news would take the edge off Amanda learning her father was helping these men.

Amanda shook her head. "My dad would never help someone like you! Someone who threatened his whole family! You're lying!"

"You're calling me a liar?"

"Damn right I am! And a thief too!" Amanda drew to within feet of the gate.

"We're survivors—you heard your boyfriend. We're not thieves."

Cole let the boyfriend comment go and Amanda hadn't seemed to notice it.

"What do you call stealing my home?"

"You found a new place."

So, they knew of the smaller ranch. That meant someone in the group had a way of keeping tabs on what was going on in the area. Interesting.

"It's not our home. This is our home!"

"Amanda has a point. She and her family live here and you knew that. You had to have figured that out by now once you saw pictures of all of them throughout the house."

Cole didn't know for certain the house contained pictures of the family, but he guessed it must. His guess was confirmed a moment later when the shorter man said, "We could have killed them all and taken it anyway, but we let them live."

"It's a good thing too."

"What? How's that?"

"It would be incredibly stupid for you to kill someone who could help guarantee the continuation of the human race."

"What the hell are you talking about?" Shorter guy took off his hat and wiped his brow with the back of his sleeve. "Not everybody died, obviously." His tone dripped sarcasm.

"That's true, there are survivors, but how many? Did you know that there's a minimum viable population level?"

The shorter man scratched his cheek as he thought for a moment, then shrugged. "Well, we've seen at least twenty people besides ourselves."

"That's it?" Cole cocked his head. "And I would bet that Amanda and her family made up a majority of those survivors, right?"

"Well, yeah, but now we can add you to the total, so twenty-one." He laughed as if he'd told a hilarious joke, and his friend laughed along with him.

Cole wondered briefly if letting these men into the gene pool was the right thing to do. A little culling couldn't be a bad thing, could it? Maybe the world would be better off if these men stayed isolated on this ranch away from any women and allow their gene pool dry up. But, they did appear healthy and had managed to survive, so, reluctantly, Cole said, "This area is going to be a magnet for people who survived the pandemic. With the dam and a reliable water source, electricity and shelter already in place, I expect the trickle of people Amanda said she's seen arrive will turn into a flood over the next several months and years."

"We don't need more people. Things are fine like they are." The taller man drew close to the gate, almost touching it.

"You might think so. Everything you ever wanted is yours for the taking."

"Sure is!"

Cole nodded. "I know, right? Any house you want, whatever is inside it, and if you need more, you just find another empty house or a warehouse and discover whatever is inside it, and it's yours. It's every person's fantasy, in a way. Although I bet nobody ever admits to it." He raised an eyebrow, giving them a sly grin, nodding in a *'am I right?'* kind of way.

Giving each other a knowing glance, the men shrugged and chuckled.

Spreading a hand on his chest, Cole dropped his voice, as though telling a shameful secret. "Speaking for myself, I had a *helluva* good time walking into a department store and plucking whatever I wanted from the shelves, piling into a dozen carts before loading it all into a truck—a *free* truck, mind you—and hauling my find back home to my family." He pantomimed chucking goods into a shopping cart and driving home the point of how much fun it was by pulling on an imaginary air horn in celebration. The men got the reference and threw their heads back in laughter.

Cole grinned in return. The men relaxed their stances, their rifles clasped loosely as they listened. That was his intended effect. The men who had stood in the distance came closer. He counted a total of seven men on the other side of the gate. Was anyone left in the house? He saw a couple were older than he was, and two looked to be barely more than teens. He nodded to them, acknowledging their presence.

He glanced at Amanda to find her listening as well, a smile teasing around her lips. He included her in the scenario. "Amanda, here, found some cattle whose owners were deceased, and she and her family survived the winter on beef that literally walked itself to her front door!"

It was an exaggeration, but even Amanda laughed. Cole ambled to the front of the Jeep and sat on the bumper. Leaning back, he crossed his feet at the ankles, propping his elbows on the hood. "Damn, that was fun!" He left out the part where he'd been shot. Or the part about the dead babies, flies, maggots, rats, and all the other horrific things they'd seen. He waited for the scenes to set themselves in everyone's head. Whatever they had personally experienced, he expected that they had all seen horrors. He finally added, his voice cracking, surprising him, but maybe it added truth to his next statement. "But most of the last year *really* sucked."

A shadow crossed the shorter man's eyes, and the taller one dipped his head, scuffing a foot on the ground before he nodded his head in agreement.

Cole remained silent, letting the images they saw in their heads coalesce and linger. Now that he knew they weren't cold-hearted bastards, he sighed and leaned forward. "Everything we got was free — none of it cost us one red cent—but I would bet every last one of us would agree that the price was too high."

The shorter man cleared his throat and slung his rifle over his shoulder. "I lost my wife and kids. I don't know how I was spared, except I'd freaked out and spent every blasted minute I could out with the cattle. I rode from morning to night, even camping out, telling Lucy that I thought wolves were killing our steers." He paused. "I shoulda been there to help her. She had to watch the kids die first before she got it. It was almost a blessing then, because she didn't want to live without them. Every time I'd come up to the house, I'd hear one of them laughing that weird, crazy laughter, and I'd hightail it back to the barn."

"It's okay, Scott." The taller man rested a hand on Scott's shoulder. "Almost same thing happened to me, only they all got it the same day. Tami died at work, and the kids at school. At least I was spared having to see them like that. But, I was out harvesting the damn beans. So, I had a mountain of beans, but nobody to eat them."

"I'm really sorry, Scott. And I'm sorry about your loss… ?" Cole raised an eyebrow at the taller man.

"Don. I'm Don."

To his left, Amanda leaned against the side of the Jeep, her eyes fixed on the ground ahead of her, tears rolling down her face. Cole hated that he'd caused her to cry, but when he heard a sniff in front of him, he turned and caught the Don swiping at his eyes.

Cole stood and approached the gate. "I mean it. I'm sorry about your families." He hoped his sincerity showed.

"Thanks." Scott drew a deep breath. "Life goes on."

"Yes, it does. As hard as it is. And this is going to sound almost callous, but I don't mean it that way. It's simply the truth. This horrible virus has given us an opportunity to start with a clean slate, so to speak."

"A clean slate? I don't get it."

Cole shook his head. "I'll explain more at the meeting. We're planning it for three days from now …"

He cast about for a location to give them, but he didn't know the area. *Damn it.* Amanda caught his eye, catching on to what he wanted.

"We're meeting at Veteran's Park, five o'clock. It's going to be a potluck, so bring food." And she gripped the bars of the gate. "And, please, I'd like to see my father. I want to make sure he's okay."

Chapter Twenty-Five

FOR A MINUTE, tension ratchetted up as the shorter man said, "No. We can't do that. We told you he's fine."

"And I'm supposed to believe you and just walk away?"

Cole put out a placating hand. "Hey guys, she needs to see her father and make sure he's okay. That's a reasonable request. You said you weren't barbarians…"

The shorter one met the taller one's eyes, and some kind of agreement must have been struck because the shorter one seemed abashed. "Okay, fine." He reached for the padlock on the chain, and dug in his pocket, withdrawing a key. "He's up in the house. His room is first—"

"I know my way around, thanks." Amanda gave the men a hard stare.

Just when Cole thought the easing of tensions was going to revert back to hostilities because the shorter man stiffened at Amanda's tone, the guy shook his head and said, "Yeah, I suppose you do."

The men parted to let her through and Cole thought about following her, but decided against it. He remained where he was, hoping to keep the men engaged.

"Like I said earlier, my name is Cole." Now that the gate barrier wasn't blocking him, he stuck out his hand to the shorter man.

"Scott. Nice to meet you, Cole." His grip was firm, his palms rough with callouses.

"Hi, Cole. I'm Don." The taller man thrust his hand out, and Cole clasped it.

The other men introduced themselves and, deciding there was nothing to see, wandered off.

Cole fought the urge to wipe his hand on his jeans. It wasn't that the men were dirty, although they had been working on the ranch, so who knew what they had come in contact with. He could handle routine dirt. He was used to working with the horses, after all, but forever in his mind was the thought of the virus. Was it still active?

Did he dare believe Holland's claim that Cole was the lone person immune to Sympatico Syndrome? None of them wore masks although he saw no signs of the virus present in any of the men. If anything, everyone was very low key, almost taciturn. He'd considered wearing a mask, but initially, there was so much distance between them and the other men that he hadn't felt the need. When the opportunity came to approach them, he wasn't about to break the fragile truce, of sorts, by whipping out a mask.

He pondered how to broach the subject of these men stealing Amanda's home. "Hey, so—" But Scott spoke at the same time, cutting Cole off.

"So, what's your story, Cole?"

"My story?"

"Yeah. You're not from around here."

"How do you know that?"

"Your accent."

"Ah, yeah." Cole rubbed the back of his neck. "I didn't think I had much of one, but I guess it's noticeable?" He slanted Scott a grin.

Scott agreed. "Yup. I'd peg you for Chicago or Detroit. Something like that."

"Close. Just north of Chicago, but actually in Wisconsin."

"Did you live here before the virus?"

"No. We only arrived yesterday." Cole took the opening to voice his concerns, but couched in what he hoped was non-aggressive language. "Amanda and her family thought we were you, ironically. She chased us down the highway until we took a stand. Once we realized we had nothing to fear from each other, we decided to stick together, at least temporarily."

It was a bit of an exaggeration as there had been no talk of sticking together, but if he could let it seem like Amanda's family and his own were together in this, they would be a force to be reckoned with.

"Us? Who is *us*?" Scott seemed skeptical of his claim.

Here's where Cole needed to make them sound formidable. "I'm with a group of men and women from Wisconsin. We battled our way here across raging rivers and through land occupied by hostile locals who tried to steal our supplies back in Kansas or thereabouts."

He gave a wry shake of his head. "This ranch belongs to Amanda and her family. Why take everything from them when you could, literally, have almost any other ranch in the area?"

Scott's amicable expression twisted at Cole's words. "Because we can. Because it has better water than any of the others. Because it's not fair that they lived and my family didn't. Let them see what it's like to suffer."

"Amanda *has* suffered. We all have lost loved ones. You have to realize that. And how do you think inflicting more suffering will make you feel better?"

"What difference does it make? Like you said, they can have any other ranch—and they did." Scott's eyes narrowed. "And what makes you think you're in a position to bring together a bunch of folks from these parts?"

"I don't know if I can, but I think it's worth pursuing, don't you? We can create a future for ourselves."

Don shrugged, joining the conversation. "Or we could all be dead tomorrow. Might as well live in the moment."

Scott laughed, but it was laced with bitterness. "Yup. We've got nothing left to lose."

Cole conceded his point. A fatalistic attitude was understandable after surviving the horror they'd all endured. "You're right. And I'm a complete outsider. Hell, I'll admit a big reason we came out here is because we hoped there'd be electricity. We were right about that."

He looked at Don, then back to Scott. The men had withdrawn, bringing their rifles up, holding them across their bodies. *Damn it*. He had to get them back. He'd intended to be completely honest and win them over by not hiding anything but he'd hit a nerve. "Listen, that's not the only reason or even the most important one. The other reason was we thought this area would be a magnet for other survivors. Right now, we—as in survivors— have *stuff*. Food, tools, clothing—basically, everything we need to get by, at least for the near future, but what we don't have are people."

Scott scowled. "We have all the people we need right here."

Despite not wanting to anger anyone, Cole couldn't hold back his reaction. "A few minutes ago, I thought you were someone with a little compassion, but I was wrong. You have none, and what's even worse, you have no common sense."

"The hell you say?" Scott's jaw thrust out, his arms fisted at his waist as if he was preparing to do battle.

Cole wouldn't back off. "A man with common sense would realize that with most of the world dead, every single life is precious. Every. Single. One." He paused, teeth clenched as frustration boiled inside of him. It was tempting to throw up his hands and walk away, but that wouldn't help anyone. He consciously relaxed his jaw and tried again. "Cooperation is not just desired, but *required* for all of us to have the best chance of long-term survival. You have to listen to reason."

"No, you listen. We're doing just fine. We have all the food we need and a good place to sleep— we don't need you."

"You may think not, but my education is in epidemiology. I studied diseases and their transmission. You said you were worried about catching the virus if you mingle with other survivors, and I can address that. It's a valid concern."

He didn't point out that they were all talking in close proximity without masks. "But besides myself, there are others with me who have medical training. Our goal is to get at least a clinic up and running and this area seemed like the most likely to have everything to make that possible. Isn't ranching a dangerous job? Accidents happen all the time. If you fight with us on this, when our clinic is up, do you think we'd be willing to help you or your men when you need it?"

Scott dropped his fists and shuffled, sending a look at Don. "We'll find someone else to help."

Cole laughed. "Have fun with that. Hospitals were the first and hardest hit. If you can find so much as a candy striper still alive between here and the Pacific Ocean, I'd be very surprised."

This wasn't going how he'd seen it in his head, but he had to keep trying. These men were key. He could feel it. From their earlier comment about knowing Amanda's family had settled at another ranch, they were actively scouting the area. He wanted to use their knowledge to help everyone, not just allow them to keep tabs on other survivors comings and goings. It also meant they must know more about who might have survived and who hadn't than Amanda's group, who had secluded themselves.

"Come on, guys. We need to share ideas. Share resources. We could form a community again. Without that, what's the point in surviving? I don't know about you guys, but I'm not ready to revert to prehistoric living conditions. Are you?" He didn't wait for them to answer. "It may not happen in our lifetime, but if our children and grandchildren survive, and that's a big if, then it'll happen in *their* children's lifetimes."

Scott shrugged. "Yeah, I guess, but by then the government will have everything worked out. This is just temporary."

He hadn't won them over yet. *Shit.* "Don't you understand? There is no government. Not anymore. Not unless *we* create one."

Don shook his head and spat to the side, taking a step back. Any second, Cole feared they'd close the gate, locking him out, and worse, locking Amanda in. He should have kept his big mouth shut. His fears were nearly confirmed when Don reached for the edge of the gate, but he didn't close it. Yet.

"Why even bother, Cole? We don't need a government. I like being free to do what I want."

"You mean like being free to force a family off their ranch just because you *feel* like it?" Stance wide, arms crossed, Cole leveled a look at Don and held it until the other man shifted his eyes. He shifted his focus to Scott. A part of his mind looked on in disbelief, wondering if he had a death wish. The other men held the weapons as he'd purposefully left his in the Jeep. And yet, here he was poking a stick in a hornet's nest.

Tension radiated up Cole's neck even as adrenaline flooded him and his body ramped up for a fight as he and Scott locked eyes.

Then Scott looked down, sweeping his toe through the dust and scattering a few pebbles. "It's not like they had nowhere else to go. I know for a fact they're living it up just a few miles away. This ranch has more water and we'll do a better job running it."

Sensing he held the upper hand, Cole took a step forward, his voice dropping low. "Did you *not* understand what I just said? You might not care about living in a state of anarchy, but I don't want to live that way and I don't want to raise my own child or see my grand-children brought up where might makes right."

He paused, noting the other men had returned and stood listening to his little speech. Sweeping a look around, including them in his next words, he stabbed a finger down towards the ground. "Right here, right now we have a chance to start over. We can't let billions of people's deaths mean *nothing*." His voice broke slightly on the last word, and he drew a deep breath. Had the other men taken it for a sign of weakness? Well, let them. He couldn't do this alone. He needed help.

Cole stared pointedly on the men's rifles until they lowered them muzzle to the ground. "Here's the reality. I spoke to someone who has seen D.C. What little government that remains only has electricity a few hours a day, and the city itself has been devastated just like every other city. There'll be no help from the government way out here for years. Are you willing to wait that long? Can you *afford* to wait that long?"

The men shuffled their feet, giving each other looks, before many shook their heads.

Cole eased back, his tone quieter, but confident. "Scott…Don… and the rest of you…none of us can do this alone. We have to work together. We can do this."

Scott and Don exchanged a look and Scott turned and surveyed his men, apparently coming to a consensus before facing Cole again. "Veteran's Park, you say?"

"Yes. Three days from now."

Cole looked beyond them for signs of Amanda, but she must still be in the house. Now would be a good time to leave. What if she didn't come out? What if someone in the house made her stay?

A movement caught his eye and Amanda appeared. Cole hid a

sigh of relief. A man hobbled at her side. Her father? When they got to the gate, she walked right past Scott and Don without a second look, hanging onto her father's arm and helping him into the Jeep.

"Hey! Where are you going, Will?"

"With my daughter. Did you actually think I'd choose you over her? You shot me!" He climbed in the rear seat on the driver's side.

Cole walked backwards to the passenger side door. "Veteran's Park. Three days from now. Five p.m."

Chapter Twenty-Six

AMANDA WHEELED the Jeep around and threw up gravel as she peeled away, the force of her acceleration pinning Cole to the back of his seat for a few seconds.

"I can't believe you still invited him to join...to join whatever it is you have planned!" Amanda shot Cole a venomous look.

"Yeah—who the hell are you and who made you in charge?" Will added from the backseat.

"I'm not in charge. If you all want to be on your own, my family will leave. There's a lot of space out here. We never have to see each other again." Cole angled against the back of the seat, one shoulder pressed hard against the frame of the car as he leaned his elbow on the window sill. He stared out the window. What had he been thinking? These people barely knew him and he didn't know this area.

They rode in silence for a couple of miles, then Will said, "Much obliged that you helped Amanda come to get me."

"I didn't do anything. I just rode along."

"All the same, I'm glad she wasn't alone and that she didn't have the twins with her. They would have started a feud for sure."

"I could have done it on my own, Dad."

Cole met Will's eyes in the rearview mirror. The older man gave his head a slight shake. "You would have tried, sweetheart, I know, but those men wouldn't have let you skedaddle out of there if this fellow hadn't been with you."

"I'm not so sure, Will. Your daughter confronted us head on yesterday and now here we are riding together. I think Amanda is a lot stronger than you give her credit for."

Amanda sent him a look that might have been a thank you, but she said, "Whatever. You're free, Dad. That's the important thing. Are you okay?"

"It wasn't bad. The shot went clean through. Don patched me up."

"Does he have medical training?" Cole was torn between hoping he did because the greatest resource they had lost was the vast wealth of human knowledge and every scrap of medical experience would be helpful, but he also couldn't help wishing Don didn't have training so that group would be more likely to join the community Cole was striving to bring together. Their threat of finding someone else hung over his head.

"I don't know. Maybe a little. There wasn't much to do but wash it and throw a bandage on it. I could have done it myself if I could have reached the wound, but I got hit right in the left cheek."

Cole whipped his head around to look the man in the face, noted that half of his face wasn't blown away, then burst into laughter when Will grinned at his surprise. "I'm sorry, I shouldn't be laughing, but—"

"Yeah, I know. The guys there were ribbing me too."

"I'm glad you find it so amusing that my dad was shot in the ass. He could have died. He could have bled to death or had the wound become infected." Amanda cast Cole a look that conflicted with her tone. The corners of her eyes crinkled as her mouth turned up at the corners.

"My apologies, Amanda, and to you too, Will." Cole chuckled one more time then said, "Look, Amanda, what I would like to do is canvas the area and find out who is living in the vicinity. Say, a twenty mile radius. That's a lot of ground to cover. Any ideas of the best way to do it?"

She pursed her lips. "We checked the fuel tank at the ranch we're staying at and there's still plenty but it's diesel so we'll have to look for diesel powered vehicles other than tractors."

"That shouldn't be a problem." Cole figured they'd be able to find them even at some car dealerships—and with luck, they could even fill up the vehicles with diesel right at the dealership and go from there.

They reached the ranch and Amanda stopped. Cole jumped out and rounded the Jeep to help Will out, but Amanda beat him to it.

"Cole? How did it go?"

He turned at Elly's voice, unable to hold back a smile at her appearance. In this warmth, she'd shed her bulky coats and sweaters they'd worn for most of the trip and in a plain T-shirt and black leggings, her pregnancy showed. Her hair curled around her face and when she came close, he smelled a light coconut scent emanating from it.

"You smell good enough to eat." He pulled her close, burying his face against her.

Laughing, she eased away. "I'm not sure whether to be pleased at the compliment or worried I smelled like a goat before."

"Be pleased. That's how I meant it." Cole grinned. "And to answer your question, it went okay. A bit of tension, but I think they'll be at the meeting."

"What meeting?"

Cole told her what he had planned.

"Do you think we have time to do that? We have to find a place of our own to live, get some kind of crops in, after we learn what grows here and planting seasons, find supplies for our immediate needs, and god only knows what else."

"I know, and I understand, but I think if we get to know survivors in the area, we can save a lot of time by learning what's available and get answers to all of your other questions."

She put her arm around his waist as they walked back to the house. "Good point. How are we going to find other survivors?"

"That's the biggest question of all." Cole entered the house, shivering at the blast of air conditioning. It felt good, but unexpected. He knew it had been on last night when he heard the fan blowing, but when he'd entered the house last night, the air outside had been cool and it hadn't been a shock. The second surprise was the tantalizing aroma of baking bread and something else he couldn't place.

"What have you guys been doing?" Cole moved to the sink and got a glass of cold water, marveling at the ease of it and vowing to never take pure running water for granted again. After guzzling most of it, he paused. If most people were dead, who was making sure the water was pure? He peered at what was left in the glass.

"What's wrong?" Elly had a glass of water also, and started examining her own.

"I was just wondering how clean this water was."

"Ah. Well, it's okay. I wondered the same thing and we figured out it's well water. It should be fine."

It tasted good and he finished it and filled another. After weeks of rationing water while driving, it felt great to slake his thirst.

"While you've been gone, Travis and I got the chickens and chicks settled in the hen house. The horses will have clean stalls to come back to after Jake and Hunter return from scoping out the land. The goats are happily cavorting in the pasture."

"Wow, you guys did a lot!"

"Yep. After all of that, I had to shower, so that's why I smell so good. You wouldn't have come near me an hour ago."

Cole laughed. "And everyone else?"

"Piper has been baking up a storm, but we're almost out of flour. I think she went to find Amanda's sister to see if there's any more around so she can bake something for them. Sophie has been washing clothes for everyone. It's a much easier task with a working washer and dryer although I think she hung some things out on a line. In this desert air, they dry faster than a machine can do it."

"Are you hungry?" Elly opened a cupboard and pulled out a loaf of bread. The aroma wafted to him. It must have been one of the fresh loaves. His mouth watered. Piper was a great baker, but conditions for perfect baking hadn't existed since the virus so to see an evenly browned loaf of bread, golden on top and darkening to rich brown near the bottom made him want to devour the whole thing. He made do with a thick slice slathered in strawberry jam. "Where did the jam come from?" It was deliciously tart.

"Smuckers."

Cole laughed. "I meant, how did you come by it?"

"It was here already and Sandy said we could have some."

After devouring the bread, Cole left Elly to help plant a garden. The ranch had a large garden already started from Amanda's group but since they'd only been there a few days themselves, there was a lot of work to do.

He found Amanda talking to her brother, Derek, out by the horse corral. "Hi Derek, Amanda. Do either of you know if my son, Hunter, has returned from his ride yet?"

"No, the stalls are still empty, so I guess not." Derek pointed to the two empty stalls he guessed had been designated for Red and Princess. There were no other horses in the other empty stalls.

Cole glanced at the stalls, unused to seeing this particular type of stable. He guessed it was open to allow more air flow in this climate and there would be no need to protect against blizzards. "You don't have any other horses?"

"Not here...back home we do." Derek scowled at his sister. "I wanted to go steal them back last night, but then you guys came and ruined everything."

"Derek!" Amanda shook her head. "I'm sorry for my brother's outburst. Apologize, Derek."

"You don't have to be sorry for me. You're not Mom and I don't have to do what you say."

"There's no apology necessary. I understand Derek's anger, but unfortunately, your horses are under locked armed guards right now. I counted at least seven men there, plus whoever your sister saw in the house when she rescued your dad."

Derek's eyes widened. "You rescued Dad?"

"That's what I came out to tell you before you started mouthing off to me. He's at the house in the big bedroom in the back."

"Is he okay?"

"Yeah. He will be, just don't bounce on the bed. He's a little sensitive on his backside."

Derek grinned. "I'm going to go find Daniel and tell him." He tore off in the direction of one of the other buildings.

"I take it Daniel is the other twin?"

Amanda nodded, preoccupied. "Derek's taking our mom's death the hardest. I don't know what to do with him anymore." She sighed. "Anyway, is there something you wanted?"

Cole nodded. "You mentioned a couple of guys from Nellis Air Force Base. Are they around here now?"

She shuffled her feet and rested her arms on the top rail of the corral. "Um, well, see...there are a couple of guys, but they aren't actually with us. I mean, they come and go in the area. They helped us with the cattle last fall but they don't come too close to anyone. They just ride in, drop off food now and then, and leave."

Cole digested that. He was disappointed they weren't here, but they would be exactly the kind of guys who could tell him what was going on and where the survivors were located.

"Any chance you might know where they stay?"

Amanda shrugged. "I asked them once, and they said mostly empty bunk houses. A lot of these ranches are no longer real working ranches. Some are more vacation spots for tourists. The bunkhouses have been abandoned as not luxurious enough for guests, so cabins are built."

"I imagine the guys think the bunkhouses are the safest." He thought about it and shrugged. "They'd probably be right."

Cole asked Amanda if she knew where any were, and she waved for Cole to follow her to the house. "I found a telephone book in a drawer in here. I can show you on the street map inside."

For the next half hour, he compiled a list of ranches culled the old fashioned way by looking through the Yellow Pages. Amanda had gone back to tend to her father and everyone seemed to be out doing chores.

"What are you doing?" Elly entered the kitchen from a hallway, leaning sideways from the weight of a full bucket in one hand and clenching a mop in the other.

"What in the world have you been doing?" He jumped up and took the full bucket from her and poured it down the sink.

"I was mopping the floors. They were filthy with dust."

"You shouldn't be doing all that hard work. You're six months pregnant."

"Seven."

Cole froze in the act of putting the mop out on the back stoop to dry. "What?"

"Jenna has been thinking I'm farther along than we thought. With the stress of the virus, I wasn't...regular, you know? So I wasn't exactly sure when I could have become pregnant. It looks like maybe the first time..." She raised her eyebrows. "Don't look so freaked out. What difference does it make? Sophie is due in a month, maybe less, and I'll be a month behind her."

"I just... damn. I wanted things to be more settled before the baby came. Is there a chance Jenna is wrong?" Cole scratched the back of his head as he muddled through the news.

"I have no idea. I just know that we need to prepare sooner rather than later. We did bring all those diapers you grabbed last fall, right?"

"Oh, yeah, we have several hundred, but we should get cloth too, right? I mean, the diapers won't last forever."

"You know what? Don't worry about the diapers. Sophie and I will figure it out. You just go do what you need to do."

"I'm going to ask Amanda to come with me. Do you mind?"

Elly laughed. "No. Why would I mind? You don't plan to get her pregnant too, do you?" The teasing glint in her eye let Cole off the hook.

"Of course not. It's just she knows the area and the guys I'm looking for will know her."

Amanda came from a different entrance into the kitchen, a tray with dirty dishes balanced in her hands.

"Amanda, I know you're super busy, but can I ask another favor?"

"Sure." She emptied the tray in the sink and picked up a sponge.

"Leave those, Amanda. I can do them. In fact, it will be a pleasure to do dishes with warm running water at hand."

"Oh, I can do them."

"I know, but this way, you and Cole can get going sooner."

She shrugged. "Fine. I'm ready if you are."

HUNTER, followed by Jake, entered the house. His dad and Amanda stood near the kitchen table, but Hunter made a beeline for the sink. Dust coated his skin and his mouth felt like mud. He should have brought more water, but he and Jake hadn't planned on being gone so long. "Hey, Dad! You won't believe this place! It's gorgeous out there." He turned on the cold water, sighing as it ran over his hands. Impulsively, he cupped his hands under the faucet, scooping water over his face, rubbing it around his neck, then slurped a few mouthfuls from his hands. It tasted so cold and fresh—not like stale water from a bottle.

"Ah, you know there are glasses for drinking?" His dad's voice made him turn around even as he wiped water from his eyelashes. "Oh, shoot. I'm sorry for the mess. I was so hot and thirsty—"

"No worries. It's Hunter, right?" Amanda found a dishtowel in a drawer and handed it to him.

"Yeah, that's me. And this is Jake—who clearly knows how to take a hint," Hunter joked as Jake opened a cabinet next to the sink, found a cup, and drank from it.

"I wasn't raised in a barn." Jake grinned over the rim of his cup before tilting it and downing the rest of the water.

Amanda took the towel from Hunter and draped it over her shoulder. With a wink at him, she said to Jake, "I practically was raised in a barn, so I know how hot hard work can make a person." She turned on the water, cupped her hands and proceeded to drink from them.

Feeling at ease, Hunter ran his hands through his hair. He felt better already.

"Hunter, I'd like you to go with me to see if we can interest some of the other survivors in the area in coming together for a meeting three days from now."

"Sure, Dad."

"If you're hungry, there's bread on the counter there." His dad pointed to a loaf wrapped in a clean dish cloth.

Jake beat Hunter to it, but sliced them each a thick piece, spotted the jam sitting beside it and handed it to Hunter. "You're on jam duty."

One of the teens, Derek, came from back in the house, eyeing the bread.

Amanda shook her head. "That's not ours, Derek."

His face fell, but Hunter edged Jake out of the way and cut the boy a slice. "Here. It's okay. My cousin, Piper, makes the best bread ever."

Derek took it, but not before requesting permission from his sister, who nodded.

Hunter handed him the jam. "Try it with this. It's the bomb."

"Derek, do you want to go with us? We could cover more ground if you go with Hunter, and I go with Cole."

Hunter stuffed the last bite of his bread in his mouth, grabbed a glass, and washed down the bread with a long gulp, giving his dad a sly grin. "Let's go. I'm ready."

"Okay. Derek, I'll take the Jeep, you can take the pick-up." Amanda tossed a set of keys to Derek, he motioned to Hunter. "Come on."

Jake looked at Hunter's dad. "What about me?"

"If this meeting comes about, we're going to need a lot of food to share. It might be the only thing that will entice people to show up."

Hunter nodded. "Good point, Dad. While Jake and I were out, we came across an empty house along one of the backroads. We didn't go in because it was getting late, but it was definitely abandoned and looked like it's been untouched. It had a mailbox out on the road. It's pretty out of the way and might be worth checking for supplies."

Amanda nodded. "I have a map in my Jeep. I should give it to you guys anyway. Derek knows the area, but he'd just gotten his license when the virus hit. He hasn't driven a lot."

"I'm a good driver."

"Did I say you were a bad driver? No, I didn't." Amanda headed out the door, tossing over her shoulder to Derek as he caught the screen door behind her, "And it's not like there's much traffic to contend with. You just have to go slow to find a path through obstacles."

Chapter Twenty-Seven

HUNTER RODE SHOTGUN with Derek driving. His dad had taken the radios from their vehicles so they had a means of communicating. He'd also given a rundown about some Air Force guys they were looking for. It seemed like a wild goose chase, but Hunter was up for it.

"So, you're seventeen?" Hunter opened the map and as they passed roads, he noted where they were and was able to pinpoint the ranch they were staying at, and then find the house on the backroad. It looked as if the road ended at a canyon.

"Yeah. Just turned. I'm not really sure what the date is anymore."

Hunter nodded. "Yeah, I know. Kind of hard to keep track of dates when there's no reason to. But, my dad has kept track since day one, so he'll know the exact date."

"I could find out here. We still have electricity and all, so, like, my computer still has a calendar, but with no internet, I don't use the computer much. It's not like I can Google anything."

"I haven't used a computer since the beginning. In fact, I fried mine the day before the virus hit. I was dreading telling my dad." Hunter laughed. "Looking back, that seems like such a minor issue. You know?"

"I guess."

"Anyway, we agreed to follow your sister to the first few houses and see if anyone is around. They're trying to find a couple of military guys?"

"Oh yeah. I've seen them before. I think they're the ones who drove the steers on to our ranch."

"Really? What makes you think that?"

"Well, I've seen them on dirt bikes tearing up the highway. Those things don't use much fuel and can get by just about any obstacle. They're way better than a car or even a truck, for getting around now. I want to find one for myself."

"That's not a bad idea."

"Yeah, so, after the stray cattle showed up, I rode out and saw tire tracks in the dirt. Tracks that were too small to come from a car, plus they made super tight turns."

"Why would they drive the cattle on to your ranch and just leave without telling you guys?"

"I guess they knew we were alive and we'd take care of them? After we butchered a couple, Amanda made up a package of beef and left it out on the road in a big orange cooler for them. The meat was gone, but none of us heard anyone. We think they took it. It was my sister's way of thanking them."

Hunter squinted to see the road sign of an intersecting road, found it on the map and marked how long it had taken to get there on a separate notepad he'd taken from his truck before leaving. "So, what's with you and your sister?"

"What do you mean?" Derek sounded defensive, his hands tightening on the steering wheel.

"This morning, before she and my dad left to get your dad, I heard you two talking out by the horses. Sorry, I didn't mean to eavesdrop, but I was taking care of Red and I guess you were right on the other side of the wall." Derek had sounded angry and defiant. Hunter wouldn't normally ask questions, but these weren't normal times and he didn't want his family to be caught in some kind of family drama going on with Amanda and Derek.

"It's nothing. She just thinks she's in charge now and I don't agree."

"Who do you think is in charge?"

"My dad."

"And Amanda doesn't let him take charge?"

"No, it's not like she does anything to stop him, but he doesn't do much."

"I don't understand. I thought he was shot?" He wondered how much they expected a wounded man to do.

"That just happened in the last week. Before that, Amanda still acted like she was in charge. She wouldn't let me and Daniel go anywhere. She practically kept us under lock and key."

"Sounds like she kept your skinny ass alive."

"Nah. I'd have been fine. Not sure about my brother but I have street smarts."

Hunter swallowed a chuckle. "Street smarts?"

"You know what I mean. I know how to take care of myself."

"Hmmm…well you sound a lot better off than I was last year. I had no clue, but I had to learn quick."

Derek shot him a look then refocused on the road and evaded a desert tortoise on the pavement. "Why? What happened?"

"I was out west, well, west for me. I was in Colorado at college and my dad called me and told me to get home. Basically, told me not to stop for anything and just drive. This was just before it got bad. It's complicated, but Elly had given him a heads up."

Derek's eyebrow rose but he didn't ask about that. "And?"

"And…I ran out of gas in the middle of nowhere, but luckily my dad had told me to get a bunch of camping gear before I left, and I had a bit of food. I found more at a farm where the owners had died. That's also where I got the horses. And Buddy."

"That's your dog?"

"Yeah. He saved my ass a few times too. And kept me from going insane. I felt like I was the only one left alive. I had to cross several states and I wasn't even sure that when I got there that my family would still be alive. I'd have given anything to already be home with them when it hit."

"But your mom didn't die."

"Not then, no."

Derek turned and stared at him long enough for Hunter to motion for him to turn his attention back to the road. Even with no traffic, it wasn't wise to look away for too long.

"When did your mom die?"

"When I was about six."

"Wow. That sucks."

"Yeah. It does. Every other kid I knew had a mom and my dad never re-married so I never even had a stepmom."

"Elly wasn't there?"

Hunter laughed. "No. I told you it's complicated. I'll tell you about it later, but I think we're at the first stop."

Derek followed Amanda's Jeep down a winding drive. "I think I know this place. A friend from school lived here." There was hope in his voice, but then it faded when they saw how overgrown everything appeared. That in itself wasn't a good indicator as survival didn't require perfect lawns, but a set of bleached bones in the middle of the drive was a pretty good bet nobody was there. The bones had to have been there a while to be so clean and white. It wasn't from a human. It was too big. Maybe a horse or cow, but as they drove past, Hunter saw bones cracked in half. Either the animal had died from coyotes or wild dogs, maybe even a mountain lion, or they had fed on the remains. If people had been around, Hunter couldn't see the animals coming so close to the house.

Amanda swerved to the right and did a U-turn, shaking her head at them as she passed by. Hunter sighed. It could be a long afternoon.

It wasn't until the ninth house that they found anyone alive. A man and a small boy. The man came out on to his front porch with a rifle in the crook of his arm.

His father stepped out and Hunter held his breath. Why did his dad always have to be the one to take the risk? He rolled down his window so he could hear the conversation.

"… Veteran's Park. You know where that is? Three days. At five p.m."

"I want you off my property. *Now.*"

His dad backed away, arms raised. "Look, mister. I know it's hard to trust other people and I know you might be worried about catching the virus, but feel free to wear a mask. Nobody will think twice about it. I'll probably wear one myself. But there will be food there."

The barrel of the rifle lowered a fraction. "Food?"

Amanda put one foot out, standing to look over the door. "Yeah.

I have beef, and we'll see what other stuff we have. If you have something to share, that would be welcome, but if you don't feel comfortable with that, just come as our guest. The important thing is that we get to know each other. You know out here, neighbors have always depended on each other. We need each other now more than ever."

The rifle lowered still more and the man put a hand on the child's head. "My son hasn't seen any other kids in a year. He said you guys were ghosts because we thought everyone was dead."

"No. There are more survivors than you think." His dad pointed to Derek's truck. "That's my son and her brother. I think we have about twenty-five people at the ranch, with both of our families combined?" He looked to Amanda for confirmation.

She nodded and said, "Plus those guys on *my* ranch."

"And those two Air Force guys. So counting you two, there are at least thirty-seven of us alive right around here." His dad's voice softened. "And some are children. We have three with us. Two boys and a girl. They'd love to have another kid to play with."

The young boy's eyes opened wide as he looked at his own father then back to Hunter's dad.

The man straightened his shoulders, the rifle inching up, but there was no threat in his voice when he said, "I'll think about it."

"Okay. Hope to see you there, but no matter whether you go or not, if you need anything, we're just down the road."

He gave a noncommittal nod. Amanda gave the man the address but he didn't write it down.

Hunter called out to his dad. "Why don't we split up? I feel like we're wasting gas just following you."

"Are you armed?"

Hunter patted the butt of his handgun tucked into a shoulder holster. "Always."

Today he wore a tank top with loose button down shirt over it. He found it was actually cooler to keep the sun off his skin than to be completely bare. The loose shirt covered the gun, but it was within easy reach.

Amanda retrieved something from the back of her Jeep and came up to Hunter's window, throwing an uneasy glance at the man, who remained on the porch as if they intended to storm the house. She called to him that they were just getting ready to leave.

She thrust a can of red spray paint at Hunter. "Here, mark the front doors with an X if the house is empty. We can come back later and check for supplies. If you can, write the addresses down, too. We're going to go west and you guys can take this road, go south and then take a right. We'll go the opposite way and we'll be covering a large loop. There will be a gas station on your left so we can meet there. Say, in about an hour?"

Derek nodded. "Yeah."

Amanda turned to go back to her Jeep when Derek shouted, "Be careful, Amanda."

She paused in the act of opening her door, stared at her brother for a moment, before nodding. "You too."

Derek rolled up his window and didn't look at Hunter. They drove south, inspected several more homes where all they found were bodies and death. They made their Xs, and if the houses didn't already look ransacked, they added a smaller S to make it easier to determine where there might be supplies. Hunter noted the addresses for future reference.

The quiet in the truck grew awkward with only the sound of Hunter's pen scratching on the notepad to break the silence. He picked up his story where he'd left off after finding Buddy. "My cousin, Trent, died just before I got to the island—that's where we went to stay away from all the sick people—he would have been almost your age now. Maybe a year younger. I miss him so much. Growing up, my dad and I spent a lot of time at my cousin's house. All the holidays, birthdays, you name it. They always had room for us. Piper's like a sister and Trent was more of a brother than a cousin. I even lived there when my dad's job took him away from home for months at a time."

Derek seemed lost in thought but then said, "My dad could have been in charge, but he's not like your dad. He just sat in the house. I'm not even sure he'd have noticed if I would have died in the beginning. He watched television hour after hour until it went off the air, and even then, he stared at the screen when it was just that white fuzzy stuff."

"Snow?"

"Is that what it's called? I never saw it before, but yeah. He finally started acting like he cared if we lived or died about two months ago."

"And who took care of things before that?" Hunter knew the answer even before Derek replied, but he let the boy say it anyway.

"Amanda..."

Hunter didn't reply and just pointed out the next house. This one looked like someone might be living there, so he told Derek to beep the horn so whoever was there would know they weren't trying to sneak up on them.

A man ambled out from a garage, wiping his hands on a greasy rag. "Hey there!"

Hunter paused before slowly opening the passenger door. He didn't get out, only putting one foot on the driveway. He studied the man, wondering if his friendly demeanor was real or if he was sick with the virus. He took out a mask and told Derek to put on one as well. "Hello, sir. My name is Hunter and this is Derek. We're going house to house looking for survivors."

"Hey, Hunter, I'm Garret." He tucked the rag in his back pocket and tipped his head to see Derek. "How's it going, Derek?"

The man sighed as he focused on Hunter. "Well, I can save you some trouble. I'm the only one on either side of this road for a mile each way. I checked myself a few months ago when I figured it was finally safe to leave."

"Nobody else is here with you?"

"Nope. I'm divorced for twenty years now. I'd have been dead too, except I took a few days off to paint my living room, had my music blasting, got a little drunk and when I was done and sober, the world had ended."

"How have you managed all alone?"

"It's been damned hard, I'll tell you. I felt like Robinson Crusoe or something." He jabbed a thumb over his shoulder. "I planted a shitload of vegetables out back, mostly at the wrong time, but I kept them watered and rigged up some shade to keep them from drying up. I babied those carrots and potatoes until I had a decent crop for a single person. Shot some rabbits, fished on the little creek that ran through the back of my property until it dried up last summer. It's coming back now, and so are the fish. But, mostly, I dressed up like one of those Hazmat guys and raided every freezer and pantry in those houses. You won't find a thing to eat in any of them."

"So, you haven't seen or spoken to anyone in all this time?"

"Nope. I saw a couple of guys on dirt bikes go by a few times, but by the time I got outside to flag them down, they were long gone."

While the man was friendly and talkative, he wasn't acting crazed as those who'd caught the virus had. More likely, he was just lonely and rambling after not talking to a living soul for nearly a year.

Hunter exchanged a glance with Derek. "You think that could be them?"

Derek shrugged. "Maybe."

The man looked confused. "You talking to me?"

"No, sir. We know there are a couple of guys who were rumored to have been from the Air Force base riding around on dirt bikes. They seem to have been helping people out now and then, but they don't stick around for a thank you. We just want to let them know about a meeting we're holding three days from now. It's to get all of us survivors together so we can help each other. Are you interested in going?"

"You bet I am." His face lit up like Hunter had told him Christmas was coming early.

After telling him where and when, Hunter asked him to spread the word if he happened to see any other people before the meeting.

They left, doing a quick check on the other homes in case Garret was mistaken, but saw no signs of life. They made an X, but didn't add an S to any of the doors.

At the last one, they found human remains scattered near the front door along dozens of beer cans, empty bottles of whiskey, and crumpled packs of cigarettes.

Derek stared at the scene before backing away. "This is crazy. I knew people died, but…I guess I thought Amanda exaggerated, you know? But she was right." He spun and fled to the truck.

Hunter took a quick look around, decided any supplies from this house weren't worth the risk and returned to the truck to find Derek, his knuckles white on the steering wheel, his body shaking as he stared straight ahead at the house of death.

Last summer seemed a lifetime ago when Hunter had been forced to come to terms with the scope of the tragedy, but it seemed as if Derek was only now realizing the depth of what had happened.

He gave Derek a few moments to process it all before he asked, "Are you okay?"

There was no reply for perhaps thirty seconds. Then as if something had broken loose, Derek, eyes watering, his nose running, sobbed about his mother's death, his friends gone forever, his high school graduation, college, all of the things he'd planned in the next few years. "Everyone is gone—why do we even bother? Why? What's the point?" He pounded on the steering wheel before wrapping his arms around it and burying his head in them.

Hunter sat motionless. What could he say to this boy he barely knew? What *should* he say? The radio beeped and his dad asked them where they were and if everything was okay. "Ah, yeah, Dad. We're fine. Just give us a few more minutes, okay?"

Derek came up for air, looking for something to wipe his nose with, finally fishing a napkin from the crevice between the seat and the console. It was probably leftover from some fast food run a year ago. When he finished, he looked drained; his eyes red-rimmed, still sniffing. "I'm sorry, man. I'm such a wuss."

Hunter shook his head. "No, you're not. You're a survivor, same as me. And like my dad. You think we haven't had our own moments when we ranted and raved about the fairness?"

Derek looked at him askance. "Yeah, right."

"For me, it came after finally reaching the island and finding out Trent had died. All that I had gone through to get there seemed pointless. I was so happy to see my family, but then Trent was dead and, like you, I wondered why he died and not me and what was the point of going on? Everyone else was dead so we might as well be too. And my dad, he blamed himself for Trent's death."

Derek's head was bowed as he picked at the leather cover on the steering wheel. "So how did you get through it?"

Hunter thought back. He'd had Sophie to help him, and she'd had her own demons to work through that he tried to help her deal with.

His dad had had Elly, and even Sean had been there after Steve's death. "I talked it out with those closest to me. I think my dad did too."

He let that sink in then added, "From what I can tell, Amanda would do whatever she could to help you. And you have your twin. He might not be where you are yet, though, if he hasn't seen any of this for himself. When he does, he'll need you there to help him."

"Yeah. Maybe. But…still, the world sucks now. I want it to be like it was."

"Yeah. I know. I think we all wish that, but what comes next in this world is whatever we want it to be."

Derek nodded and straightened his shoulders. "Tell them we're on our way."

Chapter Twenty-Eight

OVER THE NEXT TWO DAYS, the group canvassed the area and on the morning of the meeting, Cole looked over the list of survivors they'd spoken to. It was a very short list. Not including their groups, there were only twenty-seven other survivors. Only four of them were under the age of twelve. Five were teens, and the others were adults of all ages.

He knew there had to be survivors they hadn't reached yet, and hoped those they had spoken to would come across them and invite them to the meeting as well. However, going by what information they had, they'd have to assume that there would be around sixty people.

"What are we preparing in the way of food?"

Elly, Piper, Jake, and Daniel had checked homes that had been marked as unoccupied to look for provisions. Usable food was mostly confined to whatever was canned as rodents or bugs had destroyed anything in bags or cardboard. That still left them with a nice haul, including a couple of canned hams, an industrial sized can of pork and beans, and three cans of Vienna sausages. They found more, including more than twenty pounds of whole wheat flour, and thirty pounds stored in a freezer at a commercial bakery. They wouldn't be using all of it for the feast tonight, but Piper and Sophie had been hard at work baking a dozen loaves of bread. Frozen vegetables hadn't survived deep freezers as well as other foods, much of it was dried up, but they had sorted through several bags and had a big bowl of peas, carrots, and corn mixed together.

Jake and Daniel had scouted out the park a couple of days ago and had bags of charcoal and grills taken from backyards, already in place. Picnic tables were rounded up and placed close together and Sean and Joe had gone out too, finding a convenience store that had paper plates, plastic ware, and napkins. Those items had all been untouched by people seeking supplies in the last days.

Another thing that made scavenging here unlike other places was that many of the homes here still had electricity going if the power hadn't been knocked out for some reason, like lightning hitting a transformer.

That meant the deep freezers held contents that were still useable. Freezer burn probably had affected some of the contents and they'd have to watch out for food that had spoiled if power had been out for a short time, then came back on, refreezing the spoiled food, but they only took from freezers that had something that would alert them if the freezer had been compromised. If there was a carton of ice cream still intact, it was a safe freezer. If the ice cream was all over the inside of a now working freezer, they passed on the food.

Elly bustled in, large bowl of what smelled like stuffing in her hands and set it on the other end of the dining room table Cole had been using as a desk. Cole's mouth watered. "Where did you get that?"

"Ah, your brilliant and resourceful niece has been saving every scrap of bread, letting it dry and then stashing it in a freezer zipper bag. So, we have several different kinds of bread—sourdough, biscuits, cornbread—all of it is now seasoned with sage and thyme and chicken bouillon cubes."

"That right there will be enough to draw folks from miles around if they could smell it." Cole rose and rounded the table to sniff the steam escaping from the bowl.

The kitchen door opened and Cole went to see who had come in. It was still weird living communal style with people they had only met a few days ago, but everyone was getting along well, so far.

"Hey, Cole. My dad has the meat ready to go." She washed her hands at the sink, then eyed the loaves of bread. "Oh, my god. I can't wait until dinner." She grinned. "And something else smells wonderful. I can't place it, but it's familiar…"

"Stuffing?"

"That's it!" Amanda sniffed again. "But there's something else too."

Piper came up from the basement door, an apron around her waist, now holding it to form a pouch. Bulges in the pouch made him look hard to guess what they could be. He didn't have long to guess as Piper emptied the pouch on the kitchen table. Cans of sweetened condensed milk, a canister of cocoa power, and, of all things, a canister of powdered hot chocolate mix covered the surface.

Piper grinned at Cole's surprise, but then turned to the oven, opened it, and pulled out a sheet pan.

Cole gaped as she set a chocolate cake to cool. "Wow! Piper, you've outdone yourself."

"Thanks, Uncle Cole." She set her pot holders aside and said, "I've been thinking, when things are a little more settled, maybe I could trade baked goods for other food. For instance, I could trade a fully baked cake for a quantity of flour or sugar. Someone else could trade me so much chocolate or vanilla. Another person could trade eggs and dairy."

"I see what you're saying. With all of the items, you could bake cakes for all of them if they don't have all of the ingredients, and you'd get to keep the extra to trade for things like beef or vegetables."

"Exactly."

"That's a great idea, Piper. I was already thinking your mom could trade her medical care for things she needed. Like how doctors used to be paid with chickens or piglets."

"Speaking of chickens, Travis tells me they are all doing well, and he, Luke, and Zoë took care of them this morning, gathering enough eggs to make this cake." Elly examined the canister of hot chocolate mix. "What are you going to do with this?"

"There's a lot I can do with it, actually. They have powdered milk, so right there, that's helpful. I could make a chocolate biscuit, for example."

Elly scrunched her nose. "I'm not so sure about how good that would be."

Piper laughed. "I know it sounds weird, but it wouldn't be much different than a chocolate cookie—which I can make when I have eggs. But without eggs, it would be a biscuit and what if I added something savory like chili flakes? That could be good with a spicy chili."

Cole thought about it and wasn't sure but in these times, unusual combinations were the norm, so he shrugged. "I'd eat it."

"Me too," Amanda chimed in. "If it's chocolate, I'll eat it." She laughed.

"Same, Amanda." Piper shared a smile with the other woman. "But that's an idea for later. I thought it would help me thicken a frosting I have in mind for the cake. I don't have butter or cream, or even powdered sugar, but I have this condensed milk, cocoa powder, a little shortening, and this hot cocoa mix. With a dash of vanilla, I think it'll make a decent frosting."

"I'm sure it'll be delicious." Elly smiled. "Is there anything I can help with now?"

"No, I don't think so. Sophie wanted to help more, but she wasn't feeling so great. She's lying down."

Elly shot Cole a worried look then asked Piper, "Is she okay?"

"I don't know...I think so? My mom is checking on her now."

Cole drew Elly close. "Why don't you see about Sophie, and then lie down for a bit yourself? We have a few hours before we have to be at the park."

She drew back, looking undecided.

"Yeah, Elly. I think everything is done for now." Amanda spread her arms. "We have enough food for a small army...er, well, I hope it's not an army, but you know what I mean. All we'll have to do is transport it to the park and warm it up on one of the grills."

"Jake said they would get one grill with a small bed of coals just for that purpose. The other grills will be for cooking the beef and grilling slices of the ham."

"Where's Hunter? Does he know about Sophie?"

Piper said, "He's out making sure the animals are all fed and watered a bit early so we don't have to worry about them while we're gone."

Amanda bit her lip. "You know, I've been a little worried about leaving this place unguarded. If everyone knows we're at the park, what's to stop them from coming in and taking over this ranch too?"

Cole thought about it. "You're right." He wondered if Joe would stay back. And maybe Mike. Both men were good with guns and both were level-headed. "I think Joe and Mike would be okay with it if we leave them some of this delicious food. It wouldn't be fair to them to take it all."

"I'll give them huge slices of cake and fill plates with stuffing and vegetables."

Amanda said, "I'll have my dad cut them two big steaks just for them."

"I have time. I could even cook up the steaks just before we leave so they can take their meal out on the deck while they keep guard."

"Okay. I'll go propose it to them." Cole left and found the men in the barn, chatting while watching a pregnant cow munching on hay. Amanda's father stood beside them, favoring his left leg, but otherwise, appearing healthy. Will had instructed the other two on the butchering of the steer they were eating tonight.

When he asked them about doing guard duty, they were a little disappointed, but agreed it made sense. They perked up when Cole mentioned the steaks and cake.

Will looked pensive. "Maybe I should stay, too. I don't want another ranch stolen from me."

Cole started to agree that three men would be better than two, but thought better of it. "Will, of course, you do what you feel is right for you, but I'm a newcomer here. I think success in uniting this community hinges on you and your family being there."

"Me? Why me? I know cattle. That's it. My wife—she was the smart one. She was like you. Amanda's like her too. You guys will do fine."

"It's not about intelligence, and you're no slouch in that department. It's about people. Even if you don't know these people personally, what you say will resonate with them. Your story of survival will be closer to their own. What I say won't carry a whole lot of weight with these folks, but you—you're their neighbor. What you do and say will matter to them."

Will looked undecided, his eyes darting from Joe to Mike as if seeking their input. Mike just nodded, but Joe said, "I think Cole is right. What he won't tell you is that he's good at bringing people together *because* he understands other people's strengths and weakness right away. He's a good guy and people will listen to him, eventually, but he could use your help in getting acquainted with them."

Cole blinked in surprise, humbled at the vote of confidence.

Shrugging, Will agreed. "But I'm no talker so don't expect me to say anything."

"I don't expect a speech, but maybe an introduction?" Cole lifted a hand, his thumb and first finger a few inches apart. "Just a short one? And I'll even give you my slice of cake—although I might follow behind you and lick the plate clean."

Will laughed. "Fine. And you can keep your slice of cake."

COLE PUT ON A CLEAN SHIRT. It was one he'd packed a year ago when they had first left for the island but hadn't ever worn. It was just a plain white Oxford. It was his go-to shirt for most occasions. Oddly, the shoulders were tighter than he recalled, and the front, looser. He changed into a well-worn, but clean pair of jeans, marveling at the softness imparted by machine washing and drying.

Elly also changed clothes, but had a harder time finding something to fit. "My belly is just too big now." She wore a pink, stretchy long-sleeved top over some kind of black stretchy pants that accentuated her new curves.

"You look great. I mean it." He smiled when she rolled her eyes at him.

"You're just saying that." But she smiled to soften the comment. "Oh, and Sophie is fine. She said she just had some tightness. Jenna said it was Braxton-Hicks contractions. All normal. She had her drink some water and lie down. She's still planning on going tonight."

Cole nodded as he rolled his sleeves up to just below his elbows. He worried about bringing pregnant women to this meeting. What if there was violence? He had no clue how tonight would go. It could be nobody would show up and they would eat and come back here.

He picked up his holster, hesitating. Would it be better to go unarmed? Would it scare others away? They hadn't discussed it but they all carried a sidearm. With no law, they had to. Sighing, he strapped it on.

Everyone pitched in loading the food, all of the lawn chairs, and Piper found a Frisbee she and Trent had packed what seemed like a lifetime ago. Cole wished they had the volleyball net they'd left at the island. He wanted a fun atmosphere. When they reached the park, he didn't see anyone but Jake, Derek, and Daniel. They had gone ahead early to get grills going, set up folding tables, and bring coolers of drinks. Cole still couldn't get over that they had actual ice. Of course, they had plenty of ice on the island all winter, but he'd missed having it last summer and fall and while traveling.

As he parked, he paused for a moment to take in the scene. They had scrounged up eight tablecloths. Four white, two red, and the last two, yellow. The colors looked festive and cheerful.

The kiddie pool that they had found the day after Travis had joined them was set up to one side, just a few feet from a hand-pump. He couldn't see if it was filled, but a blue plastic bucket lay discarded near it, so he would bet it was. It must have been something Jake and Derek had done earlier. The kids would love that.

The scene pulled memories from Cole's mind. Memories of Fourth of July picnics, block parties, and birthday celebrations with his family and neighbors when they all ate too much, got sunburned, or sprained an ankle playing softball like they were still eighteen years old. Then having a cold beer and laughing over it at the next picnic. It was difficult to accept that this picnic was different. He sighed.

"What's wrong?" Elly shot him a look.

"Nothing. Just worried how things will go."

"It'll be fine." She leaned over and gave his cheek a kiss. "I'm going to go put this bowl of veggies to heat up."

Cole nodded and started lugging pans of sliced ham to the grill to warm, and went back for the baked beans. They were already baked and the pot, still hot. He had to use potholders to carry it to one of the folding tables that was set-up for food.

Elly nodded to the spread. "I thought everyone can serve themselves buffet style."

Piper arrived with Sophie and carried a large basket covered in kitchen towels. "I sliced the bread."

Sophie brought the cake and sent Cole a panicked look when she stumbled on a stone. She recovered her balance with a little laugh. "Piper would have killed me if I dropped the cake. I told her she shouldn't trust it to the pregnant girl who can't see her feet."

Cole laughed and took the pan from her. "How are you feeling?"

She waved a hand. "Oh, I'm fine. Ready to have this baby though."

"Not yet you aren't!" Jenna approached the table, bearing a bowl of fruit. "No baby for you for at least another three weeks. Then you'll be at least thirty-nine weeks. Forty weeks would be even better."

Cole looked at the fruit. "That looks delicious."

Jenna shrugged. "It's only canned fruit cocktail, but it smells good. Sean found an industrial sized can at a school."

By quarter to five, Cole noted everyone who was coming from his group and Amanda's was there. Food was heating and the brisket Amanda had cooked over a low fire on the grill back at the ranch had been transferred to the third grill at the park. There was nothing left to do but wait for others to show up.

Cole sat in a lawn chair and Sean ambled over and offered him an ice cold bottle of beer. "*Surprise*! I found a few cases but kept it a secret."

"Oh, man. You are the best brother ever!" Cole took the bottle, twisted the cap, and watched as a sliver of mist swirled from the mouth of the bottle.

Sean took the chair beside his and held his bottle out. "Here's to a great meal and, hopefully, new friends."

"New friends," Cole echoed, clinking his bottle to Sean's. He took a long swig, closing his eyes as the carbonation prickled his mouth and slid down his throat. "Ah, that tastes unbelievably good. I don't even know this brand and it doesn't matter."

Sean laughed. "I only brought one case though. I figured you wouldn't want a bunch of drunks, but offering the people who show a nice cold beer? That has to count in our favor, right?"

"You're brilliant. And your daughter is too. That cake will win over anyone not convinced by the beer."

Beaming, Sean took another sip from his beer, then straightened in his seat. "Here comes a car."

Chapter Twenty-Nine

COLE STOOD, unsure whether to keep the beer or set it down. He opted to set it on a picnic table. Sean did the same.

The car slowed, started to back up as if they were going to leave but after a hesitation changed directions and crept forward. The driver's window rolled down to reveal a woman of about thirty. Long, dark hair framed her gaunt, tan face. "Is this the meeting?"

Cole didn't remember her but Hunter and Derek could have invited the woman. He smiled. "Yes. It sure is. Welcome."

Elly approached, her smile warm, a hand resting on her belly. "Hi. I'm Elly. Why don't you join us?"

The woman's eyes flicked to Elly's hand and where it rested, then past Elly to where Sophie sat at a picnic table. The tension in her mouth eased into a smile. She nodded. "Okay."

Before she had parked, a pick-up truck roared into the lot. Cole braced for something, not sure what, but he took a step forward, shielding Elly.

Hunter trotted over beside Cole as the truck sped into a parking spot. "I think I know who this is."

The door flew open and Hunter grinned. "Hi, Garret! Glad you could make it."

"Hunter! I wouldn't have missed this for the world. Been counting the hours." He slammed the door and strode towards them, his hand out to Cole. "I'm Garret Richards."

Cole couldn't help but smile back at the man. His enthusiasm was infectious. "Cole Evans, and it seems you've already met my son, Hunter."

"It's a pleasure, Cole. And you raised a fine young man." He turned to Elly. "Mrs. Evans?"

Elly shot Cole an amused look, then shrugged. "Yes, sir. Please, call me Elly."

The other woman approached, a young teenaged girl and a boy of about twelve following her. All three looked frightened half to death.

Cole waved Sean closer. "Garret, this is my brother, Sean." With the man delivered to Sean's care, with a beer offered and gleefully accepted, Cole turned his attention to the woman.

Elly had already approached her. "This is my husband, Cole. He arranged this meeting."

"I'm Yesenia, and this is my daughter, Margarita. Brian is…well, I guess he's my son now too."

Brian, whose Asian features bore no resemblance to mother and daughter, shot Yesenia a look, his eyes widening, then he ducked his head.

Yesenia bit her lip. "I…I wasn't sure if we should come. Someone drove down the street announcing it on a loudspeaker. I wasn't sure if it was a joke, but if it was some kind of trap…"

"Loudspeaker? That wasn't us." He turned, spotting Hunter talking to Garret and waved him over. "Derek didn't have a loud-speaker on his truck when you were contacting people, did he?"

Hunter's brows knit in confusion. "No."

Garret laughed. "That was me! I was so excited that I drove all over the place announcing it. You all did tell me to spread the word, right?"

Hunter nodded, grinning. "We did."

Cole motioned to Garret. "So it seems Garret here was the one. I'm glad he was able to reach you and that you came. What this is all about is just trying to bring the community back together. I'm going to talk a little bit more about it after we eat."

Margarita darted a look at the grills and the table. "You have food?"

All three were painfully thin and Brian raised his head, watery eyes peering at the table. "Can we have some...Mom." His voice held a note of hope and questioning that went beyond a request for food. Yesenia looked to Cole, eyebrows raised.

"Of course. We have plenty for everyone, and Brian, you look about the same age as one of my boys." He looked around and spotted Travis racing around with Luke. "Travis! Luke!" The boys stopped then ran to him.

"Yeah?" Travis panted, his eyes dancing at beating Luke.

He noted Yesenia looking at Travis's dark skin and back at Cole, understanding dawning as Cole introduced the boys to her. He continued, "Travis, this is Brian. Why don't you guys get out the Frisbee and get some snacks from Piper before we start serving? Margarita, you're welcome to join them or you can hang out with your mom."

Both kids looked at their mother, who hesitated.

Elly said, "They'll be within sight at all times."

Finally, she nodded, smiling. "Okay. But stay where I can see you."

As the kids wandered away, Luke's chatter floated back to them and Zoë ran up to them, taking Margarita's hand like it was the most natural thing in the world. Cole's heart swelled at the little girl's innocent trust and acceptance. He'd grown to love all the kids as if they were his own. Zoë removed her shoes and jumped in the pool. Margarita shrugged, and kicked off her shoes as well. Cole smiled. "Kids. They're the most resilient of all of us."

Yesenia agreed. "Yes. As you can see, Brian is not my son by birth. His family all died. About a month after the virus hit, he showed up on my doorstep. He said he'd gone door to door for days and I was the only one who answered. I couldn't turn him away."

"Of course not." Elly dabbed at her eyes. "I'm sorry. I cry at everything these days."

Yesenia tipped her chin to Elly's stomach. "When are you due?"

Cole took that as his cue to leave, so he excused himself as other vehicles arrived. To his surprise, the man who had threatened them from his front porch arrived with his son, introducing the boy as Tim. He even brought an apple pie. Where he got it, Cole had no clue, but everyone exclaimed over it and the man, whose name was Kevin, blushed and stammered that it was nothing. Before long, his son was playing with the other kids and Kevin clutched a beer.

By five thirty, the guest number had swelled to around sixty people. Two more young children joined Zoë and Margarita, splashing in the little pool, while a girl of about fourteen played Frisbee with the boys. Cole tried to remember everyone's name but managed to offer a few words of welcome to everyone.

The beer had been handed out, but a few other people had brought some and added it to the cooler. The buffet table was laden with more food than Cole recalled them preparing. His eyes widened at the dessert table.

Elly approached. "I can't believe so many people showed up." Her face wreathed in smiles, she swept an arm out at the people standing in groups. Some of the guests spoke with other guests, some with Amanda's family, and some with Cole's group. Music started playing and Cole spun to look at Derek, who had set up a Bluetooth speaker with a cellphone. The boy grinned and shrugged. "It's not a party without music."

A parking block just behind the buffet table was the perfect platform for Cole to get everyone's attention. He motioned for Derek to turn the music down. Spreading his arms wide, he drew everyone's attention. "Hello and welcome! If I haven't had a chance to meet you personally yet, my name is Cole Evans. We planned this feast to get to know other survivors and hopefully, this will be the first step in forming a community where we can help each other. But first, I know everyone is hungry, so why don't we dig in?"

Applause accompanied his suggestion and he hopped off the block.

When the guests hesitated to approach the buffet table, Piper made a show of marching up to it. "I call dibs on the first slice of ham!"

That broke the ice and a line formed as Jake and Daniel manned the grills, serving slices of ham and brisket. Several steaks had also appeared on the grill and Cole learned they had come from some of the guests, to be sliced up for anyone who wanted some. The spirit of giving had gone beyond anything he'd hoped for and his throat swelled. Thankfully, nobody chose that moment to speak to him, and he merely grunted when Jake offered him a slice of ham. Giving him an odd look, Jake set the slice on his plate along with a portion of brisket and slice of medium rare steak.

Cole found a seat beside Elly and welcomed guests to sit with them. Conversation quieted while everyone ate. Jake and Daniel claimed the last two seats as they put down their serving tongs.

A few people offered prayers before eating and then conversation turned to compliments to all the cooks, exclamations about the bread, and warnings to save room for dessert.

As people finished dinner but before dessert was offered, Cole approached the block again. He knew speaking to hungry folks would never go as well as speaking to those who had just eaten a delicious and filling meal, but still anticipated dessert.

He hopped up on the block, and was surprised when Derek handed him a microphone. "It'll go through my speaker, so everyone can hear you."

"Thanks." He must have looked puzzled because Derek lifted one shoulder. "I used to do Youtube videos so I had all the gear still in the truck." The teen returned to his seat.

Cole drew a deep breath, then startled when it blew across the microphone, drawing everyone's attention. "Whoops. Well, I guess this thing works."

Chuckles followed his blunder and Cole grinned. "Once again, I welcome everyone and look forward to getting to know all of you better. I'd like to thank Amanda and her father, Will, for allowing my group to stay with them these last few days. I don't know how this would have been accomplished without them. Amanda, if you could stand up."

She did, with a mock bow.

"And Will?"

Will didn't stand, merely waved his arm. "Too busy eatin'!"

"Will and his family are ranchers from this area. I'd hoped to have Will say a few words, but I guess he's busy."

Laughter accompanied his comment and encouraged, Cole

launched into an abbreviated account of how they had come to be in Las Vegas. "And my son Hunter had learned that electricity might still be working here, so we came out. He was right."

Nods all around as people picked at what they left on their plate and a few went back for seconds.

"I know I'm not from around here, but I can tell you first hand that between here and D.C. there's not much left. I don't want to be a downer so we won't dwell on that. We all know the situation. We have to focus now on what happens next. And what happens next will be determined by how all of us move forward from tonight. We can—"

Loud music and revving engines cut him off. He turned to find three pickup trucks, music blaring, turning into the lot. Dust flew in the air as the trucks spun their tires before peeling around the parked cars.

Anger raced through Cole. He recognized Scott and Don driving two of the trucks as they pulled up behind him, rolled down their windows and whooped and hollered as their music blasted. Each truck had two men in the cab and two more riding in the bed. All carried rifles.

Out of the corner of his eye, he saw Piper rush to cover the desserts from the cloud of dust. After the initial alarmed voices, all chatter ceased as parents drew children close.

Cole turned to face Scott's truck, one foot anchored on the first block, and planting the other foot on an adjacent block. He raised the microphone and offered a welcome. His voice carried over the music but was hard to understand. Someone in the truck playing the music turned it down. Cole took that as a good sign and repeated what he'd said, ". "Welcome, Scott, Don. Henchmen."

Scott's smirk faded as the crowd behind Cole chuckled at his dig. He hadn't meant it to be funny, but the look of confusion on Scott's face made him wish he had done it on purpose.

"Hey, you invited us, remember?"

"I do. And you're welcome to join us, but leave the long guns in the trucks. This is a peaceful gathering." Cole had looked for Scott's group and hadn't been sure if he was relieved or disappointed that they hadn't shown. But, now that they were here, he couldn't hold his anger that they had scared everyone. He waved a hand back to the people eating. "Look what you've done. You've scared the kids, sent dust flying all over the food, and have people ducking under the picnic tables, worried that you all have the virus. What made you think such an entrance would be welcomed?"

"Don't forget they stole our ranch!" Amanda's voice carried even without the microphone. Murmurs of anger and questions of why these men were invited rose behind Cole. The men in the beds of the trucks had gone from wild jubilation to abashed feet shuffling.

"We're not sick."

Cole shook his head. "I'm afraid it appeared that you all were. Too bad too, because we have baked beans, ham, brisket…" The men in the back of the trucks looked worried, darting glances at each other.

"Hey, mister…" One of them waved to get Cole's attention. "We didn't mean any harm. We thought we were just having a little fun. Most of were regular guys before. We had families and jobs." He took a gulp of air and looked away for a split second. "I… I had a daughter… before. I don't want to scare kids." His look rested somewhere behind Cole and when he glanced over his shoulder, he saw Zoë with her head buried against Elly's stomach.

Shoulders stiff, Cole stared hard at the man. "What your intentions were and what you actually *did* are not even close. You owe everyone here an apology." He swept all the men with his gaze, including Scott and Don. "If the people behind me accept your sincere apology, you can join us. If not, you'll have to leave." They were outgunned and he didn't want any shooting at all, but he drilled Scott with a look. "It's your call."

Scott stared at Cole for a few seconds, then his eyes slid to the folks behind Cole. He nodded and put the truck in park, shutting it off. His followers did the same. Immediately, the quiet had a calming effect. He hopped out, holding his hands out. "Folks…I am, sincerely, sorry." He glanced at Cole, then focused on Amanda for a few seconds, seeming to get an idea. He looked at Cole and the microphone. "May I?"

Cole shrugged and handed it to him, but didn't offer his blocks to the man. Scott tested the speaker, then said, "When I met Cole a few days ago, he asked me why I took Amanda's family's ranch, and my only answer was because I could. I'm ashamed of that answer now, and I guess Cole's question has been percolating in the back of my mind since then. I wanted to come here tonight as, I don't know, I guess to prove to myself that I was right to take over the ranch. That in this new world, it was survival of the fittest, and I thought *we* were the fittest."

Nobody spoke and the unfriendly stares focused on the man made even Cole uncomfortable.

"But, I was wrong. I just realized it. The fittest are people like you." Scott pointed at Yesenia. "I saw you once, last winter. You were struggling to bring supplies back to your house. I was sitting in a truck, just having slept off drinking too much. I could have helped you, but instead, thought about taking what you had found. If I hadn't had such a hangover, I probably would have. But, you were a lot stronger than me. Look at you. You survived with your children."

Yesenia shifted, darting looks left and right.

Cole said, "I don't think she's going to feel grateful because you didn't steal her supplies, so what's your point?"

"My point is, I was wrong. You organized this and brought all these people together. I guess that makes you the fittest." He started to hand over the microphone, but brought it back to his mouth. "Once again, I apologize. If you could see fit to let these other men join you, I'd be grateful. I'll go on my way, but please consider letting them be part of your group. They're good men. Or were, until they met me."

Cole hopped off the block and reached the microphone with one hand, and wrapped the other arm around Scott's shoulders as he addressed the group. "How about we let all of them share this feast with us?"

At first, the claps of approval came only from Elly and Hunter, then Sean joined in, and Garret. Then, Amanda stood and clapped as well.

With a smile, Cole turned and offered his hand. "Scott, you and your men are welcome here."

Scott clasped it. A contrite group went through the buffet then looked for a place to sit. Most of the tables were full, but Hunter stood. "Someone can have my seat." That prompted others to offer theirs or scoot closer together until there was space for everyone.

Cole resumed his speech, such as it was. He suggested a sheet with everyone's address and said they would make copies and send them around in the next few days. When the discussion turned to specifics, such as where they were with supplies, and who had more of one thing than they needed, but not enough of another. Cole offered another list for that. People could put down what they had and what they needed. If others wanted to share or trade, they could do that.

Dessert was announced and conversation only halted long enough for cake to be sliced or pie to be served. As dusk fell, a few people started their cars, the headlights allowing the party to continue. People had been hungry for more than just food. They'd been hungry for company, for laughter, and for sharing stories of hardship and triumph.

Cole noticed a lot of hugging and tears, fears of the virus overwhelmed by the need to connect with other people. He worried about the disease, but for now, he was convinced it had gone dormant. Diseases were like that. The Spanish flu had ravaged the world for a few years, then disappeared. He prayed Sympatico Syndrome had ended as quickly as it had arrived.

Elly strolled up to Cole as he spoke to one of the men who had ridden in the back of Scott's truck. Cole smiled at her and wrapped an arm over her shoulders as he nursed a beer. "Guess what, Elly? This is Dave. He was a pharmacy student before the virus."

"No kidding? Did Cole tell you about the clinic we want to start? He and I will run the lab, Jenna will probably help train more nurses, and I'm sure a pharmacist would be a welcome addition."

"Oh wow. That would be awesome. My buddy, Ben, is a paramedic. I bet he'd love to work there too."

"Is he the one who bandaged Will?"

Dave nodded. "Yep."

"Excuse me, Dave. I need to speak with Cole for a moment."

Cole waved goodbye then focused on Elly. "Are you okay?"

"I'm a little tired. My feet hurt."

Looking around as one of the set of headlights went out, he realized the crowd had thinned. "I guess we should wrap this up."

Garret sauntered up to Cole. "I had a helluva good time, Cole. I was about to go crazy out there at my house." The man's jovial tone dropped and his voice cracked. "Thank you...for this. You saved me. I was thinking of...well never mind. I have hope now."

Cole stuck out his hand. "This wasn't me. This was all of us. We survived Sympatico Syndrome."

Elly tugged his arm. "Come on. Let's go home."

Chapter Thirty

"ONE MORE PUSH, Elly. You can do it." Cole bit his lip as he did his best to help brace her as she pushed. He'd been present for Hunter's birth, but they had been in a sterile delivery room surrounded by lights, several nurses, a doctor and an aide. A pediatrician had been at hand to take care of Hunter once he was born.

Now, it was just Jenna, Sophie, and Amanda and they were in a small exam room at a clinic that had belonged to some doctor who had succumbed to the virus. The clinic had been thoroughly cleaned and had already served as the birth site of his granddaughter, Belle.

Elly sank back against him, panting, eyes closed. She didn't speak to him or anyone. She'd already sworn at him a few times, but she was past that stage.

"I can feel the baby's head. It's right there, Elly. Next contraction, I need you to bear down as hard as you can." Jenna stood waiting to catch the baby. Sophie waited next to Elly's left side, clean towels in her arms.

"Almost done, Elly. This is the hardest part." Cole smoothed damp strands of hair from her face. Her eyes opened.

He felt her body tensing as the beginning of another contraction brought her up off the bed. Gripping her knees, she almost squatted as she bore down. Cole tried to steady her and get out of her way at the same time.

"The head's out! Hold on. Don't push." The wet sound of a bulb syringe came, and then Jenna said, "Last big push. When you're ready, hon."

Elly took a deep breath, her face scrunching with effort as she grunted long and loud.

"The baby's shoulders are out!" Sophie peered over Elly's leg, her arms out.

More suction sounds, then a loud, hoarse cry. Jenna grinned at Elly, then Cole. "It's a boy. And he doesn't sound too happy about coming out to this cold, bright world."

Unlike Belle, Sophie and Hunter's daughter, this baby flailed his little arms and legs, crying loud enough to make everyone laugh. Tiny Belle had frightened everyone when she'd been born early. Born blue and limp, her first cries had been weak. Barely louder than a faint mew from a kitten.

Elly collapsed against Cole's arm, a smile breaking through her fatigue. "He's okay?"

"He's perfect, Elly. A healthy baby boy. If I had to guess, I'd say he's about seven and a half pounds."

Sophie took the baby from Jenna, who gently massaged Elly's abdomen to help her expel the placenta. She dried the baby, set him on Elly's chest, indicating that Cole should hold him there as she tossed away the wet towels and replaced them with dry blankets. Quickly, she swaddled the baby. "Here's your beautiful baby boy, Elly."

Cole blinked hard, the little pink face swimming in front of him. He rubbed the heel of his hand against his eyes and laughed. "He's so tiny!" While bigger than little Belle, he still appeared fragile and helpless.

Elly peered at him, seemingly oblivious to the ordeal she'd just gone through as she bent and kissed the still damp, matted hair on the baby's head. "He's so precious."

Cole reached out, grazing a finger down the baby's cheek, chuckling when he turned his head to the side and started rooting. Elly's eyes flew wide. "What do I do?"

Sophie reached over and helped guide the baby to the breast as

Jenna said, "Let him nurse. It'll help with getting you all back together down here."

The baby latched on the third try, with more help from Sophie, who was now an expert at breastfeeding.

For several moments, nobody spoke. Mesmerized by the infant, Cole barely noticed when Sophie moved away and started cleaning up, only aware that she had done so when Elly began shaking and Sophie appeared with a warm blanket, draping it over her.

Jenna no longer stood at the end of the delivery bed, and had somehow managed to change the linens without Elly having to move. With a push of a button, the bed went from almost a chair to a regular bed, with the back raised for Elly to lean against. And even more incredibly, Jenna and Sophie had somehow managed to change the sheets with Elly still in the bed. A few half-rolls in each direction, and it had been accomplished.

"What do you think we should name him?" Elly gently broke the seal as the baby seemed to lose interest in nursing, but his eyes were wide as he blinked up at her.

Cole edged to the side to get another look at him. "I have no idea." Many had run through his mind, but he hadn't voiced them out of fear that picking a name would jinx the birth. That something would happen to Elly or the baby. She hadn't spoken of any names either.

She smiled into the baby's face. "Now that he's here and I can see him. I think I have the perfect name for him. Fox."

Startled at the choice, Cole tilted his head, watching the baby's eyes. He leaned in closer, and the baby, seeing the movement, shifted his look to Cole's face. "Fox…"

The baby blinked, his body jerking slightly as if in response. His legs kicked the blanket. Cole grinned. "Yeah. I think he likes it. *Fox*. With a big brother named Hunter, you're in good company with a strong name."

Elly smiled at Cole, then dropped a kiss on Fox's head. "Welcome to this new world, Fox."

Epilogue

"I'M GOING to go deliver this beef to Garret after I'm done at court. Do you have anything you want me to take?"

Elly came from the kitchen, one arm around a squirming Fox as the toddler fought to get down. In the weeks since he'd learned to walk, that's all he wanted to do. He kept them all on their toes. He probably wanted to find Belle, but Cole knew she was napping. "Yeah. Piper baked up an extra loaf of bread and wanted you to send it. It's on the counter. And ask him if he has any more potatoes."

With a head-start on growing potatoes at the beginning of the pandemic, Garret had become the main source of them. Willingly trading them for other goods. Wisely, he'd saved most of his first harvest, subsisting on canned goods he'd taken from empty homes, and used his first harvest to increase his second one, giving him enough left to plant while leaving him surplus to trade.

As the unofficial peacekeeper, in addition to helping on the ranch that now, effectively, was theirs after Scott and Don had vacated Amanda and Will's family ranch, and putting in hours helping Elly get a biology lab going, Cole was kept busy settling disputes. Most of them were minor, thankfully. Someone didn't feel a trade was fair and sought out a neutral third party. For some reason, he was the one most turned to.

At first, he'd gone along and helped settle matters to keep the peace, but some weeks, he'd had to drop what he was doing four or more times to go hear both sides. Now, he set hours at an abandoned office and people started referring to it as the courthouse. Twice a week he went in to arbitrate between ten a.m. and two p.m.

Anyone who had a problem could come in on those times and Cole would hear them out. Often, both parties would eventually agree upon an outcome with him only guiding the conversation. Afterwards, more often than not, both parties also left him payment in the form of food, or goods.

Sometimes he got a bottle of whiskey, other times, a chicken, but he didn't set a fee and accepted whatever was offered. He'd tried to decline at first, but Garret, Amanda and Will convinced him that his time spent away from his other duties should be compensated, so reluctantly, he took the offerings. Consequently, with the number of chickens he'd received, their ranch had grown into a chicken farm.

With the abundance of eggs, Piper was able to create baked goods that were sought after by other folks, and she and Jake had moved into a house next to an abandoned bakery. Jake put his diving skills, learned over many summers at his dad's house in Florida, to good use when he and another diver succeeded in cleaning the intake pipes on the Hoover Dam from being clogged with mussels. It had been the biggest threat to their electrical supply. A couple of Dam employees had survived the virus and had trained a few others, so electricity still flowed unimpeded. Sean had taught Hunter some basic electrical skills and the two of them, with another man who had arrived from Arizona, repaired broken power lines.

Their world had returned almost to normal. The population had grown, as Cole had predicted, when survivors migrated to the Dam area. Last fall, an unofficial count had their numbers close to three thousand people. He guessed another five hundred had taken up residence since then. Housing wasn't an issue, but food always was a worry. In the spring, nearly every man or woman who could sit a horse scoured the hills in the area for cattle that had wandered away in the first days of the virus. Everyone who participated in the round up was entitled to a share of the cattle collected. Those too old to ride but who helped in other ways, such as preparing food for the cowboys, were also given a share.

Cole had gone along, as had Hunter. Each of them received ten steers for their efforts. Sean hadn't needed to since he was often paid with calves when he got someone's power up and running, or fixed their air conditioning. He gave Hunter a share of what he received, but since Hunter was still learning, he didn't get a full share.

Between what Sean received and, what Jenna accepted when she created the clinic and treated everything from cuts and scrapes to heart attacks, his brother's family was doing well.

Belle and Fox weren't the only babies delivered. Thirty more had either been born in their new community, or were newborns when their families arrived searching for other survivors.

As Cole walked to his car, one that ran on electricity, since that was much easier to come by than gasoline, he scanned the skies. A few pilots had settled in New Vegas, as some had begun calling the area. The first time he'd seen a plane overhead, he'd marveled at it with everyone else. It seemed like a miracle. Now, he was more apprehensive. It was one thing when it was a local flying, but another when an unknown plane approached. That had occurred several times and nobody knew who was in the planes. He hoped that eventually, they'd be able to trade with survivors in other areas, but for now, they were all on their own.

A buzz from the air made him look east. It wasn't a plane this time, but a helicopter. As it came closer, Cole froze, his hand on the door handle.

The helicopter flew past, but low, and looked to be landing somewhere a mile or so up the road. He hopped in the car and took off in that direction.

He wasn't the only one drawn to the helicopter's landing and he nodded to several men who parked alongside the road as the helicopter's rotors slowed. It had landed in the middle of their main road. That irritated Cole already. While most people walked or rode horses to conserve fuel, the road was used every day for people to deliver goods and livestock to other parts of the community. Jenna's clinic was on this road and so was his court.

It had to be an outsider. Even with the Air Force base so close, helicopters were unusual because the local pilots didn't know how to fly helicopters. So, when a helicopter had been spotted months ago, it had been news. Someone had gotten out of the copter, asked a few people who were close at the time of the landing what the name of the town was, who was in charge, and other questions.

Cole had spoken to the people questioned. Nobody had given the man any names, but one person had said that Cole's name had been brought up. He had pretended not to know who the man was talking about, telling Cole at the time, "He looked like military, you know? They weren't around to help us so I don't owe them shit."

The helicopter door opened and Cole wasn't surprised when Holland stepped out. Damn him.

Well, he couldn't hide forever. Might as well see what the guy wanted. Cole straightened his shoulders as he approached the man.

"Holland?"

The man turned to Cole, surprise splashed across his face. "Cole Evans? I did not expect you to greet my arrival." He smiled as if they were long lost friends and approached, his hand extended. Cole ignored it.

"What do you want? If you want me to leave with you, forget it. This is my home now."

"And a fine job you've done creating it."

"It wasn't me. It was all the local folks, and the amazing survivors who have flocked to the area."

"Yes, I'm aware of what this place is like. You see, we got word of this community back east."

Cole opened his eyes wide in surprise. "Really?"

"Yes. And we sent someone out here to scout the area to see if the story was true. It was, and your name popped up."

"That's not how I heard it. I heard someone was asking for me, specifically."

Holland waved dust from in front of his mouth, spitting to the side. "Sorry. The helicopter must have stirred up a lot of dust. Why don't we go somewhere more comfortable to talk."

"Here is fine."

Holland sighed. "Okay. Well, nobody is here to take you away. Instead, I'm here to offer you a chance to make the vaccine right here. I even have some key information for you. Your medical record from when you were infected, along with a sample of the virus you were exposed to—before it was modified to create Sympatico Syndrome. With your antibodies already in you, it's possible you could make a vaccine with this."

Cole's jaw dropped. "How did you get all of that?"

Holland grinned. "I tried telling you I wasn't a bad guy. I was just determined to get a cure. I haven't yet, but you are the key. We can't ever let this virus destroy us again." He put a hand out. "Will you help me?"

"I'm no expert on creating vaccines. Hell, I'm no expert at all. I had an idea how to make one, but no clear way to go about it under these conditions."

"I have a couple of people to help with that. Good people from the CDC. What's left of the CDC anyway. They're coming out even as we speak and should arrive tomorrow."

Cole didn't see a downside. They did need a vaccine and with others' guidance, they might be able to create one. He owed it to his family to try. He didn't want Fox or Belle or any other children to have to face the same virus in the future.

He took Holland's hand, clasping it firmly. "I'll help."

Sympatico Syndrome Survivor List

From Infection and Isolation:

- Cole Evans—Former epidemiologist with the Navy. Retired a year or so before the pandemic.
- Hunter Evans—Cole's son. Was away in college when the pandemic struck. Made his way across the country. Age 20 at beginning of series.
- Sean Evans— Cole's younger brother. Had his own business as an electrician.
- Jenna Evans—Sean's wife. Worked as an ER nurse prior to pandemic.
- Piper Evans—Daughter of Sean and Jenna. Age 17 at beginning of series. Was a senior in high school.
- Trent Evans—Son of Sean and Jenna. Age 14 at beginning of series
- Elly Jackson—Epidemiologist with CDC. Knew Cole from prior mission to Africa to treat people with Ebola.
- Jake—18 year old who teamed with Elly on the streets of Chicago during the pandemic. Lost his mother, who was a doctor. Parents divorced. Dad had lived in Florida.
- Sophie—18 year old girl who lost entire family. Hunter helped her escape from bad guys. Is approximately seven

months pregnant at the beginning of Invasion. Hunter is the father.

- Joe—had been a long-time friend of Cole's uncle, who had left Cole the island in a will. Lived in town on mainland near island. Joins with Cole's group. Has many handyman skills.
- Luke—8 year old boy whose mother had died. He survived with his younger sister. Found by Elly and Jake.
- Zoe—Luke's younger sister. Approximately five years old.
- Steve—With a group of friends who survived the pandemic, show up to find help for his friend, Mike.
- Mike—Seeking treatment for a bad cut on his hand that had become infected.

Acknowledgments

I'd like to thank my amazing beta readers, Vickie Boehnlein, Win Johnson, and Lala Price. I couldn't have published this without them. They gave me valuable feedback on what worked and what didn't work from a reader's point of view.

Thanks also, to the Antioch Writer's Group, where I've received lots of encouragement and critique.

And finally, my daughter, Maggie, who helped me brainstorm several aspects of this novel, and who, as a teen herself, and budding writer, gave me feedback to make sure the teens in this novel sound like actual teens.

Afterword

If you have a moment, a review of Invasion would be fantastic and greatly appreciated. It would also help other readers decide if this book is something they might enjoy.

Invasion: A Post-Apocalyptic Survival Novel

Join my MP McDonald's Newsletter list and get a free copy of:

Mark Taylor: Genesis
(The Mark Taylor Series)

When Mark Taylor witnesses the drowning of a little girl whose death appeared to him in a photo taken the day before, he discovers that the camera he found in an Afghan bazaar has a strange and unique ability — it produces photographs of tragedies yet to happen.Tragedies that he is driven to prevent.

Wary of his new super-hero like power to change the future, Mark keeps the camera a secret--even when it means risking his own life. But with only 24 hours to act, what if he fails to prevent the greatest tragedy his country has ever experienced?

Afterword

About the Author

M.P. McDonald is the author of supernatural thrillers and post-apocalyptic thrillers. With multiple stints on Amazon's top 100 list, her books have been well-received by readers. Always a fan of reluctant heroes, especially when there is a time travel or psychic twist, she fell in love with the television show Quantum Leap. Soon, she was reading and watching anything that had a similar concept. When that wasn't enough, she wrote her own stories with her unique spin.

If her writing takes your breath away, have no fear, as a respiratory therapist--she can give it back via a tube or two. She lives with her family in a frozen land full of ice, snow, and abominable snowmen.

On the days that she's not taking her car ice-skating, she sits huddled over a chilly computer, tapping out the story of a camera that can see the future. She hopes it can see summer approaching, too. If summer eventually arrives, she tries to get in a little fishing, swimming and biking between chapters.

M.P. McDonald loves hearing from readers, so feel free to drop me an email telling her your thoughts about the book or series.
www.mpmcdonald.com
mmcdonald64@gmail.com

Contact Me

I love hearing from readers, so feel free to drop me an email telling me your thoughts about the book or series.

Email Me

Or use my contact form on my website:

http://mpmcdonald.com/contact/

Please checkout my Facebook page. I post updates and tidbits about my current projects. I love interacting with fans on the page:

M.P. McDonald Facebook

Printed in Great Britain
by Amazon